By:

NATHAN ROTEN

Edited by: Jordan Roten & John Hudspith

Cover Design by: Damon Za

Interior Layout by: 12stone Press

ISBN: 0990637816
ISBN-13: 978-0-9906378-1-3

Find out more at:

www.AegisSeries.com

Keep in touch with Nathan at:

www.NathanRoten.com

DEDICATION

To Anna Gray, Sam & Eliza. I hope you know how valuable and loved you are. Such great things are in store for you. Daddy loves you.

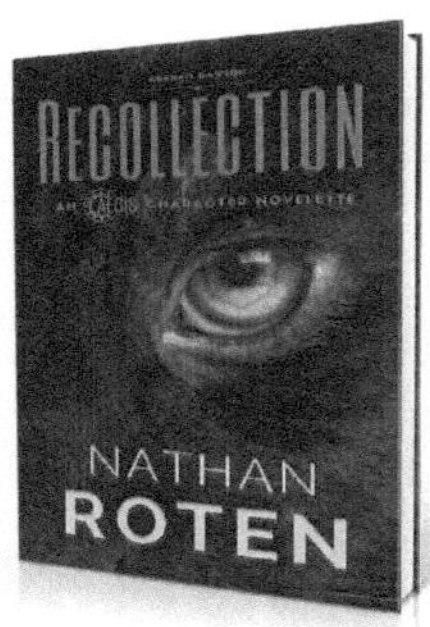

FREE DOWNLOAD

WITNESS THE NIGHTMARE THAT STARTED IT ALL

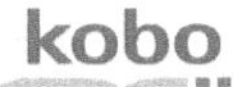

Sign up for the author's New Releases mailing list and get a FREE copy of RECOLLECTION - An Aegis Character Novelette - and witness the nightmare that sent Graham into the woods as a small boy.

Visit the website below to claim your copy today!

NathanRoten.com/free-book

Contents

FLASH FORWARD

Present Day

"Get away from me, or I swear I will use this!"

It was getting dark outside. Thick fog hovered overhead, making it hard for Graham to see anything, let alone what the man coming at him was going to do next. Graham knelt in the wet grass, panting. The others stood close by waiting to see what was about to happen next.

"I am disappointed, Graham. Murder isn't your thing."

"You have hurt us enough for it to be self-defense," said Graham in shallow breaths. He was dizzy from the pain. The metal blade in his hand was multiplying into three as his eyes crossed. He drifted to the side a bit and then forced himself to refocus. His wrists were still glowing, though they were fading with each attack.

"There's a big difference between close combat weapons and long range weapons." The veiled figure extended his hand, firing a blast of light from his palm. The light hit the knife, sending it spiraling into the air. "Now you know the difference."

Graham recoiled from the attack. The knife had taken the bulk of the hit, but his hand was stinging from the aftershock. As he pulled his hand to his chest, his heart sank into his gut. There was no way he could win.

"Fight back!"

Graham remained motionless.

"I said fight back!" Another glowing blast hit the ground in front of Graham, sending dirt and rock into the air.

Graham wanted to fight, but he was so fatigued that it took all his strength to remain upright on his knees and not succumb to the dizziness.

"Fine. Have it your way."

The man reached out and shot a blast of light from his hand, just in front of the silent figures huddled together to Graham's right.

"STOP IT! Why are you doing this?" yelled Graham.

The man did not respond. He just stared into Graham's eyes as his hand illuminated again.

"Hit me! Leave them out of this!" Graham's chest tightened and cramped as he yelled.

"You need to fight. You should be able to use your full strength by now, but you are still holding back. First you can't control it, and now you can't use it." The man lowered his illuminated hand to allow Graham time to think about it. "Does everyone have to get hurt before you let go?"

Graham's mind was numb with the pain surging through his body. He could not focus. He could hardly even breathe. Trying to stand back up, he braced on one foot, but it gave way, sending him back onto his side. Exhaustion had taken full effect.

No. It can't end this way. I will not let it end this way. Closing his eyes, Graham pressed his face against the wet grass. In his mind, he saw a wave of black smoke. He heard the voices screaming to keep away, and then his own screams filled the air as the light surrounded him. Taking a deep breath,

Graham let the memory empower him.

As his eyes opened, he braced his weight on his hands and pushed himself upright. His head was swimming, but he forced himself to focus. In slow movements, he swung his legs around so that he was on his hands and knees. His wrists began to glow again as he painfully got to his feet. He clenched his jaw and made eye contact through the fog. His fingers curled up into fists, making the light around his wrists intensify.

"Yes, now you are beginning to understand." The man on the other side of the fog took a step back into a fighting stance. "Now we are getting somewhere." The chill in the air caused his breath to form white puffs of vapor as he spoke.

The pain that had wracked Graham's body subsided. He felt his energy levels rising with his anger as the light around him grew brighter.

"This ends now!"

A Survey Of The Crowd

4 days earlier...

Graham sat atop Building 14 as he did every Saturday morning. It was a crisp 55 degrees outside and the leaves of the trees were just beginning to trade in their formal summer green shells for their true vibrant colors of yellow, orange, and red. Saturday was the busiest day for the Wellington Market, with all the vendors pouring into the city after stocking their carts and stores throughout the week. Not only did sellers of produce, clothing, meats, exotic animals and rare objects come from all over the region, but customers with eager eyes came from even farther away to buy these eclectic treasures.

The Wellington Market was the largest market on the eastern side of the United States. Perfectly positioned between three main highways criss-crossing around the small town of Portfield, it attracted sellers traveling in the northeast. The market was modestly built with only two rows of buildings stretching over a 1/4 mile. The buildings were facing each other with a simple cobblestone road holding them apart.

Each building was labeled with a number, ascending from West to East. Most of the buildings were a single story, made of wood, stone or brick, but there were three buildings that stood tall and masterfully crafted with elegant architectural skill. These three were made of large stone blocks, seven stories high, with steep roofs and ornate carvings embellishing the corners of the rooflines.

After climbing the narrow, rusty metal ladder in the alleyway between Buildings 14 and 15, Graham had assumed his usual position between two stone gargoyles perched as overseers of the western side of the market. Graham stood a modest 5'6" with short, sandy blonde hair and a slim athletic build. His eyes shifted from building to building. They matched almost perfectly the deep blue hue of the morning sky as the vendors finished setting up their shops. He slowly slid his raggedy green backpack off his shoulders and dropped it to the ground, creating a cloud of fine dust around the base. Graham took hold of the small zipper and opened the right side pocket of his backpack. Plunging his hand in, he fiddled around for a second or two until he felt the plastic cylinders tucked at the bottom. As he continued surveying the crowds of people, he removed his plastic binoculars from the pocket and proceeded to lie down on his belly with his elbows braced against the two stone gargoyles. Reaching into his sweatshirt pocket with his other hand, he took out a small rubber ball and rolled it around rhythmically between his fingers.

As Graham put the binoculars to his eyes, his nose was hit with all the different scents of the market. Fresh pastries and brewed coffee from Collins Café & Bakery were the first to come. His stomach began to growl with hunger, reminding him he had skipped out on breakfast. The eastern breeze carried the aroma of citrus and berries from Mrs. McKay's produce stand at Building 2. Familiar scents swirled around him: leather, clay pottery, animal fur, and finally came the best fragrance of all. Wood. Not just because there was a carpentry shop near the end of the market, but from the woods that encapsulated Wellington like a hidden treasure.

Graham's grip tightened around the binoculars. *Today I will find you. I just know it.* Armed with eager anticipation and a quickened pulse, Graham peered through the binoculars in search of answers. For *Him.*

His first inclination was to stare down the freshly baked pastries his belly demanded, but after deciding that it would make matters worse, he shifted his gaze to the sitting area of the café. The first thing Graham noticed was an older couple holding hands under a red umbrella as they ate their spinach and cheese scones.

He focused in on the middle-aged man behind the couple in a brown overcoat, bending down to tie his golden retriever to the nearby lamppost. *I wonder who this guy is? I haven't seen him here before.* Once the leash was firmly knotted, the man sat down to a cup of steaming black coffee. He then removed a small gold coin from his pocket, tucked it in between his first two fingers, and proceeded to let it cascade over his knuckles like a waterfall.

This can't be him, Graham thought to himself. *He doesn't fit the description I heard Ms. Winstone giving.*

After another five minutes or so, Graham gave up on looking through Collins Café & Bakery and decided to work his way down the line of shops leading east. There were so many people to sift through, his mission seemed almost impossible. A bit overwhelmed yet undeterred, he made his way down the road, looking far enough past his own building to where he could begin searching in a zig-zag pattern between the stores on each side of the street.

He shifted over to the Bengal tiger and the monkeys at the front of the store. He was so entranced with watching the animals move around, that he nearly forgot what he was doing. Blinking his eyes a few times to refocus, he looked again for people around the animals, only to notice that there weren't any. *How does this guy stay in business? I've never seen him sell a single animal.*

Getting back on track, Graham looked next door to the leather smith. *Maybe that's how he stays in business*, he chuckled. Looking inside the store, he quickly saw there was nothing and nobody. He continued to profile every person walking through all sixty buildings of the entire market, but after hours of searching, he was forced to admit that there was absolutely nothing worth his attention. No one matched the description. No strange happenings. Not even a quarrel broke out at the pub.

Mumbling under his breath, Graham's heart sank at the thought of another wasted morning. *I have to find this guy. I have to!* He threw his binoculars down and tightened his grip around the ball. In his frustration, Graham slammed his fist down hard on the ledge in front of him. As he did, a burst of light sparked around him, shooting outward. Small pieces of gravel and trash defied gravity as they hovered around him for a brief moment before being hurled through the air with the dispersion of light. Graham immediately panicked and dropped down behind the ledge, rubbing the hand he had slammed against the stone. *Get it together, Graham. You have to get it together or people will get hurt.* He closed his eyes as the memory took over.

He was in the woods with two other people. He felt an overwhelming sense of fear and anger. Screams filled the darkness followed by a blast of bright light. Graham's eyes opened and his head jerked in reaction to the light. He was sweating. *What did I do?*

Graham let a few minutes pass, in case anyone below saw the burst of light. He wanted to stay for a while longer, but he knew he had to get back before Ms. Winstone noticed that he was missing. With a half-hearted sigh, Graham put the binoculars back in the pocket, picked up his backpack and made his way back to the rusty stairs.

As Graham grabbed the railing of the ladder, he looked up to the field separating the market from the edge of the forest. A bolt of adrenaline rushed through his veins, causing him to freeze. A figure in a long coat holding a thin walking cane in his right hand stood in the middle of the field, a small stone's throw away, and was staring directly at him.

Graham started to panic again at the thought of his unnatural abilities being discovered, but he forced himself to keep calm. He slowly let his backpack slide off his shoulder so that he could retrieve his binoculars as his mind kept cranking out questions. *Maybe this is him. Could this be Cavaness? He doesn't look huge to me. No, this guy doesn't match the description. It can't be him.*

A thousand questions reeled around in his mind upon seeing this stranger in the field. Graham glanced down for the zipper, but as soon as he looked back to the man, he had vanished as quickly as he had appeared.

What the…he was right in the middle of the field! He couldn't have gone anywhere. Graham grabbed the binoculars and swept the field with his eyes. He wasn't quite sure if he wanted to find this guy or not, but part of him couldn't shake the hope that if he did, he would finally find answers. After a few moments, he let out his breath and relaxed a little. After giving it some thought, Graham's sensible side began to kick in.

Maybe it was just my mind playing tricks on me, or maybe I'm getting a little lightheaded from not eating this morning. There is no way a person could have just disappeared. The field is just too wide for anyone to have run to the woods or the market that fast. He kept his inner monologue going until he was convinced that it was nothing. Trying his best to shake it off, he put the binoculars back into the side pocket and lifted his backpack onto his shoulders.

Putting his foot on the top rung, he could see the roof of Greenwood Orphanage towering over the sea of maple trees that surrounded the market.

Home Sweet Home.

Greenwood Orphanage was the only home Graham had ever known. Established in 1773, it was one of the oldest and most respected institutions for abandoned children in the northeast. Their highest priority was education. Going beyond the physical needs of the children, skilled tutors were hired to help them in each subject they were currently studying in school. Subjects including, but not limited to: Mathematics, Science, Literature and History, in which they were currently learning about Portfield's famous contributions to the Underground Railroad.

The building itself stood three stories tall, the exterior with arched rectangular windows stretching uniformly across the outside. The green ivy crawling up the walls was just finishing its climb over the final row of windows. The orphanage was an architectural delight to look at, though the beauty had faded with time. The main entrance was the width of a football field with a steep gable roof setting it apart from the two wings that expanded at a slight angle on both sides. Over the ridgeline of the wings, you could see chimney stacks standing tall every so often with three black pipes protruding from the top of each stack. Though the paint cracks were visible through the thick ivy coat and the walls seemed as though they were trying to escape from one another, it was a relatively cozy place to be.

The inside of the building was set up with two main wings, one for the boys and one for the girls. Holding the two wings apart were the dining room, kitchen and main living room area called the Commons. It was the most ornate room in the entire orphanage, featuring a massive stone fireplace as the main centerpiece, which held a large portrait of the founder over the wooden mantel.

Graham always had a hard time going back. It was so crowded there all the time. Maybe that was one reason he always came out to the market on the weekend. He could be alone, with all the room in the world, just him and his thoughts. He could take solace in his withdrawal to the rooftop without having to worry about hurting anyone.

Jumping from the next to last rung, Graham's feet hit the ground. Looking up again toward Greenwood, he finished his train of thought. *Home sweet home. Just me and my 87 brothers and sisters.* Now, walking back toward the edge of the forest, Graham shook off the feeling of disappointment, forcing optimism to the surface. "Next week, then, Cavaness. I will find you next week."

BACK AT THE ORPHANAGE

Graham walked back through the woods, until he came to a large stone arch covered in moss. He stopped for a moment, running his hands along the big chunks of rock. He remembered being lost in the woods as a child and finding this structure. It was his beacon of hope. It was his sign that he was not going to die in these woods. It was also his little secret. Orphans did not have many personal belongings, and this was one of the things he could call his own. Although he longed to stay there, Graham knew he had to keep moving.

Now back on Greenwood property, he made his way up the steep gravel road and past the three ancient willow trees on the front lawn of the orphanage. As he crested the hill, Graham noticed a thin and wiry boy stealthily making his way out of the side entrance of the parlor room. Weighing in at 105 pounds, 5'3" tall with jet black hair, greenish-hazel eyes and small button nose, Damien was Graham's best friend. Since leaving Peru as a small child, he never seemed to lose the golden, South American tan.

"Que haces? Porque eres tan descuidado! Ms. Winstone has been looking for you for over three hours!" said Damien. "You

never stay gone this long. What is going on?"

"I know, I know… it takes a while to search all of Wellington. I was going as fast as I could," replied Graham. "Now let me by, I need to get back inside."

Graham had already lost control once today; he was not going to do it again, especially in front of Damien. He had to get away.

"Hey, wait!" Damien grabbed Graham's arm and pulled him back. "I don't know how much longer I can be your watchman, Graham."

"Look, Damien, you and I both want to find out what is going on. Both of us cannot go to Wellington, and I know my way around the woods surrounding the market much better than you do. This is what we agreed on, right?"

"Yes," Damien murmured as he rolled his eyes.

"Good, it is settled then." Graham pulled his arm from Damien's hand and continued quickly toward the door.

Damien wasn't going to let Graham walk away again. Sprinting after him, Damien again stopped Graham with a hand to his chest.

"Listen, I don't know what your deal is right now, but we need to talk. How about you try talking to me for once instead of avoiding me like the plague."

Graham took a deep breath to hide his frustration. He knew Damien was getting tired of being pushed to the side, but over the past few months, his unexplainable power had become increasingly more difficult to control and hide. He was only trying to protect his best friend, but he recognized that Damien was not about to let him walk away without some answers.

"Fine. Maybe when Ms. Winstone's friend comes over again, we can find out more about this mystery person. Her last conversation didn't exactly give us much to go on. It's like I'm looking for a ghost. The only thing I have to go on is the fact that there's a huge guy in town named Cavaness, who can do things normal people can't."

Glad that Graham was finally talking to him, Damien tried to concentrate on what Graham was saying, but the fear of being reprimanded by Ms. Winstone kept him on edge.

"We both need to be in on the conversation, so we don't miss anything, ok?" whispered Graham. "We need a plan. I only got the final part of their conversation last time."

"*Sí*," replied Damien. "Now, *vamos*, we need to get back inside. I don't want you to get in trouble. Why don't you go to the west wing and act like you have been hiding there? If I see Ms. Winstone, I will tell her that we have been playing hide-and-seek."

"Hide-and-seek? What are you talking about? We are *fifteen*, Damien. We don't play hide-and-seek."

"Hey, it's the best I've got right now. You have any better ideas, amigo?"

Graham thought for a few seconds and realized he could not come up with anything better, so he reluctantly agreed. He put his two fingers to his forehead and flicked them toward Damien as a salute before easing his way back through the rusty storm door of the parlor room. Damien breathed a sigh of relief and decided he would just go back in through the front door, as if returning from looking for Graham's hiding spot outside.

As Graham made his way through the parlor, he poked his head through the doorway into the commons. Seeing no sign of life, he made his way past the leather armchairs and the giant fireplace.

"Stop looking at me, Alexander," breathed Graham, addressing the portrait overtop the aged wooden mantel as if he were alive. "You give me the creeps every time I walk by you." There was nothing overtly disturbing about the portrait. It was only a picture of the founder of Greenwood from the chest up. He was in a coat and vest, looking slightly upwards like most people do in portraits. A small grin could be detected underneath his large beard, and he had the air of a man who took great pride in what he stood for. He actually had a kind face, but there was just something about it that was unnerving to Graham.

Moving on, Graham finally made it through the commons, stopping at the threshold of the main hallway between the two wings and the dining room. On each side of the door leading to the dining room, there was a grandfather clock positioned to give scheduled rings for each wing. One for the boys and one for the girls. Just past the clocks were two wide staircases leading to each floor of the wing of the orphanage. The main level was for staff. The second level was lined with study rooms, utilities and offices. The only thing on the third floor was bedrooms.

The gongs of both grandfather clocks signaled that it was study time. *Perfect! I'll just walk in there with the others as if I've been here the whole time.* He darted up the staircase. Graham looked down the hallway and noticed for the first time that it was strikingly bare. Every twenty feet or so, there was a gap between doors with blank wall space, in front of which was a small table with a vase or small sculpture on top. Above the table hung a portrait of either a prominent past staff member or nature scene.

After seeing a few kids in the first three rooms, he decided to keep moving until he met a group of kids to mingle in with. He turned to walk back, but immediately tripped, falling flat on his face. His cheeks turned red with embarrassment as he stood up. With a slightly bruised sense of pride, Graham looked behind him to see if anyone had noticed his clumsiness.

Hoping to see a vacant hallway, he turned around, only to be greeted by the large, round belly of Mr. Kobble. It felt like an eternity as Graham's face plunged into that rounded gut. He could feel the large buttons of Mr. Kobble's vest against the bridge of his nose as he took in the overpowering smell of a woodsy cologne. As Graham tried to recoil and flee the scene, Mr. Kobble grabbed him by the shoulders with his strong, stubby hands.

"There ye are, lad! Werd has it Ms. Winstone has been searchen fer ya," he belched in his rich Scottish accent. "Better that I find ya than her, ya know. She is a bit cross today."

Graham forced a small grin and politely nodded.

"You've seem'd like a ghost these past few weeks, Mr. Graham. Wha'dve ye been up to that makes ye so scarce round 'ere?"

Mr. Kobble guided Graham past the sculptures, beyond the staircases and through the middle section leading to the office of Ms. Winstone, the Head Matron of Greenwood.

Graham's first response was to begin talking and let his imagination fill in the details. "Well, I've been seeing rats running around my bed at night, so I thought I could follow them back to their colony."

As he was saying this, Graham knew this was a horrible excuse for a story. He mentally kicked himself. *Colony! Rats don't live in colonies, you idiot. You can do better than 'colony'.*

Still in full stride, Mr. Kobble replied, "Well, it's a good thing we have ya 'round, Mr. Graham. Can't be hav'n colonized rat families eat'n all yer grub, now can we," he said with a slight grin and a hint of sarcasm. "Well, here ya go. I suspect Ms. Winstone is done with her afternoon tea. Now's just as good a time as any."

Mr. Kobble removed his right pork chop of a hand from Graham's shoulder and balled it into a fist. With minimal effort, but huge impact, his booming knocks on the door caused Ms. Winstone to let out a small shriek of surprise.

"Ms. Winstone, I've got a little fella here that I believe ye want to see."

"You found Graham?" Ms. Winstone replied, still a bit frazzled.

"Yes, ma'am."

"Wonderful. Please show him in."

Mr. Kobble opened the door to reveal Ms. Winstone sitting at her desk with her fingers interlaced, forming one big fist that rested on the desk top. "Thank you very much, Oliver. I will take it from here."

"Yes, ma'am." With a quick nod of the head, Mr. Kobble gently closed the door.

Now completely focused on Graham, Ms. Winstone held out her hand toward the empty chair in front of her desk. "Please, sit."

Graham followed orders and took the seat. He noticed that the room was strikingly bare. The craftsmanship of the rest of the orphanage flowed into her office with its ornate woodwork and 18th century charm, but Ms. Winstone never added any of herself to it. All the walls were bare, except for one, which held the yearly picture of each group of children housed at Greenwood. The rest of the room seemed like a metropolis with stacks of papers and folders towering like high rise buildings. There was not even a single photograph of Ms. Winstone or any family members.

Without any pleasantries, Ms. Winstone got straight to the point.

"What are you doing?" she asked with an intense stare.

"Well, er, um…."

"Let me expand. What are you doing when you leave here every Saturday?"

"I just go to be by myself, Ms. Winstone."

"And what does one do by one's self?"

"Nothing specific. I guess I just go out so I can be alone. I don't like being in crowds. It makes me anxious, and since this place is filled with people, I have to go somewhere where I can be by myself." Graham understood this would get him in trouble, but he never could conjure up good lies. The rat colonies proved that. "I… go into the woods."

Not surprised by this news, Ms. Winstone kept probing. "Is that all you do? Go into the woods?"

Graham's gut sank. *What do I tell her? If she knows I go to Wellington, she'll never let me leave the building again, but if I lie, she will know, and I will never leave the laundry room.* Storylines raced around in Graham's head in a flurry of non-creativity until his conscious calmed the storm and prevailed.

"No, ma'am," Graham let out with a sigh.

"And what exactly is it that you do, Graham?"

"I go to...Wellington."

"Wellington? That is more than seven miles away! What on earth do you do there?"

"It's not that far if you go through the woods, and I don't go out on the street. I always go up on a rooftop balcony by myself. I just like to watch everyone go about their day."

Ms. Winstone sat silent for a moment taking the story in. After some reflection, she got out of her chair and walked over to the wall of photographs. As she looked over the faces of each of the children, she chose her next words carefully.

"I would have thought you learned your lesson years ago after getting lost in those woods, Graham. You nearly gave me a heart-attack being gone for so long." Still looking over the faces of the children, she softened her tone. "Graham, I am responsible for the welfare of each and every child in Greenwood. You know that, right?"

"Yes, ma'am."

"Then you know Wellington is a gathering place for people coming from many different walks of life. Some people are good-natured. Others enjoy mischief. Some even find fulfilment in hurting other people." Ms. Winstone turned to face Graham. The crow's feet at the corners of her eyes softened a little as her typical facade of non-expression gave way to a slight compassionate smile. "Life is very different outside these walls and I don't want you to experience the bad side of it. Not yet. Life throws all sorts of unknowns at you that will take you down paths you never knew existed." She paused for a moment, either for reflection or dramatic effect. Graham could not tell which. "Innocence is a perishable gift, and I want you to keep yours for as long as you can."

Graham didn't know what to say. The first thing he

struggled to process was the fact Ms. Winstone was being nice. Caring, even. It wasn't that she was unusually evil– she was just strict all the time. Catching her smiling was like spotting a unicorn. The second thing he had issue with was the thought of being banned from his place of happiness and solitude. It was his safe haven, and the thought of losing it was unbearable. The turmoil he felt inside was evidently etched into his facial expressions, because Ms. Winstone immediately took notice.

Ms. Winstone's strong suit was discernment. That's why she eventually climbed the ladder to the big chair at Greenwood. Having been brought up under the motto of 'spare the rod, spoil the child', she was never any good at finding the line between outward displays of compassion versus strict compliance to the rules and the swift discipline of folly. As she took in the expression on Graham's face, other questions came to mind.

"I've never noticed your absence until just recently. Now, it seems as though you are gone more than you are here. What keeps you away so long?"

"Um… I just get caught up in looking over the market, I guess."

Ms. Winstone's partial grin disappeared as she squinted down at him.

"No, it is more than that, isn't it." The two stared at each other, each trying to guess what the other was thinking. She analyzed the situation until it dawned on her.

"You heard me talking about Cavaness, didn't you?"

Graham's eyes widened. "I, um…well…"

"That's it. You wanted to see if the rumors were true."

Ms. Winstone sat back down in her chair and relaced her fingers. Knowing now what Graham was truly after, her grin returned along with the crow's feet at the corners of her eyes. "Are you seeking out Cavaness because of the stories?"

"Ummm…"

"I know Cavaness. He is skilled in many areas, but magic

is not one of them. He has a reputation around town for that sort of thing, but I assure you, his methods are not mystical. Magic does not exist outside of fairy tales, Graham, and chasing it is even more foolish than believing in it."

Graham let his head fall as he looked at the floor. *No, I won't believe that. If this guy is anything like the stories, then I have to find him. I don't care how foolish I seem.*

Ms. Winstone's gaze never left Graham's face. "Don't believe me? Well, I suppose I will have to set up a little meeting with you and Cavaness so you can see for yourself. I am having a friend over tomorrow evening who is close to Cavaness. I'll see what I can do, so we can put all this nonsense to rest."

Ms. Winstone studied Graham's face, peering into his eyes as if they were windows into his thoughts. "Graham, I am not exactly deaf, you know. During our evening rounds, Mr. Kobble and I can hear you scream in your sleep. You have a vague past. Foggy memories can produce a strong desire for answers. In your pursuit for understanding, repressed memories and experiences can bubble up to the surface in dreams. It is a way for your mind to cope. Whatever you're dreaming about, dear, you are looking for real-life answers, not magic remedies. If you want help, all you need to do is ask. As a matter of fact, I remember a former guest here that—" Just then the dinner bell sounded, cutting off the conversation.

Ms. Winstone let the ringing stop before speaking again. "We will talk about this later. For now, I expect you to understand that you are not to go to Wellington. I know you love it there, but it is simply too dangerous. Also, you must learn to confide in someone, Graham. All orphans struggle with trust, especially when the people who were supposed to provide love and care abandoned them. I get it, I really do. Your parents may not be here, but I am. Mr. Kobble is here as well, and we are not leaving anytime soon, so if you need anyone to talk to, then you can rely on us to listen. Now, I suppose all of your game-playing has made you work up quite an appetite."

"Yes, ma'am." In Graham's disappointment, that was all he could muster. The mention of his parents made him cringe. *If she only knew...*

"Well, why don't you go get yourself ready for dinner. I can smell the fresh biscuits coming out of the oven now."

"Yes, ma'am."

Graham's stomach rumbled as he stiffened his legs to stand up out of his chair. As he turned around and grabbed the door handle, Ms. Winstone's voice followed him out with one final reply.

"Remember, Graham, putting yourself out there may indeed expose you to pain, but it also opens you up to the good things in life like love and companionship. Those who reach out for help usually find it."

Without turning around, Graham gave a light nod of his head and continued out the door. He did not want to talk to anyone. He made his way to dinner and sat at the long dining room table in a daze as Damien ranted on and on about one of the kids who was pranked by being blasted with the 'broth bath', which meant that someone had put chicken bouillon cubes in the shower head. Every so often, Graham would nod or give an *'uh huh'* or *'yep'* so that he seemed like he was following the story. Finally, the gongs of the grandfather clocks gave their bedtime chimes.

Saved by the clock, Graham made a quick escape to his room. Neglecting the normal bedtime routines or any form of hygiene, Graham pulled off his shirt and jeans to slip into his ragged, white t-shirt and a pair of torn mesh shorts. Once in the safety of his bed, he grabbed his small rubber ball and tossed it above his head. Tossing the ball mindlessly up and down was his nightly routine to help clear his mind. After about ten minutes, he felt the first tug of exhaustion. He put the ball back on the small table beside his bed. Then, pulling the covers over his head, he willed himself to sleep.

Control…Cavaness, you have to help me control it… he thought to himself as he drifted off.

NIGHT TERRORS

A warm breeze blew through the leaves as the couple walked along a wide trail in the woods with their two-year-old boy. The dad wore jeans and a blue button-down shirt. He walked hand in hand with his wife, who was wearing a yellow and white summer dress. The little boy reached out his hand as the mom took hold of it.

"Climb?" the boy asked.

"Yes, dear, you can climb."

The little boy giggled as he began walking up the fallen tree trunk. As he got near the end of it, he looked at his dad.

"'ump? Peese j…ump?"

"Yes, Graham, you can jump." The dad took hold of Graham's hand as he squatted down and leapt from the fallen tree. The boy giggled as his feet hit the ground, followed by his stomach. His dad smiled and dusted off his jeans and orange t-shirt, gently setting him back on his feet. Not wanting a good tree trunk to go to waste, Graham tried to go back to do it again, but his mom and dad kept hold of his hands as they continued down the trail.

"I love you, baby boy," the mom said.

"Ouve ouuu," the two-year-old Graham replied.

The couple strolled along for a few minutes until they saw a clearing under a cluster of oak trees.

"There's a little open area right over there to sit down for lunch. How about it, Graham? Are you getting hungry, son?" the dad asked.

"Eat!" Graham eagerly replied.

"Yes, eat. You need to eat so you can get big and strong like Daddy." The dad raised his arm and flexed his bicep. He belted out a laugh as Graham tried to imitate him by curling his arm. "I love you, son."

"Ouve ouuu, Da-di…..Eat?"

The dad smiled. "Yes, eat." He rustled his fingers through the little boy's hair. "You know, you are a special little boy, Graham. You make Mommy and Daddy very happy and very proud."

The small family spread out a blue plaid blanket and set out a wicker picnic basket. The mom popped the latch and removed two ham and swiss sandwiches cut perfectly from corner to corner, and one smaller **PB&J** sandwich that was one slice of bread folded over on itself. Following the sandwiches was some fresh fruit and some white linen napkins. Graham grabbed the first thing he could reach, taking a huge bite of his peanut butter and jelly sandwich, then another and another. The dad and mom both unwrapped their sandwiches, completely unaware of the large wave of smoke approaching quickly behind them.

Graham sat and stared as the wave got bigger, towering over the tops of the trees, resembling a tidal wave from a hurricane. As it moved closer, the trees began to bend, and then disappear in the billowing wake. Feeling the growing intensity of the wind, the dad turned around in shock. In an instant and with one swoop of his arm, he swiftly tucked his wife and child behind his back.

"STAY BEHIND ME!" There was a controlled urgency in his voice; the type of tone that left no room for objection.

Graham huddled behind his father, feeling his strong arms push him closer to his mother. "No matter what, stay behind me!" It was hard to hear him over the roaring of the wind and the terrifying wall of swirling black smoke.

In a moment of unanticipated fear and anxiety, Graham cried out in a loud squeal. Flashes of light shot all around the family, penetrating the huge wall of smoke.

"I'll die before you take them!"

More flashes of light streamed before Graham's eyes, followed by loud, blood curdling shrieks from the mom. Graham sat there unable to process what was going on. Without thinking, he simply reacted with more wailing as the entire forest was enveloped in blinding light. Graham's scream lasted for what seemed like an eternity, then nothing. Silence overtook the noise as darkness eclipsed the light. Graham's head began to swim. His little body began to shake until he fell on his side and went limp.

With a jolt of adrenaline, Graham sat straight up in his bed, snapping out of the nightmare. Big beads of sweat streamed down his face. In a split second before it all came crashing down, Graham noticed everything around him suspended in mid-air, as if all his belongings were being held up by invisible strings. The small metal night table with the cup of water, his treasured rubber ball, a picture frame, miscellaneous books and notepads, and even his footlocker full of clothes were all hanging like marionette puppets. He caught a quick glimpse of it all before it collapsed around him. With resounding thuds of his wooden footlocker, followed by the hollow ring of his cup hitting the wooden floor, Graham realized that once again his nightmare had caused this freakish, unexplainable reaction. This time, however, he had caused an actual earthquake.

All the kids were beginning to wake, looking around as they sat up like statues in their beds. The entire orphanage was shaking. A large crack formed in the floor, just under Graham's bed. The quake lasted for a few moments and then slowly dissipated. Mr. Kobble ran into the room to check on the children.

"Easy there, lads. It was just eh tremor. Ev'rything is alright now. We may feel a few aftershocks, but I believe the worst is behind us."

All the boys in the room began to squirm. This was the first time something like this had happened. Mr. Kobble quickly made his way around the beds checking on each boy individually. Seeing that Graham was covered in sweat, he became concerned. "Yer really shaken, Mr. Graham. Do ye need some water to calm the nerves?"

"Nn…no sir. I'm fine. I'm just not used to the building shaking like that. I'm fine. Really."

"Alright, lad. If yer sure."

Mr. Kobble gave Graham a few pats on the back, stood up and checked on the other children, and then made his way into the next room.

As Graham sat there, drops of sweat dripped off the end of his nose while his lungs gasped for air. He felt like he had just run a marathon. His lungs huffed and his head swirled with pain and confusion. His eyes darted back and forth over his scattered belongings. He held both sides of his head, trying to ease the pain with deep breaths to control his panicking lungs.

"Mom…Dad," Graham whispered in a quivering voice.

The pounding of his head echoed his throbbing heart. *What did I do?* A wave of guilt washed over him, crushing his spirit. He gritted his teeth, trying to keep his emotions at bay. *What did I do to you? I'm sorry. I am so sorry.*

With his head still pounding, Graham twisted his legs to the side of the bed and slowly put both feet on the ground. The scenes in his head were still reeling from the nightmare, and the earthquake still had him a bit disoriented. Graham pushed his knuckles down into the firm mattress, standing to his feet. His legs were a little shaky, but after taking another deep breath, he grabbed the rubber ball from the floor, and quietly made his way past the other beds to the window in the far corner of the room. Fortunately for him, the other boys in the room were mingling together, talking about the thrill of it all. This allowed Graham to retreat and be alone.

Graham's sorrow for the fate of his parents slowly began to morph into self-pity. Graham crossed his arms on top of the windowsill, and placed his chin on top of his arms. As he rolled the ball around mindlessly in his hand, he peered into the darkness of the storm clouds, letting out a small sigh. It was a cliché stormy night; the type of weather that mimicked the emotion he held inside. As rain began to pelt the window, Graham stared off beyond the cliffs to the small outline of the lake in the distance. He lived in a large building surrounded by people, yet, at this moment, he felt completely alone. Worse yet, he felt like a freak. He didn't want to push people away. To the contrary, he wanted just the opposite, but his dream was a constant reminder that when he let people get close, they got hurt. He could not let that happen. All he wanted to be was normal. The burden of his unexplainable secret was beginning to crush his soul after years of holding it all inside. He wondered if he would ever feel happy again.

Hopelessness began to overtake him until he was reminded of his chat with Ms. Winstone. In his mind, he heard the conversation play over and over. Graham could see the seriousness in Ms. Winstone's eyes.

"Whatever you are dreaming about, dear, you are looking for answers, not magic remedies. If you want help, all you need to do is ask."

Maybe it was time to reach out to someone, but not just anyone. It had to be Cavaness. There must be some truth to the rumors. If he couldn't help, then who could? It was a longshot, but it was one Graham had to take, however terrible the odds were. He lifted himself from the windowsill, and with it, his spirits. Hope was not something Graham was used to feeling. It was refreshing what a small dose of hope could do. Graham resolved himself to focus on the benefit of talking to Cavaness rather than to reflect on his problem. This gave him a warm feeling of contentment, which ran throughout his entire body. *I'm going to find a way to talk with you tomorrow, Cavaness. And when I do, maybe you can tell me what is happening to me and how to control it.*

Holding on to that thought like a lifeline, Graham crawled back under his covers and immediately drifted off into a heavy, dreamless sleep.

5

DINNER AND A GUEST

The following day flew by. Before they knew it, most of the afternoon had already come and gone, and dinner was being served. Graham and Damien sat at the first of three long tables that stretched out almost the entire length of the dining room. The meals here were never quite enough to fill you up; however, you also never went without one. Tonight, Graham pushed some mashed potatoes around a thin slice of beef and a little pile of green peas. He could not get the conversation with Ms. Winstone out of his head, especially her last remark. *'Those who reach out for help usually find it.'*

Damien looked over at Graham. "Heard you got a pretty good tongue lashing, amigo. You ok?"

Coming out from his daze, Graham looked at Damien. "Oh... yea. Don't worry about me. I don't really want to talk about it. Let's concentrate on tonight. Mr. Kobble will be roaming the halls after lights out, so we need to be careful as we sneak downstairs."

The two of them talked briefly about logistics, then scarfed down the remainder of their food. After dinner, all the children had to immediately go up to their rooms and clean up before lights out. Since Graham and Damien did not share a room, they parted ways at the entrance to their bedrooms with a mutual nod in anticipation of the night's events.

"When I see the headlights of our guest's car, I'll knock on the air vent screen. Got it?"

"Claro," Damien replied.

"What?" Graham said. "I don't know Spanish, dude. Speak English."

"*Claro* means that I understand. I know two languages Graham. You need to diversify. If I can learn your language, you can at least learn a few simple phrases in mine," said Damien, rolling his eyes.

"Whatever. Stay by the vent. I'll talk to you soon."

"Claro," Damien replied with a smirk on his face.

Graham smiled back, and then disappeared into his bedroom.

"LIGHTS OUT!" belched Mr. Kobble with his hands cupped around his mouth. "Sleep tight, y'ung lads. May yer dreams be as pleasant and refreshing as a Scottish spring."

This was his little saying every night. Though he was often abrupt and spoke without a filter, his goodnight wishes hinted at his tender heart for the young kids of Greenwood.

Graham lay silently, hardly able to keep still. The thought of finally getting some answers sent sparks through his nerves. Not wanting to wake his roommates, he just laid in bed facing the window and let his mind run free as he continued listening to the heavy footsteps of Mr. Kobble pacing up and down the hallway.

"I can set up a meeting with him if you like." Ms. Winstone's offer only fueled Graham's enthusiasm. As he tossed the small rubber ball up and down, Graham's mind continued to roam. He could barely hold back his excitement as he pictured

someone to help carry his burden. Someone else that could not only explain the levitating and the light, but also help him control the outbursts. It was all too much. The thoughts and questions continued to multiply in Graham's mind until his focus was thrown off by a bright flash of light from outside.

He's here! Graham mouthed as he got up from the bed.

Graham fell to his knees and crawled over to the nearest air vent. On the other side of the wall was Damien's cluster of kids. Not knowing if the other kids were asleep, Graham gave three light knocks on the metal vent cover. A few minutes passed and then he heard the faint thud of feet on the floor, followed by three knocks from the other side.

"Everyone asleep?" whispered Graham.

"Sí. I could hardly hear your knocks over the snoring," replied Damien.

"Good. The headlights of the car just came up the driveway a few minutes ago. We need to move fast. It's been about twenty minutes since Mr. Kobble gave his goodnight wishes. The coast should be clear."

"Ok. I will peek my head out first to see if the hallway is empty. If it is, I'll knock twice on your door."

"Got it."

Damien stood up and tiptoed across the room and grabbed hold of the antique doorknob. Before turning it, he took in a deep breath, shaking his head from side to side. "I hate drama," he muttered.

With a few creaks, a sliver of light appeared from the hallway. Damien poked his head out, squinting and letting his eyes adjust before proceeding. The hallway was empty. Damien swiftly made his way to the entrance of Graham's room and rapped twice on the door. Within seconds, Graham emerged with the same tilt of the head and blinking of the eyes.

"Great day, that's bright!" Graham whispered.

Once they had both got used to the light, they treaded as lightly as they could down the hall. Greenwood was an old building, and the floors loved to creak and crack, even with the lightest of loads. Arriving at the staircase, they turned and looked at each other in eager anticipation.

Keeping all their weight on their toes, they dashed down the stairs, trying to displace their bodyweight by holding on the handrail. Now nearing the ground level, they gave a quick glance to the left, then to the right at the bottom of the staircase. Satisfied with the vacant halls, they bolted down the final stretch of hallway to the safety of the parlor room. Gasping for breath, they both sat in the darkness, trying to keep their panting to a minimum as they let their heightened pulses calm down to a normal pace.

Graham looked at Damien with a wide grin on his face. "We made it! Man, what a thrill, huh!"

Damien countered Graham's grin with a scowl. "I hate thrills."

Ms. Winstone and her guest had already exchanged pleasantries by the time Graham and Damien were able to listen in. Graham leaned through the doorway so that the murmurs of Ms. Winstone's conversation became recognizable words.

"How much longer do you have in town, Chase?"

"I haven't quite decided when I will leave. I suppose in the next three or four days. I have a few more things to do at Portfield Manor, and then I will make my way back to Glendale."

"What on earth are you doing at Portfield Manor? Wasn't that place condemned after the fire all those years ago?" asked Ms. Winstone.

"*Was* condemned, Ms. Winstone. Not *currently* condemned. I have been hired as the Groundskeeper of Portfield Manor. It is not the most elegant of jobs, but it pays the bills. The Manor was built shortly after Greenwood and has remained in the Alexander family since its completion. It has not served a purpose for the community since the early 1900's, but I guess it holds a certain sentimental value, so the family wants it kept up."

"Chase, you are no longer living here. Please, call me Olivia."

"Yes, Ms.... um, Olivia," he said with a smile.

"Some say that the place is haunted, you know," said Ms. Winstone. She leaned in toward Chase like a storyteller at a campfire. "The children here tell tales of that place almost every night. They say it is villainous. Of course, I do not believe in such nonsense..." she trailed off, waiting for a reaction. After a moment of silence, she smiled. "But there is no denying the reputation that place has."

Damien looked at Graham. "Ms. Winstone actually smiled. She never smiles. I wonder if it hurt using those new muscles?"

Graham chuckled. *Like a unicorn.*

They both snickered as they turned their attention back to the conversation at hand.

Chase was amused and intrigued by the stories, though of course he already knew about them. They were the same ones he and his friends told while he was a resident here. Enjoying the nostalgia, he decided to just keep quiet and let her continue.

"All sorts of emotions come with the changing of seasons, especially as the chill fills the autumn air. The leaves fall from the trees and the moon shines bright, casting mischievous shadows. It's a breeding ground for spooky stories and heightened imaginations." She leaned in conspiratorially. "The children tell stories of unexplained light coming from the house, with shadowy figures moving throughout the abandoned building at the top of the hill. Even I can admit that strange noises wake me up every so often, and I find it a bit strange to see the trees bending and shaking all around that place as if someone or some*thing* is tromping through the forest."

"I assure you, Ms. Winsto… er, Olivia, that I would remember crossing paths with a ghost or goblin." Chase grinned. "The only thing to fear there is the loneliness of a large, empty house."

"Well, that is reassuring, Chase. It suits you to manage a home, you know. You always did have such a keen eye for detail and a strong ability to handle situations. Speaking of situations… have you had any more relapses with the nightmares?"

Graham's eyes widened in excitement. He lunged forward, almost to the point of falling into the room. He had to be sure he did not miss a single word. Damien looked over to see the expression on Graham's face.

"You ok, amigo? You look like you have seen a ghost."

"Shhhhhhh," replied Graham. He waved his hand dismissively at Damien, trying to focus on Chase's reply.

"I'm doing just fine. Cavaness has helped me immensely. It was hard at first, but over time, I learned why I was having them in the first place. Once I knew that, I was able to cope. I haven't had one in over five years now."

Olivia stood up and placed her hand on Chase's shoulder. "That is lovely, dear. Just wonderful. I am glad to hear it. You gave us all quite a scare over the years with the screams and cold sweats." She walked past Chase, placing her cup of tea on the marble countertop to the left of the fireplace. Once placed, she made her way to the huge portrait over the mantel.

Chase watched Ms. Winstone as she placed the cup down and walked over to examine the portrait of Mr. Alexander. The cup of tea and matching saucer teetered on the edge of the countertop. He watched the swaying cup as gravity overtook it. The tea fell over the edge and began to spill.

It must have been at least fifteen paces from where Chase was sitting to where the teacup was falling, but in a single blurred motion, Chase ran over to catch the cup, placed it back on the countertop, and returned to his seat before the next word could come out of her mouth.

"Oh, my!" said Ms. Winstone, turning. The force of Chase's rapid movement caused a breeze to run through the room. "There's a draft in here. Did you feel that?"

"No, ma'am. Not a thing."

Graham and Damien stared at Chase with wide eyes and wider mouths.

"Impossible," said Graham. "I hardly saw him move, but I know he did. No one can move *that* fast."

"*Este es loco!* How did he do that?" replied Damien.

He's like me, Graham said to himself. *The nightmare, the unexplained ability. I have to talk to him!* Graham stood up from his kneeling position and began to walk into the commons. "I've got to talk to him right now."

Damien reached for Graham. "*Eres loco?* Get back over here! You are going to get us caught!" Despite his best effort, Graham was out of reach.

While still in mid-conversation, Chase twisted his head toward Graham's direction as if he had heard their conversation. Graham froze. Within a millisecond, he saw the same blurred movement and the door slam shut in front of him.

"What on earth was that?" said Ms. Winstone, startled by the sudden noise.

"I don't know," Chase spread his hands. "The door back there slammed shut. I suppose the draft you mentioned earlier created a cross breeze through here and caught the door."

"Strange. Very strange. Are you sure? We have had a few incidents with children sleepwalking during the night. I'd better go check." Ms. Winstone left the portrait and walked over toward the parlor room door.

The vision of laundry duty for the next ten years ran through Graham's mind. They looked at each other with their hearts pounding in their chests. Their guts sank and they were both paralyzed with fear.

"We are sure to get caught this time," whispered Damien.

As Ms. Winstone's hand grasped the doorknob, Chase intervened.

"It was nothing. I happened to see it slam shut from the corner of my eye. I am confident it was just the wind."

Chase stood up. "I think I'd better call it a night. Thank you very much for the tea and conversation. It is always good to see you, Ms. Winstone. Thank you for your dedicated service to both myself and to the children of Greenwood. This place is one of the few beacons of light here in Portfield."

"How very nice of you to say. Thank you, Chase. Be safe in that house. Oh, and please give my best wishes to Cavaness when you see him at Wellington tomorrow."

"Yes, ma'am. I'll be sure to pass along the message over lunch."

Ms. Winstone and Chase both continued into the hallway until they disappeared around the corner toward the front door.

Graham and Damien took this as their chance to get back upstairs. They ran into the hallway and up the stairs, being careful to listen for any other footsteps along the way. They quickly made it back to the entrance of Graham's section.

"I'm going to Wellington tomorrow, even if it means I have to do laundry for the rest of my life," said Graham.

"I am coming with you," replied Damien. "After what I saw tonight, there is no way I am missing out on this, even if it means more drama."

"Tomorrow then," said Graham.

"Tomorrow."

An Invitation

Graham and Damien stood at the edge of the forest. Graham gently punched Damien's shoulder.

"You ready, amigo?"

Damien looked back at Graham. "From what I saw last night, I want to see this guy just as bad as you do."

"Okay then. Let's get a move on."

The two set off into the woods. They jogged through the forest, ducking under branches, hopping over logs and zig-zagging through the foliage.

"I can see why you come out here. It is amazing!" said Damien.

Twenty minutes passed before they came to the huge stone arch. Damien stood in its massive shadow, his mouth open in awe.

"What in the world is that?"

"I'm not sure, exactly. It looks like the remains of some sort of building. I don't know how long it's been here, but it looks ancient. If I'm not in Wellington, I'm here."

Damien walked over to the arch, taking in the beauty of the structure. It stood roughly twenty feet tall with big stones stacked in random order. Lush green moss hung over it like a shawl, and the sunlight gave it a lifelike glow.

"Who in the world would have built this thing in the middle of the woods like this?" asked Damien.

"I dunno. Someone who wanted to have it to themselves, I guess," replied Graham.

Graham punched Damien's shoulder again. "Better get a move on. We don't have long. This Chase guy said they would be meeting during lunch. I hope we haven't missed him."

The two picked up their pace and made their way past more trees, down a bank, around a large cluster of rocks and over a small creek. Every so often Damien would notice a small ragged piece of white cloth tied to a tree branch as they passed by. Damien looked inquisitively at the tattered strips of cloth, wondering if they were how Graham first learned how to navigate the forest. After sidestepping a large cluster of rhododendron bushes, they found themselves on the edge of Wellington.

Standing at the rear of Building 14, Graham began to give the layout of the market to Damien. Pointing to the left, he began with Ms. McKay's stand, and then worked his way down the line. Pointing slightly to the right, he said, "That is where we are going to start. Collin's Café. There are only four places to eat here, and Collin's is the most popular."

Graham took hold of a metal rung and told Damien to follow. "Usually I go all the way to the top for a good view, but we need to be able to get down fast. Let's go to the first story balcony."

As they climbed the creaky ladder and stepped out onto the balcony, Damien ran his hand over one of the gargoyles.

"Wow. These look so real."

"Come on! We don't have time to look at those," Graham said, even as he remembered how enthralled he was the first time he had seen the lifelike statues.

Graham pointed across the street to the patio of Collin's Café.

"Start looking over there. You know what Chase looks like. The only description I have of Cavaness is that he's very big with a black goatee." Pulling his binoculars from his back pocket, Graham continued. "I will check down here at O'Mally's."

The two looked intently through the crowd of people eating lunch. Most of them were nearly finished and were beginning to stroll up and down the cobblestone road to let their food settle.

"Come on, come on, come ON!" Graham mumbled. "You've got to be around here somewhere."

"Graham, look!" said Damien. A tall, thin man in a long coat was walking into the café. "That looks like Chase!"

It was hard to see his face with all the umbrellas set up in the patio.

"Maybe," said Graham. "Let's see if we can catch his face as he walks out."

The two waited in anticipation as they watched the man walk through the line, order a drink, and make his way out to the patio. He was just at the edge of the table, ready to take a seat. Graham focused intently on the man through his binoculars. As he sat, his face was finally revealed.

"Ahhhhh! He has got to be at least 40 years old! COME ON! WHERE ARE YOU?" Graham shouted in frustration.

"*Calmate.* You are going to give us away. I want to see this guy, too, but you have got to cool the engines a little."

"Cool the jets," Graham replied.

"What?"

"The saying is cool your jets, not cool your engines."

"Whatever. I have never seen you like this before. What's with you?"

Graham's grip on the binoculars almost cracked the lenses. He could feel the blood pooling in his cheeks as his anger grew. *I cannot miss you this time.* He felt Damien's gaze bore into him, knowing he was waiting for an answer. Graham did not want to answer his question, but he knew

Damien was hard-headed enough to get it out of him. More importantly, he realized that if he did not calm down, he might accidentally hurt Damien with his powers. Taking a quick breath to relax, he put the binoculars down and faced his friend.

"Fine. I've been having nightmares. I've had them for years now, and after hearing Chase talk about his nightmares last night, this is the only shot I have to get some answers. Special powers or not, if Cavaness helped Chase with his dreams, then maybe he can do the same for me."

Damien just stared at Graham. "Why didn't you ever tell me? We all got stuff we deal with, amigo. We are orphans. We could write books."

"You wouldn't believe me even if you wanted to," said Graham with a huff.

Graham thought of his parents being attacked by the black smoke. He could hear the yelling and screams and see the intense light flash around them, before darkness closed in. *I killed them.* Just then, something caught Graham's eye. He peered through his binoculars to look more closely at the man standing in the entrance of the alley between Collin's Café and the jewelry store. He was leaning against the building with his legs crossed and, though the shadows concealed his face, it was obvious that he was looking right at Graham. Graham met the man's stare and suddenly felt like a tiny bird precariously perched in his nest.

Dropping the binoculars, Graham immediately darted toward the ladder.

"Hey, where are you going?" yelled Damien.

Graham made no effort to reply. He just continued down the stairs, assuming Damien would follow. Damien chased after Graham, slinging his legs over the ledge to the first rung of the ladder.

"Wait up, man!"

Graham did not wait. His adrenaline wouldn't let him. Not bothering to look for oncoming traffic, Graham ran out into the middle of the street as screeching tires and loud blasts of car horns filled the air.

"HEY! Watch out, kid! Ya wanna get killed or something?" yelled a driver.

Graham fell back onto the uneven cobblestone road. Damien rushed out and took him by the arm to pull him back onto his feet.

"Gotcha. *Vamos.*" The two ran up to the edge of the patio and frantically searched the alley, but no one was there. The man was gone.

"What did you see?" asked Damien. "I know you want to find this guy, but you've got to think a little. You almost got flattened."

"I saw Cavaness! It had to have been him. He was standing right there! Damien, he was looking right at us."

"I didn't see anyone. Are you sure you saw someone there?"

"Why would I make up something like that? He was right there, Damien. Right there!"

Graham pointed to the vacant alleyway. Crowds of people gathered and stared at the two kids, still shocked that one of them had nearly been run over. Graham paid no attention to the people on the patio, nor the people walking past. He was focused on one thing and one thing only.

Cavaness.

The two boys desperately searched for any sign of the man. Graham ran down the street a little way past the café, as Damien ran the opposite way also looking for anyone who matched the description. Graham's head was swiveling so much that he was beginning to feel nauseated. He decided to go back to Damien and regroup.

Even as Graham walked back toward the café, he continued to glance behind him, just in case he missed something. He took a few more steps until he hit something hard and fell to the ground. Looking up at the object he had just run into, he saw a man in a long, tweed jacket staring at him. Graham blushed in embarrassment. He mumbled under his breath as a large hand reached out toward him.

"Easy there, little man. Are you alright? Here, let me lend you a hand." The stranger continued to hold out his hand, while keeping his other hand on top of his walking cane.

Graham was hesitant to take the stranger's brawny hand, but reluctantly accepted. With a quick jerk, the man pulled Graham to his feet.

"Cavaness?" Graham asked with an unsteady voice.

The man smiled. "Goodness, no. I am much too small to be Cavaness," he chuckled. "My name is Silas."

Graham looked him over. *Long coat, walking cane…Wait a minute, is this the guy from…?*

"You were in the field the other day, weren't you?"

The stranger brushed his hand off against his jacket. He leaned in close enough that only Graham could hear what he was about to say. "Admittedly, yes. I didn't mean to come off as rude, but one cannot help but stare at a boy that creates small quakes, surrounded by light and hovering objects."

Graham's heart leaped into his throat. He must have looked like a fool, staring at Silas like a deer in headlights.

Silas kept his warm smile. He didn't appear alarmed at all by what he had seen. To the contrary, he actually seemed accustomed to it. Maybe he knew something, or maybe it was just his sophisticated tone that made him seem so nonchalant.

"You know, fits of anger coupled with boundless curiosity can produce a whole host of odd, unexplainable reactions."

"How do you know that I'm angry, or that I have questions?"

"My dear boy, everyone has questions. I have never met a person yet who had it all together. Trust me, as a professor of psychology, I have seen it all. Well, almost." The professor smiled. "I haven't yet seen such a young person with your type of, how should I say… unique circumstances. As for the anger? Well… the slamming of your fist is a good indicator. I cannot claim to know your specific circumstances, however, I can help with the other, more unexplainable problems. You are not the only one out there who can create these unknown forces and surges. I know because I have worked with others much like you."

Graham was speechless. *Someone knows. This Silas guy knows, but he's not afraid. Maybe he can help. He seems kind enough, but he doesn't know about my parents. If he were to find out what I've done–*

Graham felt Damien's hand land on his shoulder.

"*Eres bien?*" Damien kept his hand on Graham's shoulder for a few moments as he looked around for anyone who looked like Cavaness, completely oblivious to the man speaking to Graham. Suddenly, Damien's grip tightened until it felt like a vise around Graham's shoulder.

Graham winced. "Oww. I'm fine. No need to break it off. What's with you?"

Graham looked over at Damien and saw the excitement his face.

"Damien. Hey, Damien!"

Graham waved his hand in front of Damien's face to get his attention. Damien didn't blink; he just raised his hand and pointed. Graham quickly looked in the direction Damien was pointing and saw a tall, thin boy sitting at the last table at the edge of the patio. He was hunched over with arms crossed. His elbows were resting on the table and his head was tilted, looking at them. It was hard to see his face which was partially hidden by the hood of his jacket, but they both recognized him immediately.

"Chase," Graham whispered. "CHASE!"

He looked quickly back around to address Silas, but the man was gone. He wanted to continue talking to Silas, but Chase was right there in front of them. Graham ripped from Damien's grip and began running toward him.

"Hey, Chase! I've been looking for you!"

Graham felt as though a huge weight had been lifted. With his heart pounding, he began waving his hands in a desperate attempt to get Chase's attention.

"You don't know who I am, but– Hey! Where are you going? STOP! I just want to talk!"

Graham and Damien bolted down the road, but Chase was faster. He leapt from his chair like a cat, knocking it to the ground as he took off down the street.

"Oh, no you don't!" Graham yelled.

Chase continued to run. As he approached a small wall, he placed his hands on top of it and tucked his knees underneath him, clearing it with minimal effort. Now close to another store, he took a few more strides and jumped, placing one foot on the front of the building. Then, as if using the building as a launching pad, he propelled himself to the adjacent wall, grabbing the top edge. He pulled himself to the top and stood up, looking back at Graham and Damien tauntingly.

"HEY! I JUST WANT TO TALK!" yelled Graham. Before he could continue, Chase jumped from the wall to the roof of the next store and continued running. "Come on, Damien! We have to chase him from down here."

As a soccer athlete, Damien blew past Graham with ease. "You are the one who is going to have to keep up, amigo."

The two continued down the street, keeping their eyes locked on Chase as he ran along the top of the buildings, jumping from roof to roof. Chase took a sharp left toward an alley, with the boys in pursuit. He jumped from the rooftop down to a smaller roof covering the back door of the building. With a single pounce, he leapt from the small roof down to the cobblestone road in front of Damien, letting his momentum take him into a forward roll. Then he was right back onto his feet, not missing a single stride.

"Is this guy part cat or something?!" Damien asked.

"I dunno," replied Graham, straining to speak through his labored breathing.

Glad to see Chase back on their level, they picked up their pace. A small black railing stood at the end of the alley. Chase placed his hands on the top and effortlessly swung both legs over. Fifteen paces later, both Damien and Graham made their way over the railing, but a little less gracefully.

After taking a right behind the next building, Damien and Graham searched for any sign of Chase, but he was gone.

"CHASE!" yelled Graham.

"Why are you running, man? We just want to talk to you!" Damien echoed.

After yelling Chase's name a few more times, they both hunched over with their hands on their knees, panting as if they had just finished a marathon. Big beads of sweat dripped from their foreheads as their chests heaved in and out.

"Surely that little sprint didn't get the best of you two."

Graham and Damien jerked their heads up and saw Chase three stories up, leaning over the railing of the fire escape platform with his arms crossed. His hood still hung over his head, but this time they could see the grin on his face.

"Damien, I thought you were supposed to be the star athlete." In a blur of motion, he hurtled down all three stories and stopped right in front of Graham.

"And Graham. I've been waiting to meet you for some time now."

Graham stared at Chase, scrunching his brow and tilting his head slightly to the side.

"How do you know our names?"

With a serious expression, Chase met Graham's gaze. "I know pretty much everything about you, Graham. I've watched you sit on your perch at Wellington every Saturday. I know how you sneak around Greenwood listening in on conversations that don't concern you, and I know you carry struggles which you keep buried deep down inside."

Graham was stunned.

Suddenly, Chase slapped Graham on the back and chuckled, breaking the tension.

"Lighten up, man. Ms. Winstone told me about you."

Looking over at Damien, Chase said, "*Y tú, mi amigo.*"

Relief washed over Graham like a wave.

"Thought I was a loon for a second there, didn't ya?" said Chase.

Graham was relieved, but still unsure how to respond. "Yeah, you had me going for a second."

Realizing that this was his chance to finally ask Chase some questions, to finally get some answers– Graham opened his mouth to speak, but was cut off by Damien.

"Hey, why did you run from us? Why make us chase you all the way down here?"

"Yeah, that was a bit odd, wasn't it? I guess I needed to stretch my legs, although I've gotta say, it was very hard to move that slow."

"SLOW? I could barely keep up!" said Damien, still panting.

"I may have seemed fast to you, but for me, that was a snail's pace. The real reason, I suppose, is that I needed to get you away from the crowd so I could talk to you. It's hard to have a conversation when everyone is staring at the kid who almost became roadkill."

Chase laughed again as Graham's cheeks turned red.

"Yeah, well, not everyone is a Johnny McSpeed-ster like you," Graham replied.

"Touché," Chase said with a nod of the head. "I know you're searching for something. I hate to disappoint, as I'm clearly not Cavaness, but I can take you to him, if you like."

Graham almost fell over with excitement. "Really?"

The hope emanating from Graham was palpable.

"Really, really," replied Chase. "Maybe you can even get some help with those nightmares of yours."

"How'd you kn…"

"Ms. Winstone. I think we had already had that conversation before the two of you crept into the parlor room last night. You are not alone on that one. You know, we three have one thing in common. We are orphans with screwed up pasts. Sometimes those things, those vague or horrible memories we tried to bury, force themselves to the surface."

"No kidding," said Graham.

"I don't know what you guys are talking about. I don't have any crazy dreams," said Damien.

"Well, crazy dreams or not, I'm sure there are more questions lingering in your head."

"Yeah, like how you move so fast. You're like a blur when you run," said Damien.

"All in due time. Like a good story, you need to hear it from the beginning," said Chase. "As I'm sure you overheard, I am the caretaker of Portfield Manor. You know, the place people think is haunted."

Graham and Damien leaned in closer to Chase as they listened.

"There are others who live there, but they are not ghosts and ghouls."

"Then who are they?" asked Damien.

Graham nudged Damien with his elbow. "Let him finish."

"Let me put it this way. There are two types of people in this world: those who learn and accept who they truly are, and those who choose to remain in ignorance. I know that sounds a bit ridiculous right now, but if you choose to accept my invitation, then you will find out how true that statement is."

"What invitation?" Graham asked.

"An invitation to find out who you really are," said Chase. "Every so often, we have an invitation for people like you who we see as *unique*."

"You mean broken," said Graham, not sure if he liked the way this conversation was going.

"Define it how you want, Graham, but I mean unique more in terms of being *set apart* than I do *cast aside*. You are not broken. You just can't yet explain what is happening inside. Regardless of the definition, it is your choice. I hate to be vague and cryptic, but unfortunately, I must. If you two choose to accept, then we will be at Portfield Manor tomorrow night at 3 am."

Because they were behind the final building of Wellington, Chase could easily point down the road to a clearing in the trees.

"Portfield Manor is a few miles from here. Since you are a pro at navigating the woods between here and Greenwood, I have faith that you will be able to make it to the Manor on time. You want answers? You will find them there."

With that said, Chase ran off down the road in a blur, leaving Graham and Damien in a wake of dust.

"Well, that was dramatic," said Damien. "What do you think? It sounds like a hoax to me. And why 3 in the morning? What the heck?"

"Maybe, but if this is my chance, then I'm taking it. You do what you want," replied Graham. "That is, if we make it back to Greenwood without being questioned about our afternoon. Ms. Winstone has already told me not to come back here. If she knows I've disobeyed her, I may not live to make it to Portfield Manor."

Graham and Damien turned around and began to walk back toward Building 14.

They both breathed a sigh of relief when they arrived back at Greenwood and saw that most of the kids were still out on the playing fields.

"I think we're good," said Graham. Just then, the gongs of the grandfather clocks could be heard from inside, instructing the kids to come back for study time before dinner.

"Wow, we couldn't have timed that any better," said Damien.

High up on the 3rd floor, Ms. Winstone stood at the window with a cup of tea in her hand, bringing it to her lips for a sip as she watched Graham and Damien emerge from the woods, walking over to mingle in with the other children.

THE PATHWAY TO FREEDOM

Disregarding all pleasantries, Ms. Winstone looked sternly into Graham's eyes. Whatever was on her mind immediately escaped her mouth like a bird from an open cage.

"I thought I told you not to go back into the woods. Not only did you directly disobey me, but you took Damien with you."

Without hesitation, Damien spoke.

"Graham was showing me his favorite places there. I asked him to. He told me about them yesterday, and I practically begged him to let me go see it. Please don't blame him. It was my idea, Ms. Winstone."

Ms. Winstone considered him for a moment. The boys stole a quick look at each other, hoping this would be the end of it. Studying the boys' faces, and not missing the glance they had shared, Ms. Winstone tried to decipher truth from fiction. After a moment's pause, she decided another question was more important.

"If you were so keen on seeing the woods, then what of Wellington? Did Graham show you that as well?"

Damien swallowed hard. He did not want to say it, but he

knew the truth would eventually come out.

"Yes, ma'am."

"Damien, I have no doubt that you hold a certain power of persuasion over Mr. Dawson, but my expectation was clear. Wellington is a dangerous place, especially for those who do not seem to fit in. Wellington was, and still is," she glanced at Graham, "off limits."

Damien did not know what to say. He wanted to protect Graham from any possible punishment, but Ms. Winstone's decisions were usually set in stone.

Trying to find a balance of justice and mercy, Ms. Winstone looked at Graham. She wanted to show compassion, but if she gave any ground now, the news of her leniency would soon get around to the other children.

"One week of revoked recess. You are to stay in your room or in a study hall. You eat, you study, and you sleep. Am I clear?"

"Yes, ma'am."

"Damien, since you were mostly unaware of our previous conversations, you are off the hook this time. However, I expect you to use some common sense every now and again. You should know better than to wander off into the woods and down to Wellington."

She kept a strict eye on them both.

"Now the expectation is set," Ms. Winstone added with a stern stare and a tone of finality.

The two boys sat as still as statues. Nothing was worse than a rebuke from Ms. Winstone. It was as though she addressed your very soul.

"I shall also have Mr. Kobble keep a close eye on you two once you return to recess. No more ventures into the woods… or anywhere beyond them for that matter. Now, go get ready for dinner."

The boys stood up from their chairs in unison.

"Yes, ma'am. Thank you, Ms. Winstone."

"You know I care for you both– very deeply, indeed.

Young minds are always searching for adventure and purpose in this world, especially when they feel they have none in their seemingly mundane, day to day activities. Whatever you two are really in search of, you can find it in the library, not in Wellington."

"Yes, ma'am," they replied.

At that, Graham opened the door and closed it behind them. As they walked down the hallway and up the stairs to their rooms, he could not get over the lump in his stomach. He did not like the chastisement from Ms. Winstone, nor did he enjoy the thought of deliberate insubordination, but he knew what they had to do. They had to make it to the meeting tonight, no matter what the cost.

Graham broke the silence first.

"If we really get the chance to meet Cavaness tonight, it'll be worth the loss of a month's recess. A year's recess, even. I don't care how much trouble I get in."

Graham playfully punched Damien's arm as they continued walking.

"Thanks for having my back. You didn't have to do that."

"What are friends for, right? You've saved my tail more times than I can count. I'm glad I could finally return the favor."

Damien held his fist out in front of Graham. Graham smiled, bumping it with his own. Turning the corner, they arrived at their rooms.

"See you in a few minutes," said Graham.

"*Hasta luego.*"

As everyone was cleaning up for dinner, Graham decided to roam the halls in search of the door that would lead them to freedom. Room by room, he looked along the back wall for any exterior doors, and room after room he became increasingly frustrated. So far, he could only locate five doors: the kitchen, the front door, the parlor door, and two doors at the end of each wing. With only a few options left, the next room he came to was the library.

So, this is where I'll find my life's answers, huh? I doubt that.

Amidst his doubt, Graham pushed open the door to have a look around. The library was a beautiful room. Graham had only been in here a handful of times after his spat with a fellow orphan years ago. The memory brought unwanted emotions to mind, though in his pursuit of quiet, solitary places, this would actually fit the bill quite nicely. Knowing everyone was preparing for dinner, he allowed himself to be enveloped by the solace of the large empty room.

Reading was never his first activity of choice these days, so it had been at least two or three months since Graham had visited the library. He had forgotten how cozy it was. The craftsmen had definitely spent more time in this room than most of the others. The two adjacent side walls were mostly covered with large bookshelves that reached from the floor to the top of the twelve-foot plaster ceiling. The exterior wall was all windows. In the middle of the room, there were two massive study desks stretching over fifteen feet long and six feet wide. The countertop extending beyond the wooden base enough for the reader to fit their legs underneath. Eight chairs were stationed at the desk with eight lamps on the countertop, one in front of each chair.

Looking to the outside wall, Graham searched for an exterior door, but was again disappointed when all he could see were large portrait style windows that reached from floor to ceiling. As the anger within him grew, he turned away from the desks to face the endless rows of shelves that housed countless books. Like a slow boil, however, his disappointment dissolved into curiosity as he paced back and forth, staring at the columns of books.

Graham ran his fingers along the spines, reading the titles as he went. *American History, From Darkness to Light, The Origin of*

Man, The Unseen War, and then a volume of matching history books, which filled the remaining space on the row.

He contemplated Ms. Winstone's statement about finding life's answers in here. No doubt these books answered many questions, but Graham found it hard to believe that any one of these books would hold the resolution to his nightmares that caused objects around him to hover off the ground. No, only two people on earth held that knowledge, and so far, Graham could not find a way to get to either of them.

Plopping down on his butt, Graham sat with his back to the tall bookshelf, so that he was facing one of the large desks in the middle of the room. He reached into his sweatshirt pocket and took out his treasured ball. With a heavy sigh, he began to rhythmically bounce it from the floor, to the panels of the desk, and then back to his hand. Floor. Desk. Hand. Floor. Desk. Hand. The repetition was therapeutic. His mind began to clear with each bounce of the ball. His eyes followed the path to and from his hand as he allowed his mind to trail off.

Before he knew it, he had made the tosses into a game. He found himself concentrating on different sections of the desk to see if he could hit his mark. First, he aimed at the small vertical piece of trim. Floor. Trim. Hand. He then aimed for the same piece of trim to the right. Floor. Trim. Hand.

Nailed it.

Scooting over to the next section of flat space between the vertical strips of wood, Graham aimed dead center. Floor. Desk. Floor. Floor. Floor. As the ball struck the wood, it made an odd, hollow thud, losing its velocity. Instead of returning to him, it fell from the wall and trailed off on the floor. Graham stared inquisitively at the wall and wondered at the sudden change in bouncing pattern. He swung his legs around so that he was on all fours and crawled toward the large desk. Pinning the ball to the ground, he closed his fingers around it and placed it back into the front pocket of his sweatshirt.

As Graham made it to the panel of the desk, he ran his

hand up and down the trim. It didn't seem any different than the rest. He shifted to his left and knocked a couple of times in the center of the square panel encapsulated by the trim.

Solid.

Shifting back to the panel in question, Graham reached up and knocked four times. A much different sound came from this panel, as though it was attached to air. Graham's pulse quickened. He quickly shifted to his right to knock on the adjacent square. Solid as a rock. Sliding to his left again, Graham stared at the panel, wondering why it sounded so different. Could this be some sort of door? He got up and went to the side of the desk.

Six feet is plenty of room for a secret door.

Scurrying back to the square, he grabbed the trim with his fingertips and tried to pull it open. After tugging at the vertical strips without success, he tried the horizontal pieces. Straining as hard as he could without ripping his fingernails off, he grunted and jerked, but the thing would not budge.

"Come on, ya stupid door. Just open!"

Tug. Tug. Tug. More grunting. More pulling. Nothing. He plopped back on the floor and massaged his fingers. Frustrated, he crossed his legs Indian style in front of the hollow panel, and with a heavy thud, slammed his forehead into it.

Click.

Graham heard a faint metallic noise from behind the door. As he raised his head from the panel, the door hinged open slightly, confirming his suspicion. He sat for a moment with his mouth wide open. Finally, he stretched his hand out and felt a small gust of air blow from the small passageway. He cracked the door open a little more, and grabbed the lip of the trim, which overlapped the middle section of the panel by about an inch, so that no seam could be seen. The hinges on the other side of the door were masterfully inset into the wood, so no trace of a door could be detected.

With the door now completely open, Graham noticed that

the left side of the small wooden staircase was completely covered in small lines someone had carved into the wall. The lines were in clusters of five. Four vertical lines and one diagonal line running through the other four. Someone had been counting. There had to be thousands of these marks covering the wall. The marks went from the top of each step to the ceiling as you descended the stairs.

It was then that Graham remembered the history lessons from class. Greenwood had been part of the Underground Railroad. What once had been an escape for thousands of slaves would now serve as the path to Graham's freedom. What a wonderful slice of irony. Two slices of irony, actually. Remembering Ms. Winstone's remark about finding answers in the library, Graham could not help but smile to himself.

Thanks, Ms. Winstone. You were right after all.

Beginning from the left side, Graham counted the number of sections of the desk and made note of which one housed the hidden door. He pushed the door shut and heard another *'click'* letting him know that it was latched again. He then stood up and made his way back to the library door. Back in the hallway, Graham began searching for Damien. He had walked back toward the commons and turned the corner when he saw Damien coming out of the parlor room.

Now running, Graham almost tackled Damien in his excitement.

"Whoa there, chief! This isn't the NFL. You almost knocked me down," said Damien as he began to give his report. "I have been up and down these halls. There are no doors that go outside, except the front door, the doors at the end of each wing, the kitchen door and the parlor door."

Grabbing Damien by both shoulders, Graham looked at his friend with wide eyes.

"You are not going to believe what I just found."

At The Stroke Of Midnight

"*Im-pos-eee-ble!* Inside the big desks? Do you know where it leads?" asked Damien.

"No. I didn't have time to go through the tunnel to see where it came out, but it has to lead somewhere, right? I saw thousands of tick marks on the wall. This had to be a station for the Underground Railroad. From what I remember, there were many secret passages built to help the slaves escape from the south up here to the north in order to get a fresh start. I'm pretty sure it didn't end with staying in a tunnel underneath Greenwood. If it doesn't lead anywhere, then we can just come back up. What's there to lose?"

Damien shrugged. "Nothing, I guess. So what next? Do we just wait until midnight and then sneak out?"

"Yeah, taking into account the time it takes to get out of here, walk to Wellington, and go the extra few miles to Portfield Manor, we'll need to leave our rooms around midnight, assuming the underground path isn't too long. The most important thing is that we get to the meeting and back without anyone knowing that we're gone. With this plan, no one will be able to see us leave or come back. It's perfect!"

Dinner flew by as the anticipation of the night's events built up inside Graham. He lay in bed fully clothed as he counted the chimes of the clock downstairs. He tossed his ball up and down to the rhythm and counted eleven dings. One more hour until game time. All of this sneaking around and scheming had started to fray his nerves.

The satisfaction of knowing that answers were within reach excited him, but there was something else there; another excitement that Graham could not pinpoint. It could be the thought of an adventure, sure, but after wrestling with this new and unfamiliar emotion, he finally decided that it must be what others described as *purpose*. He really believed that these answers could lead to something more; a life dedicated to something more than merely existing. Yes, that must be what was making his heart pound and flutter.

'More like set apart than cast aside.' That's what Chase had said.

What does that even mean? Graham thought. *Both seem equally as bad to me.* Tossing and turning with thoughts running through his mind like wild animals, it seemed like only a few minutes had passed when he heard the next series of chimes from the clock. Ding. Ding… Twelve chimes.

Game time.

9

PORTFIELD MANOR

Just as they had talked about before dinner, Graham made his way over to the duct and gave three knocks. Without hesitation, three knocks echoed from the other side. Damien was ready. Graham creaked open the door to the hallway and gave a quick glance both ways before stepping out. It was very dark, with only a few small nightlights spaced out every eight feet or so, illuminating their path.

The boys tiptoed down the hallway until they made their way to the staircase. They reached the bottom of the stairs without interruption, and turned the corner to the library.

Damien breathed a sigh of relief. "It is much easier to do this in the middle of the night."

"No doubt," Graham replied.

A few creaks and cracks of the floorboards later, they finally made it to the entrance of the library. They both made it inside and quietly closed the door behind them. Graham led the way to the rear of the desk, where he had been just a few hours before. Counting the squares, Graham settled his right hand on the fifth section. "This one. This is the door." Using his hand this time, Graham pushed against the hidden door until he heard the click. The door moved a few inches letting a small gust waft in Damien's face.

"*Asombroso!* This is the coolest thing I have ever seen!"

Reaching into his pocket, Graham pulled out a small plastic flashlight he had received as a gift years ago. It was a child's toy, but since they did not get gifts often, Graham had taken good care of it. He pushed the little black switch up and the hidden staircase flooded with light. The stairs were steep and covered with cobwebs. Pointing his light to the left wall, he illuminated the tick marks on the wall.

"See, I told ya."

"Wow. These were made by slaves all those years ago?"

"Yeah, I guess. This led them to their freedom, and now, it is going to lead us to ours."

Graham could hardly contain his excitement. They were going to do it. They were going on their first real adventure. This went well beyond sneaking around and eavesdropping on conversations. They were about to step into a secret tunnel, which could lead them anywhere. They were going to tromp through the forest during the darkest part of the night and make their way to a secret meeting with people who could do things that seemed impossible. This was the sort of thing you only read about in books, but tonight, it was really happening.

"You ok? Is something wrong?" asked Damien.

Coming back from his thoughts, Graham looked at Damien with a smile on his face. "Nothing. Absolutely nothing. I have never felt better."

Testing each step by easing their weight onto it, they made their way down the staircase. Graham turned around to the door, taking hold of the small strap on the back of it, and closed it. Now on the dirt floor, Graham took the lead, shining his flashlight down the path. It was pretty impressive. About every ten feet or so, thick rustic timbers braced the walls and ceiling of the narrow tunnel. Graham could almost stretch out his arms and touch both walls at the same time.

Knowing they only had a short amount of time remaining before the meeting, they resisted the urge to explore. They began jogging down the tunnel, ducking under large cobwebs and passing boxes of blankets and small barrels. Having kept count of the timber braces as they ran, Graham realized they were at least 800 feet from the stairs.

He slowed down a little to catch his breath. Damien was right beside him and matched his pace. At the very end of the beam of light, they could see the beginning of another set of stairs.

"We made it. We are at the other end!" Ecstatic, Damien took off in a sprint toward the stairs.

"Hey, wait up! You're going to break your neck running in the dark."

Graham took off after Damien trying to shine the light ahead of him so that he didn't run into anything. Noting his friend's attempt at a speedy exit, Graham was reminded of how much Damien hated dark, confined spaces— especially when they had been dark for decades. There was no telling what sorts of creatures and crawling insects were down here. Not concerning himself with testing the stairs, Damien leaped from the ground and made his way to the top. Before the word 'STOP' could come out of Graham's mouth, Damien's head slammed against a large wooden trapdoor which appeared to be part of the floor of the structure above.

"OUCH!!" cried Damien.

"I told you to wait up."

"Shut it," Damien said, rubbing the small bump forming on the top of his head. "I just want to get out of here. Shine your light up here. I can't see how to open this thing."

"Wait a second. Let's listen for any sign of life, now that you've rattled the door with your head."

They sat on the stairs for a few minutes listening for footsteps or voices. There was nothing but silence. Graham aimed his flashlight up to the door and took hold of the round metal handle, which was inlayed into the wooden frame.

Pulling the middle ring out 90 degrees, the door clicked, signaling that it was unlocked. Graham tilted his head to the left so that he could push against the door with his shoulder, but the door would not move.

"Hey, quit worrying about your little boo boo and help me push."

"I could have a concussion. Cut me some slack."

Damien continued to rub his head through his thick black hair trying to massage the bump back down as he walked over to Graham. He hunched over and put his shoulder against the door.

"On three, ok?"

"Push on three? Or count to three then push?"

Graham sighed and stared at Damien. "Really? Just push when I do."

"Fine," said Damien, still wincing in pain.

"Three!"

Graham pushed with all his might against the door.

"Hey wai…" Caught off guard with three instead of one, Damien pushed with Graham. With the two of them straining, the door began to hinge open as fine trickles of dust fell on their heads and shoulders. They got it cracked about eight inches or so, allowing Graham to see that there were no people in the room and that there was some sort of bag on top of the small trapdoor. He scoured the dark room the best he could for a few more seconds before their strength gave out. The door slammed shut again.

"I think we're clear, but there is something preventing us from being able to get out. Like a large burlap bag of food or something."

"Ya don't say," panted Damien.

"I do say," said Graham, matching Damien's sarcastic tone. "Come on, let's try again. On three."

"Three!" Damien anticipated the three instead of the one this time. With every ounce of strength they had, they pushed against the door. Six inches… eight inches… "Arrrhhhhaaa!"

They both grunted with clenched jaws. As they continued to push, they felt the bag begin to slide, carrying its momentum down the face of the door and off to the side, allowing the door to fly open.

"YES!" yelled Damien.

Graham poked his head up from the floor to see where they were and if anyone was close by. Satisfied with the darkness and silence, he climbed out, waving Damien forward. Graham moved his flashlight back and forth, surveying the room, trying to gather his bearings. He looked down at the large burlap sack that had been on top of the trapdoor. Kneeling, he shined his light on it. There was a big picture of the state of Idaho with the word 'potatoes' written in large brown letters underneath. Standing back up, Graham looked around the small room at all the root vegetables and dried leaves that hung from the large timbers on the ceiling.

"This must be a root cellar or something," said Graham.

"No kidding. What was your first clue?" replied Damien.

"Shut up."

"We are definitely in a root cellar, but where? I have never seen one near Greenwood before? We can't be that far away."

Shrugging, Graham replied, "I dunno. We'll just have to get outside and look around." They both walked over to the door. Graham was the first to step outside. A cool breeze blew over him as he took a few more steps. He was about to say how much he loved it when the wind carried the scents of the lake below, but instead, all that came out was a loud scream as the ground began to give way under his feet.

"GRAHAM! LOOK OUT!" Damien frantically grabbed for Graham, his hand finding the hood of his sweatshirt. Graham's arms flailed in the air as he tried grabbing for anything that would save him. As his body went over the side of the cliff, his neck snapped back as the collar of his sweatshirt choked him from Damien's tug. Damien pulled with all his might, falling to his back. Graham was pulled back just in time for his butt to hit the ground with his legs dangling over the side of the cliff. His head hit the ground hard behind him with a thud.

"Graham! You ok, amigo? You there?" Damien asked.

"Mmmuhh… yea, I think so," Graham mumbled.

He sat up and felt a twinge of pain in his spine. Trying to figure out what had just happened, he looked around, only to notice that they were on the edge of the cliff near the orphanage. Looking over to his left, he saw a small dirt path that led up the hillside. Looking behind him, Graham could see the stone wall that ran across the length of the cliff.

"We're below the cliff wall," he said to Damien. With his head still throbbing and his back wracked in pain, he squinted toward the wall. "Must have been the only way they could hide the entrance. The only way down here is a little goat path, if you can even call it that."

Scuttling away from the edge of the cliff, Graham turned around to his knees and slowly stood up. The pain worked its way up every vertebra as he straightened. Damien also stood up, brushing off his pants and sleeves.

Graham looked over at the dirt path and motioned Damien to follow. Though the pain in Graham's back made its presence known with every step he took, he knew they had to keep moving, or they would not make it in time. With only two feet of ground to walk on, the two put their backs and arms flat against the cold stone wall and began to sidestep their way up to the top level of the ground. Once there, they turned around, grabbed the top edge of the wall and pulled themselves on top.

Before getting off the wall, Damien turned around and pointed toward the lake in the distance as the light from the moon lay on top of the water like silk ribbons. "Man, what a view." The moon was full, the air was crisp and the scents of autumn were in every breath of the wind. Damien could not peel himself away from the glimmer of the lake below and the beauty of the landscape in front of them. Maybe it was the thrill of being out at this time of night, or maybe it was because they had almost plummeted to their deaths, but he sat there on the wall as if in a trance.

"Damien? Earth to Damien? Snap out of it, we need to keep moving."

Damien blinked a few times and then hopped from the top of the stone wall. Far off to their left, the boys could see the shadowy form of Wellington standing out against the starlit sky. Now Graham knew where they were and where to go.

"We need to hug this treeline until we're past the face of the orphanage. That's where we went into the woods yesterday."

Knowing that he shouldn't use his flashlight here, he let the light from the moon guide their steps until they reached the entrance of the wooded trail. After they entered, he waited until they traveled at least 50 or 60 feet in before retrieving the flashlight, though he could probably navigate these woods in total darkness if necessary.

Running as fast as they could, Graham and Damien bobbed and weaved their way through the woods in record time. Knowing Wellington would be a ghost town in the middle of the night, the two ran through the alley, between two buildings and onto the cobblestone street. They both were relieved as they saw the streetlamps still lit up. Glad to have light again, but not wanting to completely expose themselves, they ran over to the sidewalk and started jogging down the market. As they ran, they passed the second of the three tall, elegant buildings in Wellington. It was very similar to Building 14, which was Graham's typical perch. They could see the outlines of gargoyles along the many rooflines and corners. The one feature that made this one different, however, was the huge clock that hung three quarters of the way up its face, like a pendant gracing a woman's neck.

"2:05. I think we are going to make it!" said Damien.

"Only if we keep this pace all the way there," said Graham between big breaths. "I've got to stop. Just for a sec."

Graham slowed down and bent over, placing his hands on his knees, gasping for air. "I've got to start playing soccer with you or something. This is ridiculous."

Damien, completely unfazed by the journey so far, stood straight with an even, rhythmic pulse. "I agree, amigo. You are pretty out of shape."

Graham rolled his eyes, but could hardly give a witty response when he was doubled over, gasping for air.

All the running seemed to have worked some of the pain out of Graham's bones. There was only a small pulse of pain every so often now, but he knew it was only because the blood was flowing. If he stopped moving for too long, he would be in trouble.

"Alright, señor speedster. After you."

"Okay. If you fall behind, just follow the trail of dust and shame."

"I'll show you shame," said Graham, taking off into a sprint.

Damien immediately took off after Graham.

"Enjoy that head start, amigo!" he yelled. "I'm sure that five seconds of glory will make the defeat a little easier to swallow." He was already parallel to Graham. "I'll see if they can delay the meeting for you," he said, now two or three paces ahead.

Determined not to be completely humiliated, Graham sped up. The two played this cat and mouse game for over two miles until they came to a small wooden sign inlaid in a panel of stacked stone. In an Old English font, it read *Portfield Manor*. They were so focused on beating each other that they almost missed it, had it not been for Graham's need for another break.

"Hey, back over here!" yelled Graham.

Damien made a U-turn and ran back to Graham. "You may beat me, but it won't be to Portfield Manor. It's this way."

"Well, good thing you are out of shape, isn't it?" said Damien.

Graham tried to come back with a witty remark, but he was panting too heavily. The only thing he could muster was, "Everyone has their gifts, I guess."

After a few minutes, Graham regained his breath. Damien waited patiently. Getting bored, he took hold of the large sign, trying to shake it back and forth.

"What are you doing?"

"Checking to see how sturdy it is."

"Why?"

"Why not?"

"I don't understand you."

Not attempting to even try to understand the inner workings of Damien's mind, Graham removed his hands from his knees and stood up straight. "You're not even sweating. How are you not sweating?" asked Graham, sweat pouring down his face like a running faucet.

"I'm Peruvian. We don't sweat in cold weather."

"Whatever you say."

Staring down the road leading to Portfield Manor, they both saw why the ghost stories existed. Now that most of the leaves had fallen, the long outstretched limbs of the trees lining the road looked as if they were going to grab you. The wind picked up, creating small cyclones of dead leaves swirling over the dirt road.

"Um…you first," said Damien.

Graham tried to take the first step, but was surprised at his hesitation. His whole life he had been dreaming about this moment, yet he had a hard time taking the first step. Looking at Damien, though, his pride kicked into gear. If he couldn't beat his friend in a chase, he would certainly not back down from this.

"Alright, let's go."

Graham took off down the road, followed by Damien. Not wanting to be on a creepy side road any longer than they needed to be, they ran as fast as they could. The road curved in and out like a snake, which only made its gloomy facade more intense. The big shadows cast by the light of the moon through the bare branches didn't help either. The periodic hoot of an owl and the howls of nearby dogs, or what they hoped were dogs, quickened their pace to an all-out sprint.

About a mile in, they finally saw the form of a large house hidden in a cluster of trees. As they approached, they passed through a metal gate fastened to a tall stone wall on either side.

Still feeling a little creeped out, they made their way to the house, giving their racing hearts a chance to slow back down. The house was enormous. It was made completely of stone with an arched portico over the entrance.

"Wow, this is more like a castle than a house," said Damien as they walked up to the entrance.

Even the front door was intimidating. It was at least ten feet tall with long strips of hammered metal stretching over thick wooden planks with metal bolts holding them in place. Graham looked over at Damien, giving him a quick pat on the shoulder.

"I wouldn't be here right now if you hadn't pulled me from the edge of that cliff. You're a good friend. I don't care what they say."

"Gee, thanks. That is the nicest thing you've ever said to me."

"Go on, then. Knock."

His nerves shot, Graham grabbed hold of the metal ring lodged in the talons of a bird with outstretched wings.

BAM. BAM. BAM.

The knocks reverberated all around the stone portico. A few moments went by and nothing happened. Trying again, Graham knocked three more times. A few seconds ticked by until he heard the sound of the door unlock. Graham let go of the ring as the door moaned and creaked. The door opened to reveal Chase standing on the other side in a pair of black cargo pants and red long-sleeved shirt.

With a warm smile on his face he looked at both of them.

"Just in time, guys. Come on in."

"Just in time, guys. Come on in."

10

THE MEETING

The door creaked as it shut behind him. They all stood in a huge foyer filled with eclectic artwork. The craftsmanship of the wood finishings matched almost exactly what was in Greenwood Orphanage, though the furniture, colors and interior finishings were completely different. It had more of an antique feeling.

"You live here?" asked Graham, after looking over the room and making eye contact with Chase.

"I guess you could say that. I wouldn't exactly call it home, but it is where I live for the time being."

Just being in the place made Graham want to walk a little taller, like those of high social status. Though the outside made his skin crawl, the inside had a completely different atmosphere. There was a fire burning in the next room. He could hear the crackling, feel the radiating warmth and smell the burning wood.

Just beyond where the three of them were standing, a huge tapestry hung on the wall. It was at least fifteen feet tall and over twenty-five feet long. It had an elegant weave with a massive depiction of a sun in the center. The sun was hollow in the middle and contained within a circle, with the flares curling out 360 degrees. The deep golden hue of the sun stood in dramatic contrast with the crimson red background and the shadowing behind the sun made it seem three dimensional. Graham was so enthralled with the intricacy and level of detail that he could not look away.

"Let's go into the next room. There are a few people I think you would like to meet," said Chase.

Continuing straight through the foyer, Graham passed a skinny rectangular table with three oblong mirrors hanging over top. Each mirror was a deep cheery wood with four bowl-like indentions to the right side of the glass, like a giant had pushed his fingers into the grain of the wood. Graham peered into the mirror and saw the reflection of the tapestry, so he turned around to look at it one last time. *Was it some sort of family crest? Maybe the family just liked the sun*, Graham pondered as he followed Chase into the next room.

As they entered, Graham saw two young girls by the fireplace, both wearing jeans. The older had on a brown, long-sleeved shirt with a blue coat folded over her arm. The younger girl had on a white shirt with a green coat. Three men stood in the opposite corner talking together. All but one had on the same thing as Chase. Black pants and dark red shirts. For the first time, he noticed that just below the collar on the back of the neck, the sun symbol was prominently displayed. As he studied the small group, it was hard to overlook the fact that one of them towered over the rest. He was a big man with a weathered face, jet black hair and a goatee that extended up his jawline. A thick scar stretched along the length of his left cheekbone a few inches below his eye. He was not big as in overweight. Quite the contrary. He was all muscle, at least twice the width of Chase and more than a head taller. His clothing was different. He wore a thick black wool coat, almost military style with the chest pockets and straps over the shoulders. He wore a brown shirt underneath and rugged brown pants.

"That has to be Cavaness. Is that Cavaness?" asked Graham. This guy was definitely more in line with the description Ms. Winstone had given. He even looked like what Graham had imagined.

"The one and only," replied Chase. "Cavaness Foster. The other two guys with him are Brian Murphy and Eric Branson." Waving over to him, Chase got his attention as they walked to him. "Cavaness, these are our newest seekers. This one here is Damien. He's the soccer star I was telling you about. And this is Graham. He's the one you told me about."

Graham's ears perked up. *Wait, Cavaness knows who I am? How? Why?*

Chase noticed Graham's blank stare, and began waving his hand back and forth in front of Graham's face. "Hello? Anybody in there?"

Graham quickly refocused. "Sorry. I just didn't expect you to know who I was, Mr. Foster." Graham had to tilt his head upward to make eye contact.

"Just Cavaness. No need for the Mr.," said Cavaness in a deep, gravelly voice. His words came out like the crack of a whip. Graham had known Cavaness for about five seconds, and already he knew this was a man forged in the heat of extreme circumstances and hardened by life's trials. His words fell from his mouth like heavy stones. The overall effect was quite intimidating.

"Oh. Okay, Cavaness. How do you know who I am?"

"We'll get to that soon enough. For now, we are past 3 o'clock and need to begin." Dismissing Graham, Cavaness walked away.

Chase rolled his eyes. "Not exactly a social butterfly, is he? You get used to it, though."

Leading Graham and Damien over to the two girls at the fireplace, Chase introduced them. "Boys, here are the other guests for tonight's meeting. They are from further north. This is Kel and this is Ailey. They are from the Oak Ridge Orphanage."

Kel reached out and shook Graham's hand. She stood at least eight inches taller than Ailey with brown hair and deep blue eyes. Ailey was much shorter and younger than Kel with olive skin, brown hair and greenish-hazel eyes. Her skin was almost flawless, except for a small horizontal scar on her neck, just above the collar of her green coat. They both greeted Graham and Damien with the same mannerisms, almost like they were sisters. Before the boys had a chance to introduce themselves, Chase interrupted.

"You will have plenty of time to mingle later. For now, we need to get started. Alex is ready to see the four of you now."

"Who is Alex?" Damien asked Graham.

"I have no idea." Looking at the girls, Graham asked, "Do you two know?"

"No, nobody has mentioned an Alex yet," said Kel.

Ailey stood beside Kel with her eyebrows arched as she twisted her head in a silent 'no'.

Graham shrugged. "Well, I guess we're about to find out."

The next room looked to be about the size of the parlor back at Greenwood. As they entered, they found it completely bare, except for two sets of rectangular tables. One was narrow, placed near the back wall, and the other was out in the middle of the room with four chairs facing the back wall.

The narrow table was fairly simple. It stood about four feet tall with a slight hourglass figure. On the front side of the table, in the middle of the vertical trim, was the sun emblem again.

Chase led the kids over to the table in the middle of the room and asked them to take a seat. The two men previously talking with Cavaness entered the room and took a seat at the chairs against the back wall, along with Chase. Cavaness walked over to the middle of the small table, and placed his hands on top.

"I want to be the first to welcome you to Portfield Manor. I know you have many questions floating around in your heads. I do not believe anyone has given you a full explanation of exactly why you are here tonight. You all agreed to come here because you all have unanswered questions. Each of you have been experiencing unexplained events, and you have come here hoping that you will be given answers. In a moment, you will be introduced to a man named Alex. He will be the one to begin tonight's affairs. When he comes in, it would be in your best interests to give him your highest respect. He is not only the owner of this house and estate, but he is also the founder of our organization."

At that, Cavaness took the final seat beside Chase. Graham sat there wondering what he had just gotten into. He glanced at Chase in concern. Chase returned Graham's worrisome expression with a wink and a slight grin. For some unknown reason, Graham felt peaceful when he was around Chase.

He had never had siblings, at least not by blood, but Graham imagined this must be what it was like to have an older brother. One who always had your back, and kept a protective eye on you. Though this trip had been an exciting adventure so far, Graham really did not like the unknown. He liked knowing what was ahead, but there was no way of knowing what was about to come and it was grating on his nerves. Despite this, however, this one wink and smile from Chase poured over him. He was soothed and comforted, as though Chase had telepathically told him that everything was going to be just fine.

Graham smiled back and looked over to Damien, who was spewing his whole life story to Kel. She looked like she would rather be in solitary confinement than endure one of Damien's long rants. Ailey sat beside Kel with her chin on the table, picking at a stray string hanging from the cuff of her green coat. Suddenly, her head shot up off the table as a man carrying a silver tray walked into the room. In unison, the four grown men stood up and snapped to attention. The four kids followed suit.

Alex walked over to the table and set the silver tray on top. The tray held eight golden cylinders about five inches tall, the bottoms a little wider than the tops. Each had a golden ring at the top, one at the bottom, and small rods connecting the two. On one side, two of the rods bent outwards, forming a complete circle. The same on the adjacent side. One side held the sun emblem within the circle. The other circle was empty.

Alex let the four of them look at the golden objects for a moment or two before putting his fist to his mouth and clearing his throat. Looking into their eyes, he smiled and said, "Welcome. My name is Alex. I know you all went to great lengths to be here tonight. Though I could have spoken to your superiors, requesting your presence here, it means much more to me that you have made the effort to come."

Such authority emanated from this man. He looked as though he were only in his mid-thirties, yet he spoke with the authority of a king. It was very difficult to explain. There was a balance of force and compassion in his voice as he spoke.

"You have come for answers. I'm not sure if they can all be found immediately, but perhaps with time, you will find what you are looking for. I know that some of you have come here in the hope that you will be able to perform magic."

Damien's eyes lit up at the mention of magic. Graham knew he was thinking of Chase moving in streaks of light, as fast as a bullet from the barrel of a gun.

"Many have experienced things that they cannot explain. Others are running away from their past in hopes of making a better future. Some just want to be more than what they are now. Whatever your motivation is for being here tonight, you are searching for truth– the truth that will explain the unexplainable."

Taking the silver tray from the small table, Alex walked over to the table and set it between Damien and Kel. Two by two, he removed the golden cylinders and placed them in front of each person. Once the tray was empty, he took it and set it back on the small table.

Alex picked up one of the cylinders in front of Damien. With all five fingers spread out along the bottom ring, Alex held the object up at eye level.

"These are wristbands. They are the key to understanding what you are striving so hard to comprehend, but I'm afraid that I must disappoint you when I say that there is no such thing as magic. Magic is an illusion. It is a falsehood. What I am offering you tonight is much more than cheap parlor tricks. I am offering you an invitation to not only get answers, but also be a part of something much bigger than any one individual in this room. If you accept my invitation, please pick up your armbands now and place them onto your forearms with the sun facing up toward the ceiling."

They all looked at each other, wondering if anyone was actually going to put them on. Graham picked one up and looked it over. "What exactly do they do?"

"First the bands, Graham. Then you will get your answers. I know trust is a rare thing for you, but I'm asking you to trust me."

Graham nodded his head and slid one band on his left wrist and the other on his right. Watching the scene between Alex and Graham, the others followed suit. One by one, they all slid the bands onto their forearms and twisted them so that the sun emblem was facing up.

With a wide smile, Alex took a few steps back and raised both hands in a welcoming gesture. "Welcome to Aegis." Putting his left hand back at his side, Alex kept his right hand up and waved it slowly from right to left. As his hand hovered over each person, the sun in each band began to glow like embers. Brighter and brighter, the sun illuminated, followed by the rest of the band. For a split second, each of the kids winced with the pain of searing heat, squeezing their eyes shut and gritting their teeth. Kel opened her mouth as if to scream, but just as soon as the pain hit, it was gone, and a cool, soothing sensation followed. As the light faded, the gold of the bands melted into their skin and with a final flash of light, they disappeared, leaving a glowing stain in their skin in place of where the bands had rested.

The kids stared at their forearms, unable to process what had happened. Extending his fingers and balling them into fists, Graham flexed and relaxed his forearms. Damien traced the outline of the sun with his index finger. Ailey did the same, then turned her arms over to see the vacant circle on the underside of her forearms. After a thorough inspection of their new decor, they looked at each other, holding up their arms to show their new marks.

Damien's expression was pure excitement. He grabbed Kel's hand and twisted it back and forth to get a good look at her bands. Kel, however, was not as enthusiastic as Damien. Reading her expression, Graham wondered if she had only come here for her friend. She began nervously rubbing her mark as though she wanted to remove it from her skin.

While they were preoccupied with their arms, Alex looked over his shoulder to the four men standing behind him. With a single nod, they got up from their chairs. They passed Alex, walked around the table and stood at attention behind each one of the kids. Ailey twisted around to look at the person now behind her. Without a word, she grinned, revealing a few gaps in her teeth where the new ones had not yet grown in. The man behind her remained expressionless. Damien completely ignored them, still enamored with the markings on his arms. Kel met Graham's questioning glance with one of her own.

Once the men were in place, Alex spoke to the new recruits.

"Splendid. The catalysts have been applied successfully. It can begin."

Looking now to the men behind them, Alex signaled with his hand.

"Hood them."

As the words were being spoken, the man behind Graham pulled a black hood over his head. Everything went dark and a heavy brew of panic and confusion hit him. He could hear the other three struggling around him to remove their hoods. He struggled to get his arms free, but they were pinned to his side.

"Let go of me!" screamed Kel.

Damien reverted to his native language and spat out a long Spanish rant as he too struggled to get free from his captor's grasp. Ailey silently struggled, but her small frame was no match.

Graham began slamming the back of his head against Chase's chest.

"Let go, Chase! What are you doing?"

The pain coming from the tight grip of Chase's hands paled in comparison to the shock of electricity that came next. Grunting as every muscle in his body tensed up, Graham became lightheaded and felt his knees buckle. As he crumbled to the ground like a ragdoll, he heard the thuds of the other three hitting the floor beside him. Lying immobile on his side, Graham could hardly see anything except for a few shadowy outlines of the others lying motionless on the floor.

His body jerked as surges of electricity continued jolting through his body. *What the heck is happening?* He clenched his fists at the betrayal, but before he could react, he felt something press against his back. Another wave of electricity surged through his body and he went rigid as his throat groaned in the shock. The faint outline of Damien's unconscious form grew darker and darker. His body went limp and the wave of panic gave way to an odd sense of calmness as the world around him went black.

The Warehouse

"Graham? You ok, honey? That was a good fall! You are so brave!" said the lady. She took Graham by the hand as he stood back up and proceeded to get back on the fallen tree trunk. He ran the length of the tree, giggling as he wobbled back and forth.

"This looks like a good place to eat, doesn't it, Graham?"

"Eat!" said the two-year-old boy.

"Yes, eat," said his dad.

Graham sat eating his sandwich as thick black smoke rose up out of the ground like an inverted tornado, wrapping its misty tendrils around them.

"GET BACK! STAY BACK!" yelled his father.

Graham could not see anything through the smoke. His lungs closed tight, choking him, and he was unable to breathe in between coughs.

"Graham? You ok? Graham? GRAHAM!"

With each mention of his name, the sound of his mom's voice changed. At first she sounded like his mom, but each time his name was repeated, her voice grew younger and younger.

Intense flashes of light pierced the smoke, as if the brilliance of the sun was engulfing it. His little body was trembling. The black smoke was now swirling in circles, being diffused by the light. Graham screamed.

Graham's eyes popped open, and his head jerked up. He was in darkness. His mind raced as he tried to get a grip on reality. Through the darkness, he could see faint outlines of people sitting in chairs.

"Graham, wake up!"

He rigorously shook his head until the black hood fell onto the concrete floor beside him. He batted his eyelids to slowly take in the light, little by little.

"Graham! Snap out of it!" said Kel.

Graham looked up to see that he was no longer in the woods with his parents.

"Graham, you ok, amigo?" Graham looked over at Damien and saw the concern in his friend's face. "I have never seen you like that. You were screaming."

"It's nothing." That was a lie. Graham was terrified. "Just a reoccurring nightmare I have sometimes."

Beads of sweat ran through his hair and down the sides of his cheeks. Graham looked around him, expecting to see hovering objects crashing to the ground. He quickly realized, though, that it would be difficult for chairs and tables to hover when they're bolted to the floor. He tried to lift his hand to wipe the sweat off his face, but his hand only moved a few millimeters before being stopped by the ropes tied to the arms of the chair. Jerking his arms a few more times, he struggled against the ropes, but without success. Trying to move his feet, he saw that his ankles were in the same condition as his wrists, with thick rope securing them to the legs of the chair.

"It's useless. We've been trying for half an hour. They're too tight," said Kel.

"Well, we can't just sit here until the cavalry comes. There is no cavalry. Chase made sure that we all snuck out without being detected. Nobody has a clue where we are," said

Graham.

"Okay, what do you have in mind?" asked Kel. Her tone revealed her frustration and lack of patience.

"I don't know. I just joined the party. Give me a few minutes."

Ailey sat in the chair beside Kel. Her head was down, staring at the floor. Her silent sobs created big tears that fell from her cheeks making small wet circles on her jeans. Her chest moved in and out with the sobs, but the ropes prevented her from wiping the tears from her face.

Kel looked over to Ailey. Her anger and frustration of the moment gave way to compassion as she tried to comfort Ailey. "We are getting out of here. I promise. You know I will never let anything happen to you. Right now, let's think of how we can get out of this room, okay? Let's concentrate on that."

Ailey looked at Kel through the tears welling up in her eyes. She blinked a few times to let the tears roll down her face and nodded in agreement.

Frantically looking for a way out, Graham's eyes darted around the room for any sign of a sharp object to cut the ropes, but there was nothing. They were being held captive in a small room with concrete floors and cinderblock walls. A single, naked lightbulb hung from the ceiling casting light on their legs. They were set up in a circle facing one another. There were a few tables near the corners of the room, but that was it.

One window stretched along the wall to Graham's right. Through the grime and wire mesh imbedded in the glass, Graham could see a dimly lit hallway as the lights flickered off and on. Near the top of the wall, Graham saw a broken red orb. A siren, he realized, like the ones on top of police cars. He followed the electrical wire up through the ceiling until it culminated in a large bundle piled around plumbing lines. All the building's systems were exposed, running above the wire tracks that held only a few remaining ceiling tiles.

His mind searched for anything that could help them get

out of this place, but their captors had left them with nothing. Not knowing what else to do, Graham began to slam his back into his chair. Arching his back, he continued to ram the chair over and over, hoping that the wood would give or a bolt would come loose from the floor.

"Come on, guys. See if you can get your chair to break loose," he said as he slammed his back into the chair again.

Kel was the first to try. She wiggled her arms up and down while her hips moved side to side, trying to get the chair to rock. Damien tried next. Using his strong hamstrings, he tried to lift his butt off the chair and slam his body back down into the seat. The three of them moved, shifted and rocked until they eventually came to a stop, panting for breath. Ailey didn't move. She just sat there with her little fingers curled around the front edge of the armrest as tears continued down her cheeks.

Ailey was smaller and younger than the rest. She was only eleven years old. Never having done physical labor before, she knew that if Kel could not break her bonds, then she had no chance. She was small and weak, powerless to do anything for anyone, and being here was all her fault.

Kel looked over, noticing her despair. "Ailey, look at me."

Ailey lifted her head, looking at Kel through the strands of hair that covered her face. Another tear fell from her cheek and soaked into her pant leg.

"We are getting out of here. I promise. You can't lose hope right now."

With her lower lip quivering, Ailey bobbed her head, but she still wore an expression of guilt and doubt.

"This is not your fault. It's theirs. Chase. Alex. Cavaness. They are the reason we are here, not you. Understand? I do not blame you for this."

Graham recognized the look in Ailey's eyes. Maybe Kel had forgiven her, but evidently she could not forgive herself.

Graham felt bad for Ailey. She looked so sweet and innocent. Graham looked over to Damien, who was still trying to escape his chair, and realized he too had led him here. Damien would be safe and sound in his bed if he had not been so obsessed with finding Cavaness. Seeing both of them struggling for freedom only made his anger more intense toward Chase.

You tricked me. You knew what I was searching for and you used it to kidnap me, to kidnap us. Graham basted in the raw anger as he thought about the betrayal. *I will make you pay for this.*

Damien looked around at the rest of the group. "Well, it seems we're going to be here awhile." Looking over at Kel, he asked, "What is your story? Are you two sisters?"

It was evident that Kel didn't want to chat. She wanted out. Without looking at Damien, she swept the room with her eyes as she spoke.

"No. Not in the literal sense, anyway. Ailey came to our orphanage when she was two years old. I was six. As the Director of the orphanage answered a knock at the door, I walked over to him, asking what had been left on the doorstep. Pulling the object in, he turned, revealing a little car seat with a toddler slouched over in it, fast asleep."

Kel looked over at Ailey, who was still crying. Her eyes softened. "She was angelic. My heart sank as I stood there looking at this innocent little girl who was just left on the front steps like a bag of trash. I knew I had to take care of her. She looked so much like my little sister."

"You have a sister? Is she back at your orphanage?" asked Damien.

Kel's demeanor changed. Her body sank and her jaw tightened. "No."

Never able to read social cues or facial expressions, Damien kept on. "Where is she? Did you two get separated or something?"

There was silence for a few moments as Kel wrestled her emotions into place. "Yeah, I guess you could say that," she said, finally. "Look, we need to focus. The longer we stay here, the more time we give Cavaness and Chase to walk through that door."

"Ok, what do you suggest?" asked Graham.

"I'm not suggesting anything. I'm just stating the obvious. We're tied to chairs. There's nothing sharp in this room, and even if there was a giant hatchet lying on the table over there, we couldn't get to it because our chairs are bolted to the floor." Kel's impatience grew with each word. "So, I guess maybe I'm suggesting that we think outside the box if we intend to make it out of here." Kel jerked her right arm in frustration against the rope that held her down.

"Maybe thinking happy thoughts is the trick. If only I could click my heels together a few times, I could transport us back home," said Graham.

"Right now, I think I'd rather see a house fall on top of you."

"Well, if it got me away from you, I'd welcome it!"

"STOP IT!" said Damien. The echo of his voice bounced off the cinderblock walls. "STOP FIGHTING! We are all in the same boat here. We need to work TOGETHER!"

Graham and Kel fell silent. Graham had never seen Damien get agitated before. He certainly had never heard him yell, aside from during soccer games.

Never wanting to look weak, Graham was reluctant to say anything, but his conviction got the better of him.

"He's right." Graham paused. "We're tired, frustrated, and hungry. I shouldn't have snapped."

"And you are right. You shouldn't have," said Kel, still angry. "But I accept your apology. If we can just get out of these chairs…"

Kel tensed her wrists, pulling up with all her strength. "These stupid ropes!" Curling her fingers back, she shoved her palms down onto the armrests. As her skin hit the wood, a pulse of energy engulfed the room. The lightbulb above them flickered as the wood of Graham's armrests and two front chair legs exploded, blowing chunks of wood and splinters behind him. The force of the blast knocked Graham to his back.

Graham began to yell as he fell backwards, but the thud knocked the breath out of him. The back of Graham's head hit the concrete floor, making him see stars.

Ailey jerked her head up to see Graham lying on the ground, then flung her head around to look at Kel with wide eyes. Damien sat beside her with his mouth wide open.

"Was that you?" asked Damien, glancing in Kel's direction.

Kel was just as shocked as anyone else. "Graham! Graham, are you okay? I'm sorry! I don't know what happened."

Graham didn't move. He remained on the floor with his legs dangling over the front of the chair. His arms were spread out at a forty-five degree angle with the ropes still around his wrists. Wood debris was scattered all around him.

"Graham, please just say something! I didn't mean what I said. I was just angry. Please, get up!" Kel was panicking. She didn't know if what just had happened was even her fault, but she didn't care at this point.

"Mmm… my head." Graham groaned as he lifted his throbbing head from the floor to look around. "What the heck was that?"

"*No sé, amigo.* Your chair just exploded."

"Ya don't say." Twisting his body to the side, Graham put his hand on the ground and let his legs fall off the seat of the chair. He pushed himself up on all fours and patted the back of his head with one hand, checking for blood. He brought his hand back around to look, but there was nothing. Fortunately, the only thing that came from his tumble was a headache.

"Are you okay?" asked Kel.

"I feel like a house was dropped on top of me," Graham said. He looked up at Kel with a small grin.

With a sigh of relief, she smiled back. "Well, you can click your heels now if you want."

Graham stood up slowly as the pain in his back returned, coupled with new aches and pains in various parts of his body. Graham patted down his chest, arms, and legs, glad to see that everything was still intact.

"Was that really you? Can you make things explode?"

"No. I mean, I don't think so. I never have before. I'm just as surprised as you are. It couldn't have been me. Maybe it's part of their sick little game." Kel looked nervous. "Maybe there were small explosives built into the chair or something."

"Why on earth would they do something like that?" asked Graham.

"I don't know! Why did they lure us to that house? Why did they say we were going to be a part of something bigger, only to put black hoods over our heads and take us here? Maybe they're just freaks who enjoy scaring the life out of people."

Graham didn't want to believe it. He would much rather believe that he could finally talk to someone else who could do things that were unexplainable. At least that way, he would not be the only freak in the room.

"Well, whatever it was, I'm free from those ropes. We can figure out the details later. Right now, we just need to get out of this room."

"Agreed," said Kel, with a sigh of relief.

"Yes, get us out of these things," said Damien, jerking against his bonds.

Graham shook the ropes from his legs and walked over to Damien. Picking at the knot, he worked it loose from Damien's right hand. Flinging it free, Damien frantically began to tug at the knot holding his left arm down.

Seeing that Damien would be able to free himself now, Graham walked over to Kel. He reached out to untie the first knot. She looked up at him and met his eyes.

"Hey, I'm glad you're not hurt. Really."

"I wouldn't say that I'm not hurt," said Graham, running a hand over the back of his head. "But thanks."

Pulling the rope free, he began working on the other knot, giving Kel the ability to work on the ropes at her ankles. Figuring Kel would want to be the one to help Ailey, he walked over to the long window, looking into the hallway for any sign of Chase or Cavaness.

"The coast is clear for now, I think. Although it is hard to see with the lights flickering like that. We need to find a way outside. I was out when they shocked me, so I have no idea how far they moved us. Do any of you know?"

"No, I was out cold," said Damien.

"Me too," replied Kel, as she continued working at Ailey's ropes.

Ailey looked up at Graham with a blank stare.

"Well, I guess we'll have to play it by ear, then."

Grabbing hold of the doorknob, Graham turned it so he could peek out into the hallway. As the knob finished its turn, the flickering lights went dim, and the siren above the door activated in flashes of red light. The piercing sounds of a horn screamed through the room making everyone cup their hands over their ears.

"We have to get out of here now!" Graham yelled to the others.

Kel tore at Ailey's ropes with such intensity that her fingers were turning red. "Come on, come on!" She flinched, unable to cover her ears. The alarm was so loud that she had a hard time concentrating on the knots, and the flashing of the red light was disorienting.

Damien ran over and bent down to work at the rope on Ailey's other leg. The knot was too tight to get out with his fingers, so he knelt and began to bite at it. He jerked his head back and forth with the fraying rope clamped in his teeth until the knot gave way. One by one, they got the knots untied, allowing Ailey to bolt up from the chair. They all ran after Graham like cattle, pouring into the hallway.

With their heads swiveling, they looked for an escape route. Graham led the pack.

"Stay right here while I check around the corner."

Turning to the right, he jogged down the hallway until he reached the corner. Placing his hands against the wall, he eased his head around the corner to see if anyone was in pursuit. Graham squinted, trying to focus on the hallway as red flashes of light rotated behind him. Satisfied for the moment, he focused on the doors and windows, looking to see what their options were. There were at least eight doors lining the hall, but they all appeared to be the same type of interrogation rooms from which they had just escaped.

Damien couldn't stand still. He had to do something. He grabbed the door behind him and closed it. As the door hit the jamb, the alarm fell silent. The red light continued to flash, but at least they could all take their hands off their ears. Damien relaxed slightly before jogging down the hall in the opposite direction. He jogged about twenty feet until he reached the adjacent hallway.

Getting down on his hands and knees, he poked his head cautiously around the corner. It was hard to see anything with the fluorescent lights flickering on and off as if they were in their last stages of life. Damien's eyes widened and his palms began to sweat. He saw one large shadow and one skinny shadow grow as their owners turned the corner from the opposite end of the hall.

Damien pulled his head back so fast that the momentum sent him reeling backwards. Shuffling, he moved back from the corner and scrambled to his feet. Running past the girls, he yelled, "*Vamos, vamos, vamos!*"

Ailey and Kel didn't have to know Spanish to understand what he was saying. They could see it in his intense expression. Damien ran up to Graham, grabbing him under the armpit and uprooting him from his crouched position.

"*Vamos, amigo!* They are not down here, they are back there!"

"What?"

"Chase and Cavaness are coming down the other hall!

Move it!"

Damien's momentum lifted Graham almost completely off the floor, throwing him forward and around the corner. They ran past the eight doors, looking through each set of windows to see if they led outside, but all the rooms seemed identical to the one they'd just escaped from. As they reached the final stretch, they saw a door at the end. Beside the door was a sign with a small line zigzagging downwards.

"Stairs." Graham reached for the handle, but Kel grabbed his hand before he could take hold.

"Wait! What if another alarm goes off?"

"I don't see we have a choice. This is the only way out."

Quickly trying to weigh their options, Kel tightened her grip on Graham's hand for a moment, and then relaxed, letting go of him.

"Ok, you're right. It's not like they don't already know we're here anyway. Let's go."

Graham faced the door and turned the knob, bracing his ears for another screech of an alarm, but nothing happened. They all sighed a little, then rushed through the door. Looking down the stairwell, Graham noticed that there was not a set of stairs going up.

"We must be on the top floor. We need to find a window so we can see outside and find out where we are."

"We just need to keep moving," said Damien.

Taking Damien's advice, Graham started down the stairs with the others trailing after him. Approaching the next story down, he looked through the window in the door to see what was on the other side.

"It's too dark. I can't see anything."

"Then neither can they," said Kel.

The sound of a creaking door from the story above made the decision easy. Graham put his left hand against the wall beside the door as a brace so that he could open it without making a sound. It was a slow process, but he was able to open it silently.

Graham motioned the rest of them on. They all ducked under his arm, which was holding the door open. Trying his best to hold the door perfectly still, he shuffled to the other side and eased the door back into place. Just as the door closed, Graham saw two people come around the landing of the stairs. He ducked quickly so that he wouldn't be seen. Squat-walking like a duck, Graham waddled over to the others. He held his breath as the footsteps clapped closer to the door until they could hear the two men talking on the other side.

A deep, gravelly voice spoke first. "They couldn't have gone far. You take this door. I'll go down to the first floor. Branson and Murphy are on the other side. I'll radio in and tell them to do the same. We'll pin them in the middle."

"Whatever you say, boss," replied Chase.

"Just do it," commanded Cavaness. The booms of his footsteps could be heard all the way down to the next floor.

Graham huddled closer to the others. He could feel Kel's leg up against his, and Damien's shoulder met his on the other side. Ailey curled up beside Kel, burying her face into her stomach. They were pinned in the back corner of the room with no place to go.

"Whatever you do, don't make a sound," whispered Graham.

Graham was terrified. He took deep breaths as he tried to steady his trembling hands. They were completely exposed. They had no time to run to another room, hide under a table, or even slide behind another wall.

Chase creaked open the door, letting a sliver of light pour into the room from the stairwell. All four of them tensed up at the sight of Chase's form stepping through the door and into the room. They squeezed their eyes shut, as if doing so would help them disappear into the darkness. Graham opened one eye. He tensed up even more at the sight of Chase looking right at them. Graham's fist clenched so tight he thought he was about to draw blood with his fingernails digging into his palm. Chase stood there for what seemed like hours, staring right at them, but eventually he turned his attention to the rest of the room.

Graham relaxed a bit knowing that Chase had not seen them, until he saw Chase reaching for a switch on the wall.

Oh, no.

Chase's finger met the bottom of the light switch. Graham's heart sank knowing there was nothing he could do. The light would turn on and they would be exposed. This was it. It was over. He took in a deep breath as Chase flicked his wrist.

Click.

THE ESCAPE

Darkness remained. *Click-click. Click-click.* Chase moved the switch up and down multiple times, but it was dead.

He grunted under his breath. "Great." He took a few more steps into the pitch-black room. He held up his right hand as if motioning someone to stop, but with his fingers spread out, as if palming a basketball. A few seconds went by and then his hand began to glow a deep, yellow color. The light grew brighter and brighter until it was almost too brilliant to look at, casting large shadows on the wall of the tables and chairs scattered throughout the room. Using his glowing hand to light his way, Chase moved forward.

"Come on, guys and gals. Don't you think you're a little old for hide-and-seek?"

Graham surveyed the room. They were in a large, open space. There were a few chairs and tables, some standing and others turned over on their sides. Wherever they were, it looked abandoned.

At that moment, the room reflected perfectly the way Graham felt. Abandoned. *Like me*, Graham realized. Abandoned and hopeless, with no idea where they had been taken. Who knows how far they had been transported? They were orphans who intentionally snuck out of their rooms without anyone knowing. Help would not come for at least a few days, or as long as it took Ms. Winstone and Mr. Kobble to realize they weren't just off playing in the woods.

The light was almost completely gone now as Chase continued into the heart of the building. Still huddled together, Damien was the first to break the silence.

"Who are these people? First, he can move like lightning, now he can light up like it?"

What had originally made him want to be a part of this 'Aegis' group now sent waves of terror though Damien.

"I don't like this, Graham. This guy is some sort of freak, and I don't want anything to do with him. What do they want us for anyway? Are they going to turn us into freaks, too?"

"Keep your voice down," whispered Kel.

"I don't know what they want. But we need to concentrate on getting out of this place, okay?" said Graham, trying to calm Damien down. "Let's do that first, and then we can worry about what they want with us."

Their only option was to go back upstairs. That would be the only floor they had already searched.

"You heard Cavaness. They'll be searching this floor and the lower one from both sides. The only place we have to go is up."

They all thought for a second, and then nodded in agreement. Graham silently opened the door and let the others go out into the stairwell. He then closed the door behind him and followed them up the stairs. Going back through the third-story door again, they huddled together.

Kel wrapped her arm around Ailey as they tried to figure out what to do next. Damien turned to look through a window into one of the many holding rooms. Chairs, tables, a wall. That was it. "We have got to be able to see outside," he said.

"I know, but we're going to have to tread carefully up

here. Opening any doors could trigger another alarm. We got lucky last time. I don't think we'll be that fortunate again," said Graham.

The lights overhead continued to flicker as they ran down the hall, around the corner and past their old room. Not stopping, they continued running toward the other end of the hall where Damien had first seen Chase and Cavaness. They tiptoed past a few bathrooms separated by a dingy water fountain; its front panel had detached and was lying on the floor. The walls were stained with age and neglect, and cobwebs lined the top of the wall like crown molding.

The wall to their right ended, giving way to a large, open room. It must have been some sort of break room for the employees. There were small circular tables and chairs with a dilapidated couch in the corner. A few cabinets lined the wall ninety degrees from the hallway with a small sink and a coffee maker beside it, housing a broken glass pot.

Looking to the opposite side of the hall, Graham saw more doors, but they looked different. There was one large window beside each door with long, plastic strips hanging from the top. The blinds were twisted shut, but fortunately the hands of time had torn some of the strips from the track that held them in place.

They all ran to a different window to look into the rooms. "These are offices for the people who used to work here." Graham looked through the small gap in the hanging plastic. There was a large wooden desk with a leather chair that was on its side. "This one has a window!"

"So does this one!" said Damien.

"I think all of them do," said Kel, looking into the next office.

"Don't you go screaming at me," said Kel to the office door. She grabbed the knob and twisted it, hoping the alarm was intended only for detainees, not staff. Alarm or not, it didn't matter. It was locked. Graham and Damien tried their doors as well, but the knob would only turn slightly before the lock stopped its momentum.

"Give me a break!" said Graham. Looking over at Kel, he said, "Hey, just do your little blast thing."

"I told you, that wasn't me."

"It was you. You slammed your hands down and my chair blew in half," said Graham, getting frustrated.

Kel's face began to turn red. "IT WASN'T ME."

She stared at Graham with a spark of anger in her eyes.

"Whoa. Ok, fine. Don't tear my head off," said Graham, not wanting to rattle her cage.

Trying the door again, Graham gritted his teeth. Something was not right. *This isn't the first time this has happened to her. She's hiding something.* He had to keep a close eye on her. He had trusted Chase and look where it had landed him. Whatever companionship he felt with Kel was fading. He was not going to be fooled again.

As the rosiness that stained her cheeks began to fade, Kel looked to her side, realizing that Ailey was not with her.

"Ailey! Where are you?" Trying not to make too much noise, she whispered as loud as she could. "Ailey, where did you go?"

Graham turned around. He hadn't known Ailey for more than a few hours, but he still felt protective of her. She was so innocent. They all ran down the hall, coming to an abrupt stop as they saw an open office door. They ran through the door to find Ailey with her hands up against the outside window, looking out over the forest that surrounded them. Kel ran up behind her, throwing her arms around the young girl.

"You scared me half to death! Why didn't you come get me?" Cradling the back of her head, Kel pulled Ailey tightly into her chest. "I thought something had happened to you." Kel wiped a tear and smiled back, cupping her hands around Ailey's cheeks.

Meanwhile, Graham and Damien were looking out the window for a way out. There were no stairs on the outside of the building, at least not on this side. They were completely surrounded by trees. Wherever they were, it was isolated.

"This just keeps getting better and better," said Damien. "We are no better off now than when we were in that room."

Ailey moved her fingers in a series of three different patterns. Kel looked at her hand and said each letter she was forming. "O-U-T. Out? You see a way out?"

Ailey nodded with a big smile on her face.

"Where?" Kel asked.

Damien and Graham ran over to the girls. "You found a way out?"

Ailey walked past the window and behind the desk. She pointed to a crooked photograph hanging on the wall. It was of a man with a big beard and top hat standing on top of a building with his hands clasping the lapels of his overcoat. He had a proud, beaming expression on his face, as though he had just accomplished something incredible. Studying the photo, Graham realized the photographer was not just capturing this proud moment. Behind the man could be seen the lay of the land. There was a wide path cut out in the forest leading to a few small, cabins hidden in the woods. On the right of the picture was a clearing in the trees with a pond. Graham looked at the grinning man. Taking hold of the photograph, he snatched it from the wall to get a better look.

Taking the sleeve of his shirt and wiping the years of dirt and grime from the glass, Graham shouted "I know this guy! This is Mr. Alexander! This is the same guy who built Greenwood! There's a picture of him over our fireplace. We can't be far from Portfield if he was the one who built this place. He practically built the entire town."

Ailey grabbed the top of the picture frame and pushed it down on top of the desk. She moved her finger along the bottom of the picture. Beginning at the path in the trees near the building, she traced it past the small cabins, all the way to the top of the picture. It was hard to see because it was so far off in the distance, but as Graham leaned in for a closer look, he could see a small construction site at the other end of the trail. There was not much of a building there. All he could make out was a small outline of a foundation, with a small structure at the front. But the arches were unmistakable; this was Portfield Manor in its infancy. It wasn't just a mansion. It had been built as just one part of an entire complex.

Graham looked over the picture one last time and noticed some letters at the bottom under a layer of grime. Using the side of his thumb, he wiped away the dirt to reveal a small caption under the picture.

'Catalyst Grove.'

Looking up at Ailey, Graham grabbed the sides of her face and planted a big kiss on the top of her head. "You are a genius! How did you notice that?"

"It is remarkable what you can understand when you don't talk," said Kel.

"What's that supposed to mean?" Graham asked.

"It means that since Ailey cannot talk, her other senses have strengthened to compensate. She can usually see and notice things that we would just glance over."

Graham looked at Ailey with even more compassion now. "Thank you, Ailey."

Ailey smiled at Graham.

"I was also implying that you talk too much. Just so you know," said Kel.

Damien couldn't help but laugh. He could dish it out, but this girl was relentless.

Graham could not get a good read on Kel. He wanted to think she was playing, but she had the world's best poker face. He, however, would not play games. Her sarcasm only fueled his distrust.

Graham took the picture and abruptly slid it across the desk in front of Kel. "Okay, you don't want me to talk? *You* get us out of here."

"Graham, I was just kidd—"

Before she could get it out, Graham stormed out of the

room. Damien and Kel both started to go after Graham, but Ailey caught hold of Damien's shirt. Turning around, Damien looked down at Ailey.

"What is it?"

Ailey pointed up to another picture frame above the light switch. Damien looked up to see a drawing of the building that had all the rooms on the third floor. There was a red dot inside of one of the rooms.

You are here.

"Guys! Get back in here," said Damien.

Coming back into the room, Kel looked at Damien.

"What is it?"

"Ailey found something. A fire escape route, I think."

Damien studied all the different rooms and the red line connecting the hallways to the exits doors on all sides of the building. He kept looking around for any way to escape from the third floor without being seen on the other two levels. Damien saw four exit doors, but could see from the drawing that they all led to stairwells. He looked back at the red dot and tried again. Moving down the hall, he could see the rooms they had already passed, the break room area, what looked like more offices on the opposite side of the building, and six larger rooms on the third side. Going inward, there was a cluster of four rooms with a small hall leading to an elevator shaft. An elevator shaft! That was it! That was their way out!

"Graham! Graham! Get back in here. We have a way out!"

Graham's footsteps pattered down the hallway until he came back through the door.

"What? Where?"

"Here," said Damien, pointing to the little square on the drawing.

Graham read the word on the paper.

"An elevator? We can't ride an elevator down to the first floor. We might as well tie ourselves up and crawl in the trunk of their car."

"Not ride it. Haven't you seen the movies where people use a service ladder inside of the shaft? If we could make our way down and crack open the door, we could find a way to sneak out."

Graham thought about it for a minute. Looking over the rest of the drawing, he noticed the same thing Damien did. There was no outside escape route, just stairwells. His friend was right. This was their only way down.

Damien looked back over at Ailey with a smile and held up his hand. Ailey jumped off the ground and smacked his hand with hers.

"Way to go, *muchacha*. You just found our ticket out of here."

Ailey grinned. This was the first time she had been able to be a help instead of acting as a hindrance, and the pride could be seen in her smile.

There wasn't much time to say anything, however, as Graham and Kel were already halfway down the hall. Damien took Ailey by the hand and ran down the hall, following the others to the elevator shaft. They ran around the next corner, passing the six big rooms he had seen on the drawing. Each room had a drawing of the sun emblem on the floor, though you could hardly see it anymore because time had worn it thin. It also did not help that the rooms were littered with debris, fallen ceiling tiles, and some even had burn marks on the wall from what looked like a fire. Bundles of wire hung from the ceiling as if the wires had exploded.

"What in the world happened in there?" Damien asked as they ran by.

They turned right, making their way to the lobby area. They could see the small hallway that led to the four offices on their left. Walking into the lobby area, Graham began digging his fingers into the gap between the two stainless steel elevator doors. He pulled, trying to wedge his fingers a little deeper with each tug, but the doors would not budge.

"We need something to pry this thing open," said Graham, still struggling to make them move.

"Hold on. I'll be right back," said Damien.

Running back toward the big rooms, Damien entered one of them and began sifting through the rubble for a piece of metal. Bending over, he started to dig like a dog with a bone to bury. He threw aside chunks of plaster, slivers of wood, broken tiles, and files filled with paper. After moving a small mountain of trash, Damien saw a twisted piece of metal underneath. The heap of metal had once been a table, but it was now mangled, as if someone had wrung it out like a wet towel. Three legs protruded in different directions, with the forth leg dangling to the side. Damien took hold and twisted it back and forth until it broke free. Stumbling backwards, he caught himself before he fell over. Studying the twisted piece of metal, he inspected the two ends to see if they would fit between the doors. One end was twisted and bent, but the other end was good and flat.

"Perfecto!"

He started to run back out the door, but a piece of paper caught his eye. He knelt down to pick up the scattered papers fanned out from the manila folder, noticing big red stamped letters that spelled 'FAILED ATTEMPT'. Tucking the metal leg under his arm, Damien flipped through page after page. Each page looked the same, but with a different name at the top. The header read 'Case Study'. The person's name was listed below it, with paragraphs underneath, all with the same red stamp overtop of them. Linsey Rockwell, Alan Smith, Casey Hagan, Lacey Kelly, Jason Larkin. Name after name, they all had the same result. Damien shuffled the papers back into a neat pile and tucked them back into the manila folder. He retrieved the metal leg from his armpit and put the manila folder in its place. He then took off down the hall back to the elevator.

His suspicions were just confirmed by these papers. Man, we really are lab rats in some sort of experiment, he thought.

Getting closer to the elevator, Damien yelled to the others.

"Guys! You won't believe what I just found. I told you they were freaks!"

Entering the lobby in front of the elevator, he saw Kel and Ailey up against the back wall with a look of shock on their faces. Kel held her arm in front of Ailey, pinning her to the wall. Her other hand was covering her mouth.

"Are you guys okay? You look like you have seen a ghost or something."

Turning to Graham, he froze as he saw Graham continuing to pry open the doors.

"COME ON! OPEN!" His frustration was palpable. Graham was mad at the door. He was mad at Kel. He was livid with Chase's betrayal. Everything was wrong. The veins in his head began to bulge as he held his breath under the strain of his attempts at pulling the doors open.

Not knowing that the others were staring at him, Graham pulled for a few more seconds until, with a heavy sigh, he let go of the doors. As he turned around, all of the furniture of the lobby that was hovering in the air came crashing down.

OUT INTO THE OPEN

"Impossible." That was all that Damien could say.

Shock immediately replaced Graham's rage. Nobody had known about the levitation. He had been so careful. Now everyone knew, and worse— he could have hurt someone. The power didn't usually manifest itself while he was awake. He could only remember one other time that had happened. He was rapidly losing control. He knew they couldn't split up, but as long as they were with him, they were in danger.

"Maybe those bands did something to you." Pulling his sleeves up, Damien looked down, but there was nothing there. No marks. His wrists were completely bare.

"It's not the first time," whispered Graham.

Damien just stared at his best friend. "How long?"

Graham felt ashamed that he had kept this from him. His voice was low and sheepish.

"You know those nightmares I told you about? Well, this happens every time I wake up from one. It started years ago. The most recent one was the same night as the earthquake."

"Why didn't you tell me? I thought we were supposed to be best friends."

"We are, Damien." Graham started to get nervous. He had never upset Damien before.

"This is the kind of thing best friends tell each other. I can't believe you never told me about this."

Kel let her arm fall from Ailey's chest. She looked at Graham with a hint of compassion.

Damien threw the manila folder to the ground, spilling the papers all over the floor. "Here, I found out that we are lab rats. You were the first person *I* was going to tell."

Damien quickly turned away and slammed his metal table leg between the doors. With a few twists and jerks, the doors popped open. Oily wafts of air came out of the shaft as he stuck his head inside in search of a ladder.

"Here, I told you," said Damien, reaching around the door and grabbing hold of the rung of the small service ladder.

Kel stooped down to look at the papers. Pushing them around the floor so that she could read them, she looked at all the red stamps. Ailey knelt next to her, also trying to decipher the contents of the folder.

"They all ended in failure. What kind of failure? Does that mean they… died?" asked Kel. "Whatever Aegis was doing to them didn't work." The dark red ink of the stamp made it almost impossible to read the words underneath, and there were numerous black bars on the page concealing words. The flickering lights overhead did not help.

"We don't have time for this. We need to get out of here," said Graham. He was already in the shaft, his head poking up from the floor of the doorway. "Come on."

Kel took the piece of paper she was holding and folded it up, placing it in her coat pocket. She took hold of Ailey's hand, got to her feet, and then led her friend to the ladder. Ailey stepped over to the ladder and began her descent. Kel grabbed the ladder and followed.

Faint light emanating from the floodlights gave them just enough light to see a few feet in front of them. Hand over hand, they all climbed down the small ladder, squeezing past the elevator box hanging at the second-floor entrance, until they reached the bottom. Stepping off to the side, they saw a sliver of light coming from the doors. They were already cracked open a good three inches. Damien walked up to it, sliding his table leg silently into the gap. They all held their breath as he eased the doors open another couple of inches at a time until the gap was wide enough to stick his head out.

Damien signaled to the others that the coast was clear. Pulling his head back through, he slid the bar back between the doors and pried them open as far as he could. He put the bar down and slid it out into the lobby, then putting both hands against the doors, he pushed them open wide enough so that they could fit through.

"Come on. We need to find another map so that we can see how to get out of this place," Damien whispered.

They were in the main lobby now. There were big glass doors leading outside, but a thick metal chain was laced through the handles with a padlock. Graham realized that they were exposed and needed to move quickly. There was no telling how close Cavaness and the others were. He looked to the left and saw a few doors. "Maybe we'll find another map through there," he said.

Graham decided to go the other way and let Damien have some room. He felt terrible. It wasn't that he'd wanted to hide his problems. Actually, it was a relief to speak to someone else about it, but at what cost? Now there was no way he could keep Damien at arm's length to protect him. At least for the moment, Damien was upset enough to keep his distance. Once they were out of this crazy warehouse place, he would make it up to him. He didn't know how, yet, but he would figure out a way.

Meanwhile, Kel and Ailey were searching the rooms on the opposite side of the lobby for another floor plan. For the first time, Graham just stood there. He was tired of taking the lead, being the one to figure out what to do. For once, he would let them search for a way out. Yes, this was good. Now Graham could sit back and watch Kel. He still didn't trust her. He did not like the way she made excuses to cover up her ability to do what she did with that chair. Then again, he was hiding his secret as well– but at least he didn't lie about it. He just didn't want anyone to know. There was a difference between not telling and covering up. A huge difference. No, she was hiding something. There was something about Kel that Graham couldn't quite put his finger on.

Graham blew out a sigh, looking out the lobby doors. The morning sunshine began to flow through the glass doors, dispelling the darkness. The light glistened from the frost on the lawns like a blanket of diamonds, giving Graham an odd sense of hope. Hopefully this new morning would provide a way out of this place.

He would have kept staring out the doors, continuing to let the prospect of hope build him up, if it weren't for a blur of movement flying by out of the corner of his eye. Before his mind could process what it was, he heard Damien scream.

"AHHHH! GET OFF ME! LET ME GO!"

Kel and Ailey both sprinted down the hall after Graham toward Damien. They both came to a stop behind Graham. Chase walked out of the small office backwards, holding Damien by the throat with his left forearm. His right arm was extended with his fingers spread out and slightly bent, just like they'd been earlier, with his hand and forearm engulfed in light. This time the glow looked more like a yellow flame, and he had it extended toward them. Behind his hand, they could see his wrist glow with the same golden flare that theirs had when they'd first put their wristbands on.

"Easy there, trigger," said Chase, addressing Graham.

"Let him go, Chase," Graham replied in an impressively calm voice.

"Leave me. Take the girls and get out of h–" said Damien, being choked by Chase's arm against his throat.

"Aww. That's just the sweetest thing. You're going to make

me cry," Chase said. Damien struggled against Chase's arm, but with every movement, the grip around his neck would tighten, choking off his air supply.

Kel stepped out from behind Graham, still keeping Ailey at arm's length so that she was protected behind them.

"Graham said to let him GO!"

"Well, I can see who has been deemed the leader. Congratulations, Graham. Why don't you come over here and show me what you've got?" Moving his hand directly in front of Graham, the glow of the fiery light began to grow in intensity. "Let's see, how does that saying go? 'Strike the Shepherd and the sheep will scatter?'"

"No, Graham! Get out of here! You need to…rhuuu-ahhgg." Chase tightened his arm again. Damien could hardly breathe at all.

Graham was livid. "I trusted you, Chase. You manipulated me from the beginning to be a lab rat in your sick little experiment. We will not be a sacrifice so that you can glow brighter or move faster, or whatever your plan is. I said LET HIM GO!"

The sound of his voice carried through the halls and the whole building shook. Everything that was not anchored to the wall or ground lifted, hovering in mid-air. The debris and trash that littered the hallway floated around Graham like dust particles suspended in a ray of light.

"NOW!"

As he yelled the last word, everything that had been suspended flew horizontally across the room, smashing to pieces as they crashed into the adjacent walls.

Kel, Ailey, and Damien all flinched and ducked their heads, but Chase didn't move. He just stood there with arched eyebrows.

"That is an impressive party trick. I see the hovering problem has moved beyond your night terrors. That's good. That is very good indeed."

"Leave him alone!"

Kel pulled her right arm back then thrust it forward as if chucking a heavy rock. A power surge shot from her palm toward Chase, but with a gentle flicker of his hand, he fired a quick blast of light, deflecting the energy that came from Kel. The blast was sent crashing into the front door, shattering the windowpanes. The concrete entrance glistened with shards of glass, almost matching the glimmer of the frost that lay over the grass and trees.

"Oh, we've got ourselves a Pusher. Cavaness will be thrilled."

In the intensity of the moment, Chase's grip had evidently become tighter, because Damien's face was pale, and his body was starting to go limp. Looking down, Chase relaxed his grip, allowing Damien to breathe.

"*Lo siento, amigo.* I don't want you dead." Chase looked directly into Damien's half opened eyes and asked, "Do you have anything to show me?"

Not hearing a word Chase was saying, Damien focused on staying conscious, taking in big gulps of air. Even if he could do something special, he was too weak to do anything useful.

Scared of all the noise and yelling, Ailey had been hiding behind Graham and Kel, with a handful of each of their shirts clutched in her hands to cover her eyes. Feeling the tugging of her shirt, Kel jerked, as if she had felt a surge of power through her body. At the same time, Graham felt a bizarre tingling in his left arm. The two looked at each other to confirm the other felt the odd sensation. Their expressions both confirmed that they did. Somehow, they knew what the other was thinking, as though a new instinct had taken over. Graham pulled back his left hand as Kel pulled back her right, and at the same time they both threw their arms forward, sending a blast of yellow light toward Chase and Damien. It hit them with such intensity that it knocked them both back six feet. The two fell to the ground with a loud thud.

Graham and Kel just stood there, unable to comprehend

what they had done. Expecting Chase to get back up, they both pulled their hands back again, ready to attack, but neither Chase nor Damien moved. Ailey let go of their shirts and shuffled back a few steps. Her eyes were wide and her brow was furrowed. She looked as though she was scared of her own friends.

The power drained and the tingling in Graham's arms faded away. Kel began patting her arms, chest and stomach trying to figure out where the power she felt had gone. Graham pumped his arm forwards and backwards, trying to 'shoot' another blast from his hand. Nothing happened. Ailey stared at the two with the tips of her fingers curled in between her lips. She looked terrified.

Graham glanced over to see Chase and Damien still lying flat on their backs. Scenes of his parents screaming at the darkness flashed through his head as he looked at his unconscious friend. Graham watched Damien's chest rise and fall with each breath, relieved that he was at least alive. He fought back the dread of hurting Damien, knowing that it was now or never. He ran over to his friend and put his hands under his armpits. Kel ran and helped pick Damien up so that they could sling him over Graham's shoulder. Graham slowly stood up from his squatted position and walked toward the front door. He could still feel the twinges of pain from his near fall off the cliff, and his more recent fall from his chair.

Kel ran back over to Ailey and grabbed her hand. She took a few steps toward the door, but was jerked back. Ailey would not budge. Her eyes were still filled with the terror of seeing two people knocked unconscious by a wave of light that should have been impossible. She did not need words to express what was going on in her mind.

"I know you're scared and confused, Ailey. I am too, but we have to keep moving. I promise I'll try to explain when we get some place safe, okay?"

Not waiting for a response, Kel ran toward the door, almost dragging Ailey behind her. The glass crunched beneath their shoes as they ran out of the front doors. They ran quickly out in the open, looking around for a clear sign of where to go next. The road was too risky. That would be the obvious choice, but they knew the others would look there first. No, they had to find another way.

Ailey ran to the right a few feet, looking at the treeline. It was like she was studying it. She ran further down, stopping again to look at the surrounding trees.

"What is she doing?" asked Graham.

"I don't know, but whatever she's doing, I'm following. Like I said earlier, she notices everything," replied Kel.

Ailey continued her pattern of running and stopping until they were halfway around the building. Suddenly, she started jumping up and down in excitement. She waved them on and pointed at the edge of the forest.

"What is it, Ailey?" asked Kel, looking at the tall pine trees. "I don't see anything. Do you want to climb the tree to get a better look?"

Ailey gestured no. Moving her hand back and forth, she kept pointing into the forest, and then pointing back to the two trees. Looking at Kel, she put the tips of her index fingers together and drew an imaginary square in the air.

"Box?"

Again Ailey gestured *no*. She made a small rectangle with her index fingers and thumbs and twitched her right index finger like she was clicking a button, then she traced the rectangle in the air again.

"Picture? Picture frame?"

Nodding yes, she pointed back to the forest.

"You saw this in the picture from that office?"

Ailey smiled again. Graham looked up at the trees and noticed that they were two large maple trees. The other trees surrounding them were pines.

Ailey tugged at Graham's shirt. She held her hand up with her fingers straight and wove her hand through the air like a snake moving along the ground.

"The path!" said Kel. She grabbed Ailey and by her shoulders. "Is this the path that led back to the manor?"

Her head bobbed up and down again.

"You are kidding. I don't see a path anywhere. You remembered what kind of trees were beside that path in the picture?" asked Graham.

Again, Ailey nodded.

Shrugging his good shoulder, Graham said, "Okay, let's see if you're right."

Graham walked over to the two maple trees, now stripped bare from the autumn winds. Grass and undergrowth had grown up to waist height. It was hard to navigate through while carrying someone on your shoulder. Kel went first, trying to bend some of the saplings to the side, making it easier to let Graham and Ailey pass. After they got in twenty feet or so, the underbrush began to clear away, revealing a small trail. Or at least what used to be a trail. Flowers and small saplings had almost overtaken it, but Graham could still see where the constant use long ago had worn a permanent path in the ground.

"You saved us again," said Graham, wincing between grunts caused by the heavy load slumped over his shoulder.

Ailey pulled her head into her shoulders in a shy, thankful reaction as her cheeks became slightly rosy. Visible puffs of white fog came from her mouth in the cold air.

"Do you remember where the trail led through the forest? Do you think you can lead us to one of those cabins?" asked Graham.

Ailey nodded.

"Wait, we can't go to the cabins. Once they realize we didn't follow the road, don't you think that will be the next place they look?" asked Kel.

"If they even know it's here. That picture was pretty old. They may not realize how big this compound is," said Graham.

"I don't know if we can take that chance," said Kel.

Graham stood there for a moment. It was freezing outside. It would be hours before the frost melted away, but he would rather freeze to death than get caught again. Looking into the trees, he conceded. "You're right. Our best bet is in the woods."

Kel and Ailey looked at Graham, and with a nod of agreement, they took off into the foliage. As they walked through the brush, Graham thought of ways to keep everyone safe. Who knew what was ahead. In case they had to run, they needed to have a plan.

"I think we need to lay down a few ground rules, so that if we get separated, we all know what to do. First, I think we need to agree on where we are trying to go. If we can't go to the cabins, then we need to aim for something else, like that large clearing in the trees. If they come and we have to run in different directions, then that's where we'll meet up. Next, if we can keep tabs on the trail, then we should try to stay off it and in the foliage, so they can't track us. I don't know how far back these woods go, but we won't last one night out here in the cold. We have to be sure we aren't getting lost."

Kel reached down and placed both of her hands around Ailey's, cupping them in hers. She blew between her thumbs, trying to warm Ailey's hands. She then removed her coat and draped it over Ailey's shoulders.

"Here you go. Better?"

Ailey nodded as she continued to shiver in the cold morning air.

"Ailey, do you think you can bounce back and forth between us and the path to keep us on track?" asked Graham.

"What are you doing? She is not going near that path." Kel was getting angry, and she made no effort to hide it. "She's eleven! What if she gets caught? Are you willing to risk her life, because I am not!" Kel wrapped her arm around Ailey as if protecting her from Graham.

Graham kept calm, even though his first instinct was to yell back. "Kel, she is the smallest. She can move in and out of that brush without making a noise. Plus, the extra movement will keep her warmer."

Kel kept her cold stare.

"You know I'm right, so lay off with the staring. I still haven't figured you out yet." Graham was running out of breath, grunting with every step. "We've got to stop for a minute. I can't carry Damien much further."

Graham looked around them for a place to lay Damien down. Just beyond a patch of holly bushes, he spotted a couple of fallen trees.

"Let's go over there behind the trees. We can rest for a minute or two until I can catch my breath."

Ailey and Kel pulled back some branches to let Graham pass through the brush. He crouched down until Damien's legs touched the ground, letting his back flop against the trunk of one of the fallen trees. Damien's head flopped back and hit the trunk making his head rebound back against his chest.

"Oh, sorry, amigo," Graham said. He moved closer to Damien's face and waited to see the small clouds of white fog puff from his mouth.

"Good, at least you're still here," said Graham.

"Graham, about earlier..." said Kel.

"What about it?" said Graham.

"You don't talk too much. I was only trying to lighten the mood a little."

Graham sat silently waiting for Kel to continue, though he really did not want to hear what she had to say.

"I mean, you do tend to get a little bossy, but that's beside the point."

"Oh, really. And you're a perfect little gem?"

"No, I didn't say that. Look, you got us out of that warehouse, and for that, we are grateful."

"But...?"

"But what? I'm trying to make amends here. Why is it so hard for you to accept it?"

"Because you lied about your power," Graham blurted.

"My whole life people have lied to me, except Damien, and look at him. He's unconscious!"

"Look who's talking! You made everything around us hover!"

"Yeah, well at least I didn't lie about it! I just didn't say anything about it. There is a difference!"

"Are you kidding me? Hiding it… lying about it. What difference does it make? Sometimes what you don't say is just as wrong as what you do say, so get off your high horse, Graham! *We* are on the same side here."

Graham opened his mouth to react, but no words came out. He had never thought of it that way before. Was he really lying by not saying anything?

"I…I…"

"That's right. You, you. That's all you care about, isn't it? Well, I've got news for you, Graham. You're not the only one with issues and secrets you'd rather keep in the dark."

"Would you two pump the brakes for a minute? Geez," Damien mumbled under his breath as he held a hand to his head. "What in the heck happened? I feel like burnt death."

Graham twisted around. "Damien! You're alive!"

"Yeah… why wouldn't I be? Was I almost dead or something?" Damien closed his eyes again, wincing with every movement as he shifted his body against the log. He took a moment to clear his head, then opened his eyes to see where they were. "I'm in the woods? We are in the woods? How did we get in the woods?"

"It's a long story, and trust me, you won't believe how we got out here."

"I never believe what you say anyway."

"Well, at least you still have your wit intact. You had us scared, man. Very scared."

The mention of fear must have jogged Damien's memory, because he shot to his feet, pointing at Graham and Kel with one hand still gripping his throbbing head.

"You shot bright light from your hand! Both of you! How

did you– there was light and wind and… pain. Ow! My head!"

Damien crumpled back to the ground. "Your wrists were glowing. Chase's wrists were, too. Guys, those bands are real." Damien looked up from the ground and made eye contact with the others. "I think we are officially part of their experiment."

Graham pushed his sleeves back to his elbows, exposing his forearms and wrists.

"There's nothing there, Damien. Are you sure you saw them glow? Maybe the force knocked you silly."

"I know what I saw. I saw the same glow coming from Chase's wrist when he had me in that headlock. I think it's an energy source. It felt like he was draining the life out of me. Maybe they drain energy from others to make themselves stronger or something. Whatever those bands are, I think they are why you did what you just did."

Damien looked down and started rubbing his wrists. "Whether we like it or not, they're a part of us now."

He's The One

He moaned a bit before he found the strength to sit up.

A huge form was standing over top of Chase, slapping his cheek with his hand.

"Wake up, kid."

"Oh, man. What happened?" asked Chase. "Uhh, my head." He used the palm of his hand to massage his temple as he sat up straight.

"I don't know, you tell me. I just felt the building shake," said Cavaness. Taking a look at the debris and the smashed door left behind by the blasts, Cavaness said, "Looks like we've got some strong ones."

"Yeah, they're strong alright. We've got an interesting mix this time. I'm pretty sure the little one's a Bridge, and you'd be happy to know that we finally found ourselves another Pusher."

Cavaness stroked his goatee as he listened to Chase. "It's the older girl, isn't it?"

Cavaness held out a hand to help Chase to his feet. Chase stood slowly so that it didn't make the pounding in his head worse. Once he was fully upright, he tipped his head side to side, cracking his neck.

"Yes, although you won't get much out of her right now. She's pretty weak."

"If she was weak, then who did all of this?"

"It was a combo. The little girl, Ailey, was cowering behind the other two while I held the Latino boy hostage. I saw it before it happened. They both felt the connection, but I've never seen that level of strength before."

"So, it's him. Isn't it?"

"100%. No doubt in my mind. Graham is the one we've been searching for."

"I hope you're right. You know what happened to the one before him when we jumped to this conclusion. We must be certain. We're lucky to have even found him first. Who knows what the others would do with limitless power."

"It's going to take some time. There's some sort of block with him. The power is there alright, but it's like there's a cork in the wine bottle. Something is holding it back. It only begins to build up, then stops. He's going to have to learn how to pull that cork loose."

Cavaness looked out beyond the mangled front door to the woods beyond the parking lot.

"Sometimes a corkscrew isn't enough. In some cases, it's better to let the pressure build up inside until it forces the cork free."

Cavaness shoved a manila folder into Chase's chest. "I went back upstairs to have another look around. They found the files. It still amazes me that every time, though our guests are so eager to flee this place, they find time to snoop around."

Chase smiled. "Graham mentioned being lab rats when he confronted me. I figured they found something. It's all coming together then, isn't it? Which file was taken this time?"

"Casey Hagan."

"HA! The Casey file? That ought to do the trick."

"Yes, I imagine it will."

The anticipation of what was to come made Chase forget the headache. He always got a little nervous when it was time for the hunt. He knew it was necessary, but it never did make it any easier. He walked over to where Cavaness was standing and handed him a small frame.

"They found the picture of Alexander as well. I found it lying on the desk with the dirt wiped from the glass."

Cavaness took the small frame from Chase and stared at the path winding through Catalyst Grove. "Now it really begins."

Jittery, Chase started rubbing his hands together as he thought about the next stage. "You ready for the hunt?"

Cavaness thought for a moment. "I've got a better idea. Go get Murphy. We're going to need an eye in the sky."

"You got it, big fella."

Cavaness rolled his eyes and looked back outside. Holding up a hand, he said, "Wait. What did you get from the Damien kid?"

"Not much. It was hard to get a read on that one. Maybe we can funnel them to the ravine and see what happens."

Cavaness thought for a moment. "Alright. It's a longshot, but there's only one way to find out."

Chase nodded in agreement, and then took off down the hall in a blur, leaving Cavaness standing by himself.

Looking back down at the picture, Cavaness exhaled. "What do you think? Is our search finally over?"

Alex stepped out from the shadows behind Cavaness.

"Graham is exceptional, there is no denying it. I have never seen levels that high after the application of the catalysts, but only time will tell if he is the one for whom we have been searching." Alex put his hand on Cavaness' shoulder. "Time and trials will always be the best agents for uncovering one's true nature. Just stick to the plan."

"Yes, sir."

THE CASEY FILE

Damien got to his feet.

"Can you walk?" asked Graham.

"I think so. I'm a little shaky, but I am okay."

Kel took Ailey's hand and began walking back toward the path. "Good, we need to keep moving. If Damien is awake, then Chase is, too."

Graham quickly briefed Damien on their plan. Damien nodded in agreement. They all made their way back down to the path. They followed it for a while until they could get a good sense of where it was leading, and then ducked back into the trees, keeping to higher ground.

"I think we can keep following the trail from here and stay hidden." Feeling a little safer now that they were deeper into the woods, Graham turned to Damien. "Hey, I'm sorry I didn't tell you about my problem. I can't control it and I didn't want you to get hurt, but I know that's no excuse. I should have told you."

"Yes, you should have," replied Damien. "But I get why you didn't. I'm sure it was hard keeping that big secret to yourself."

"Yeah, it has been pretty terrible. I guess it should make me feel special and unique, but it doesn't. It makes me feel like a freak. I'm scared to be around other people all the time. The last time it got out of control, people got hurt. I guess I didn't think you would stick around if you knew. I don't know what I was thinking. I'm sorry. We're all in this together now, so no more secrets."

"Good. It's settled then. Now, what was that blasting all about?" asked Damien. "That was awesome!"

"I don't know. For a minute, it was like I could do what Kel did. My arm started to tingle, and it was as if something inside was telling me what to do next," said Graham.

"Same here, but I've never been that strong before," interrupted Kel. It was evident from her demeanor that she could not believe she was openly talking about being able to move things without touching them. Her face relaxed as she told them how good it felt to be able to finally speak freely, knowing that what she was about to say would be accepted.

"Sometimes things close by would fall down beside me. Most of the time it was a drink or something like that. Everyone thought I was so clumsy, but I would rather them think that than know the truth. Lately, though, bigger objects have been moving." Kel coughed and continued. "About two weeks ago, I sat down in a chair to eat breakfast and the chair beside me fell over, scooting across the floor a couple of feet."

Graham was still skeptical. As she continued to talk, he felt as though she was explaining his exact emotions. The confusion of not knowing what was going on, and trying to play it off like the abnormalities were a normal occurrence. The fear of rejection. It was as if he was listening to his own inner thoughts speaking through Kel. Did she really have that good of a read on him? Was she trying to gain his trust?

"At first, it would only happen every couple of months, and it was very subtle. My cup would move an inch or two as I was eating or something. But lately, it's been more frequent. The chair was the most intense I've ever seen it. I've certainly never made chairs explode before." Kel looked over to Graham. "When it happened I really didn't think it was me. Honestly. There's a big difference between knocking a chair over on its back and blowing it apart."

Graham graced her with a smile. He would figure out how to deal with this later. For now, they had to deal with their other, more imminent threat. He ducked under a low branch. Once he passed underneath, he lifted it up and let the others pass. Ailey ran ahead of them, making her way down closer to the path to be sure they were still following it. A few minutes later, she shuffled back up the hill giving a thumbs-up. The frost was almost completely gone now. Their breath no longer produced white puffs, and because of the constant walking, they had all stopped shivering. Once Kel had told her story, Graham couldn't help but wonder how Chase knew about them. If he and Kel had kept it hidden so well, how did Chase and Cavaness know? Before he knew it, Graham was thinking out loud.

"So, somehow they found out that we could do things others couldn't. How could they possibly know? We've kept it hidden," said Graham. He thought about the man who saw him at Wellington, but surely he did not say anything. Besides, Chase already knew at that point.

"Maybe Ms. Winstone told Chase before we got downstairs," said Damien. "If she knew about your nightmares, maybe she knew about the hovering, too."

"I don't know. I think she would have said something. She's never been one to hold back."

"Well, they had to know somehow," Damien said. He turned to Kel next. "Did anyone see you move things where you are from?"

"I don't know. Maybe. Ailey knew. Maybe a few others saw it, but they never said anything," said Kel.

Graham rolled his eyes.

Damien arched his eyebrows and shrugged his shoulders. "And why did they take me? I have never experienced anything like you two. Why bother with me?"

As they continued to ask questions, Kel remembered the piece of paper in her pocket. Continuing their trek through the woods, Kel walked over to Ailey, reached into the pocket of her coat that was still draped around Ailey's shoulders and pulled out the folded document.

"What is that?" both Damien and Graham asked.

"It's a case file from that folder you found," Kel said. "I grabbed it before we climbed down the shaft. I thought it might give us some answers."

Kel unfolded the paper and began reading from the top.

Case File

Date: [redacted]

Subject Name: Casey Hagan

Age: 17

Gender: Female

Conducted By: [redacted]

Description: [redacted]

[redacted]

All previous subjects have been unable to produce any results, even under extreme conditions. Casey Hagan was the first to accept the new concept called 'The Catalyst.' Once the bands had been set, numerous attempts to activate were conducted without success. [redacted]

[redacted]

All previous subjects have been unable to produce results, even under extreme conditions. Casey took over 18 hours to escape from the warehouse room, where she then fled into the woods towards Portfield Manor. [redacted] Casey was found in the West Wing of the Manor warning that [redacted]

Flames erupted from her wris[redacted]

This is the final report before [redacted] to arson. [redacted]

Kel looked up at the rest of the group with fear in her eyes.

Graham and Damien both stopped walking. "Ms. Winstone mentioned a fire that broke out at Portfield Manor years ago. It must have been Casey!"

They all started to rub their wrists at the thought of being enveloped in flames.

"What do we do now? How do we get these things out of us?" asked Graham.

"I don't think that's an option," replied Kel. "I think they were designed to be permanent."

"Great, so we really are lab rats," said Graham.

"I think the more important question is what experiment we are lab rats *for*," said Kel.

Graham gritted his teeth. *Ten bucks says you already know.*

"I am telling you guys," Damien cut in, "when Chase had me captured, I felt like the life was draining out of me. I think they are finding ways to take energy from other people to make themselves stronger. You saw his hand. It was surrounded by a glowing flame, but there was no heat. It was some sort of energy coming from inside."

As they continued to walk, they heard loud, thunderous cracks above them. They looked up to see small balls of light litter the sky like fireworks, but they did not fade away. They remained, blanketing the sky overhead like a cloud of mist.

Murphy stood on top of the old warehouse, his hand stretched out in front of him at chest level. Thousands of tiny beads of light shot from his hand like shotgun pellets, peppering the skyline above the forest. Once he was satisfied with the covering, the light ceased to fire from his hand, but he kept it outstretched as if commanding the beads of light to stay in place. Carefully surveying the forest in slow sweeping movements, Murphy used his throat mike and earpiece to communicate to the others.

"You want to keep moving southeast. I can't tell how far off the trail they are, but they seem to be sticking close by."

"Roger that, Eagle One," chimed Chase through the earpiece.

"Stop calling me that. We are not in the military. We don't have to speak in code. My name is Brian Murphy."

The headset crackled to life again in Murphy's ear for a second. "No, I like Eagle One better."

"Ugh."

"Hey, at least it isn't Tinker Fairy. Be thankful," said Chase.

"You're an idiot, you know that?" said Murphy.

"Yeah, but you love me anyway. Just trying to lighten the mood. I think we can all agree that this is our least favorite part."

"You're right about that. I despise the extraction stage." Murphy continued to survey the landscape until he caught a glimpse of movement. "Chase, keep moving eastward. You're closing in on them."

Murphy pulled out his earpiece so that he could concentrate. He had a unique capability to form these small balls of light and use them to detect the energy in other people, like an infrared camera. Each ball was its own sensor, giving him a live feed of everything that was happening beneath them. As he looked through the woods, he could see yellow forms running. He grabbed the dangling earpiece and stuffed it back into his ear.

"Chase, you are about 200 yards from the target. Looks like your little Latino buddy is still alive and kickin'. All four of them are running about thirty feet to the left of the trail."

"Got it, Eagle One. I'm in pursuit."

"I'm not Eag– you know what, forget it. You've got it from here. Eagle One, out."

Murphy shook his head in response to his new nickname. He held his hand out a little longer to be sure Chase was on the right track and then closed his fingers, letting his hand fall back down to his side. As he did, the small beads of light faded to a vapor and vanished.

Graham's legs were burning. His lungs were on fire. They had been in an all-out sprint since the lights appeared in the sky. Kel was able to keep pace, but Damien was way ahead of them, even with Ailey on his back. Once the orbs overhead faded away, they let up a little.

Graham came to a stop and slouched over, putting his hands on his knees, trying to catch his breath. Kel did the same. They were doubled over, concentrating so intently on their lack of endurance that they didn't notice Chase leaping from limb to limb rhythmically and silently in the trees above them.

Damien turned around after noticing that his friends were not with him. He started walking back toward Graham and Kel.

Chase continued leaping like a cat from one tree to another without a sound. His movements were so swift and precise that the limbs he jumped to barely moved under his weight.

"Catch your breath, amigo," Damien said to Kel. "You too, amigo, but only for a few minutes. I don't think those were fireworks earlier, and I don't want to stick around to find out what they really were."

Graham and Kel kept panting. Damien let Ailey down from his back and waited patiently as Graham and Kel caught their breath and stood up.

Chase sat perched in one of the trees like an owl. He

watched and studied them until he was ready to break the silence. "I gotta tell ya, this is giving me warm fuzzies all over. They knock you unconscious, almost killing you, yet you're still looking out for them. The virtue of your loyalty is inspiring. Seriously, I've got goose bumps."

The sound of Chase's voice hit them all like a sucker punch to the gut. Graham whirled around to confront him, but didn't see him anywhere.

Chase let out a small whistle. "Up here, guys."

They all looked up just in time to see Chase's glowing hand. A bolt of light sprang from his palm, connecting with a small tree to their left and uprooting it with ear-ringing sounds of cracking wood and grenade-like explosions.

They all fled in panic. Forgetting all sense of direction, they just ran.

"Ah, ah, ahh… not that way," said Chase.

He pulled his hand back again. Pushing his arm forward and snapping his elbow straight, another blast of light came from his hand, making a small cluster of trees explode upwards next to Ailey. Ailey stumbled sideways, clamping her hands over her ears and shuffling away from the explosion.

They were all disoriented. The panic inside was scrambling Graham's thoughts, making it impossible to act on a simple decision, like what direction to run. This must have been what war was like. Explosions, fear of walking into the unknown, the pursuit of the enemy, and the uncertainty of life itself. There was no time for the mind to process anything. Instinct kicked in. It was all the body could do. Fight or flight were the two options, and flight was winning by a landslide.

They clustered beside each other and ran together like a pack of wolves. Damien had the sense about him to grab Ailey after the second blast, knowing that he was the fastest one. His mind flashed back to being held in a choke hold by Chase as Ailey's grip tightened around his throat in reaction to the explosions. He didn't dare move her arms, though. He could hear her sobs as her face pressed harder into his shoulder blade. He just concentrated on the rise and fall of her little chest against his back and counted her breaths, helping him focus.

Satisfied with the outcome, Chase fired off one more blast for good measure, and then stopped. "There, that ought to do the trick," he said, watching the others disappear into the distance.

They continued to run as fast as their legs would take them. Graham could hardly think of anything but the pain in his legs, chest and back. As his legs moved on auto-pilot, he tried to busy his mind as he ran. He pictured Chase up in the tree, wondering how long he had been there, watching. He probably had been there for a while, silently mocking them as they had stopped to catch their breath. Graham's mind kicked into high gear. *He's just toying with us. This is pointless! There's no way we can outrun Chase. He can move as quick as lightning. If he isn't pursuing us, then we must be heading exactly where he wants us to go. It's his sick little game.*

Graham stopped the others. Through heavy breaths, he said, "If he wanted to hit us, he would have. If he wanted to capture us, he could have. I think he is funneling us, making us go where he wants. We need to break off in a different direction."

Kel could barely speak through her panting. "Okay… but…where?"

There were trees and bushes everywhere they looked. It was impossible to know where they were or where they had come from.

"I don't know. Let's try there." Graham pointed to the right, about ninety degrees from the direction they had been running.

Damien agreed. "We are far from the trail now. It's as good of a direction as any at this point."

They all picked the pace back up to a fast jog. They traveled about a hundred feet before the ground in front of them began to shake, erupting in a mountain of dirt. The ground moved upward like a giant wall. They all fell backwards, landing on their backs. Ailey hit the ground and rolled to the side, just in time to avoid being crushed by Damien. The wall of earth sprang upward until it was at least twelve feet tall.

"Where do you think you are going?" The words from the deep, gravelly voice weighed them down to the ground like anchors.

Turning around, they saw Cavaness standing a stone's throw away from them, with his glowing hand aimed at the ground. They all pushed against the ground with their hands and feet, shuffling backwards in an attempt to retreat.

Cavaness kept eye contact with Graham, bringing both hands up in front of his chest with his palms facing down toward the ground. As if trying to push the air into the forest floor, he pushed his arms straight, and a pulse of energy shot into the dirt. They immediately felt the ground beneath them shake. Another wall of earth burst from the ground in between Cavaness and where they lay.

"RUN!" yelled Graham.

In mid stride, Damien grabbed Ailey by the arm and flung her up and around his back. They sprinted away from the wall of dirt, dodging and weaving through the trees until they came to a long row of thick shrubbery. Not knowing what was on the other side, they sprinted through, tearing pieces of clothing and drawing blood from the pricks and prods of the small branches. The ground on the other side of the shrubs took a steep decline.

Damien was the first to tumble. Graham and Kel were not far behind. The hill seemed endless as all four of them tumbled down the embankment like small coins bouncing down a staircase. Side over side and head over heels, they continued to fall toward a large ravine. Each one scrambled for anything that would help them stop falling, but there was nothing to grab onto. Kel fell into a small patch of bushes. As she hit, the obstruction slowed her momentum down just enough to steady her pace and allow her to shift over on her back.

Waves of panic closed Graham's throat and stiffened his muscles as he caught a glimpse of the trees near the bottom of the hill and the huge gap in the ground beyond them.

Instinct kicked in as Kel pushed both arms in front of her. A strong pulse of energy burst from her hands and penetrated the ground in front of them. The earth shook and rumbled, then exploded twenty feet beyond where the blast had entered the ground. Small trees blew out of the earth, the force of the blast propelling them through the air. They corkscrewed toward the bottom of the hill, then crashed to the ground, creating a bridge over the gap of the ravine.

The kids continued to tumble side over side until they spilled into the huge crater made by Kel's blast. Graham fell into the crater, and then bounced out, but at a much lower velocity than when he entered. Each taking a few more rolls, they eventually came to a stop, mere inches away from the exposed root systems of the trees now bridging the ravine.

The disorientation of the fall made Graham nauseated. The whole forest was still spinning just as fast as his stomach was churning. Graham and Kel got to their feet with weak knees, looking around for Damien and Ailey. They, too, were struggling to stand without falling back down. Graham wobbled over to Ailey to help her to her feet. Grabbing her left side with her right hand, Kel found Damien laying between the two trees that provided the way over the ravine. Limping and wincing from the sharp pain in her side, she walked over to Damien. He was turning over onto his hands and bracing himself against the trunk of one of the trees. He twisted his head slowly, trying to level out his equilibrium.

Graham and Ailey ran over to the fallen trees where Kel and Damien were. Graham wrapped his hands around Ailey's waist and lifted her on top of the fallen tree.

"It's not a big tree, but it should hold us," said Graham. *It's going to have to.*

Still holding his head, Damien did the same on the second tree. The two trees were farther apart on their end than on the other side, but they were still close enough where they could hold out their hands and balance one another. Damien leaned to the right to take hold of Ailey's hand. Her grip was shockingly strong for an eleven-year-old. Damien made eye contact and said, "On three, okay? On three we will start together."

Ailey agreed.

"One… two… three."

On three, Damien held his left foot out in front of him and waited for Ailey to do the same. He timed his steps with hers taking the first few steps with ease. Damien's eyes bounced back and forth from the tree to Ailey, making sure she was ok.

"You are doing great, *chica*."

Ailey smiled, but did not take her gaze from her tree.

Kel looked at Damien with a hint of jealousy in her eyes. She had noticed that Damien took to Ailey right off the bat, but why? Ailey was her responsibility. She should be the one holding her hand.

Graham tried to read Kel's expression. Why was she staring at Damien like that? Was she scheming? This split second allowed Graham to think about what just happened. Cavaness had just pushed some kind of energy into the ground, making it erupt. Kel had just done the same thing to these trees. *This can't be a coincidence. What if she's one of them? It would explain her secrecy, but what about Ailey? She would not abandon or hurt her.* Graham didn't know what to think or feel. As he stepped up on the tree behind Damien, he could hardly stand the thought of holding his hand out, waiting for Kel to place her hand in his. Kel reached over and took hold. Her hand was soft– much nicer than his rough hands. They were like silk. Come to think of it, this was the first time he had ever held a girl's hand before. Graham felt his cheeks blush a little. *Come on, Graham. Get it together. She could be the enemy and you are literally running for your lives. Deal with this later.*

"Are you okay? Still dizzy?" asked Kel.

"Uh, yeah. Still dizzy from the fall," lied Graham. Better to seem dizzy than give away his distrust or awkward romantic feeling. "You ready?"

"Yes. Right foot first?"

"Sure." Graham held his right foot out to time his steps with Kel. Looking ahead, they saw that Damien and Ailey were about three quarters of the way there. Graham and Kel were able to take their second step before they felt the ground shake. They both looked back just in time to see the ground under the roots of their trees give way and crumble underneath, as beams of light poured from the cracks in the ground. Before losing his footing, Graham saw Cavaness at the top of the hill with an outstretched hand. He had just fired another wave of energy into the ground.

The trees fell a couple of feet before hitting the ground. The descent of the tree combined with the jolt of the roots was all it took. The tree only fell a foot or two, but it seemed like a mile and lasted an eternity. The two pair of kids tried to steady themselves against one another, but it was too much. Damien and Ailey were about to make a leap for the other side, but they lost all traction when the tree dropped beneath them. The roots falling back on the uneven ground made the tree roll to the side dumping all four of them over the edge of the ravine. Clawing for the tree, they screamed as they fell into the darkness.

Uncharted Waters

The descent only took seconds, but it felt like an eternity. Grabbing at air, they tumbled toward the water below as the walls of the ravine amplified their screams. Graham's vision was limited in the darkness with no way to know which way was up or down, and no way to tell when to brace for impact. All he could do was hopelessly fall into the sheet of black with an overwhelming sense of dread. To Graham, it felt like hours, but in reality, it only took seconds before he plunged into the icy water.

The sting of the frigid river contracted every muscle in Graham's body, forcing him into the fetal position. The river was deep enough so that he did not hit ground or rock.

Paddling upwards, or the direction they hoped was up, they all eventually bobbed back up to the surface as the current swept them downstream. Kel came to the surface first, followed by Damien, then Graham. Graham noticed Kel looking around for Ailey.

"Ailey! Ailey, where are you?" A few moments passed without response. "AILEY!" Kel was in full panic, to the degree where she could hardly keep her head above water.

"She is not a good swimmer! Oh, please God, where is she?"

The three of them frantically looked around, but it was almost impossible to see anything in the darkness.

"THERE! Over there!" screamed Damien. "I see movement!"

Graham and Kel looked ahead to see little arms flailing against the current. Kel went face first into the water, swinging her arms in perfect strokes. She swam to Ailey in seconds, grabbing her under her arms. Ailey looked up to Kel with a mixture of relief and panic in her eyes.

"It's ok. I've gotcha. You're going to be ok," said Kel, pulling Ailey close to her chest.

Ailey pulled away so that she could look directly into Kel's eyes. Shaking her head 'no', she pointed up to the sky. Everyone looked up and saw that the walls of the ravine that were once parallel with each other were now moving closer together. The river was about to go underground.

"Oh, no," whispered Kel.

"Grab onto each other!" said Graham, bracing himself.

They paddled through the water toward one other, each finding an arm or a shoulder as they passed the threshold of the cavern entrance into complete darkness. It took every ounce of energy they had to time their breaths so that they could inhale air between the waves of water hitting them in the face.

It was as if they were in rapids. The current grew stronger and the river began taking twists and turns. Kel was able to keep her grip around Ailey, but the jerking back and forth tore her away from Damien, and Damien away from Graham. The river turned to the left, then took a sharp right. They were like pinballs slamming into the cavern walls. All they could do was tense their bodies and anticipate the next impact. After a few more turns, the riverbed dropped a few feet, making them all plunge back under the water. Graham's arm hit the jagged cavern wall, ripping his shirt and throwing him into a barrel roll. He put his arms out straight in an attempt to steady himself until he resurfaced.

Damien was somehow able to keep his head above water the entire time. He didn't even have to kick his legs or arms to remain afloat. For some odd reason, he felt abnormally comfortable in the river, outside of the freezing temperature.

At the bottom of the drop off, the current slowed down, allowing Kel and Ailey to come back above the surface. They both coughed up water and wiped their eyes. It was still too dark to see ahead, but Graham felt very uncomfortable in the sudden calmness of the water and the silence that filled the cavern.

"Damien, Kel, Ailey… are you all there?" asked Graham. The echo of his voice carried through the cavern, making it seem like there was a crowd of people.

"I'm here, amigo."

"Us, too," said Kel.

"Thank God." Graham paddled toward their voices. He could tell from the splashing water that they were doing the same. Now together, Graham continued, "Are you guys hurt?"

"I don't know. Define hurt," said Damien.

"We're not fine, but we're not hurt either," said Kel.

"Okay, at least we have that going for us." Ignoring the gash in his arm, Graham kept working on a game plan. "I think we need to swim over to the sides to feel for a place to get out. Maybe there's another cavern or cave we can crawl into."

The plan must have sounded good, because they all started to paddle away. Graham started making his way to what he hoped was the cavern wall. Arm over arm, he swam away from the others until his hand hit rock. Turning back around, he cupped his hands around his mouth. "Just yell if you find something."

"What?" yelled Damien.

Raising his voice, Graham repeated, "I said yell if you find anything."

"Speak up. I can't hear you," Damien yelled.

The sound of crashing water was so far off in the distance that it was hardly noticeable at first. It wasn't until Graham had to repeat himself for the fourth time that he became aware of the increasing noise. The current was growing stronger.

Graham's heart skipped a couple of beats as he realized what was ahead.

"Guys, we have to find a way out NOW!"

The urgency in his voice was enough to carry over the noise of the waterfall ahead.

"Why is the water getting faster?" yelled Damien. "I think we may be going through some more rapids or something."

Kel swam to the side of the cavern like her life depended on it. The crashing of the water was so strong now that it made her head hurt.

"It's not rapids. It's a *wa-ter-fall*. We're about to go over a waterfall!" yelled Graham.

The same wave of panic that Kel experienced hit Damien as well.

"Graham! I think we're about to go over a waterfall!"

"I know! That's what I just said!"

Graham could scream all he wanted, but it was pointless. The pounding of the water was now too loud. Kel clawed at the sides of the cavern with one hand, holding Ailey tight with the other. Graham and Damien both tried to swim against the current, but the force was overpowering. There was a light ahead that looked like an open mouth waiting to consume them in one bite. In a flurry of strokes, they pulled and clawed against the current, but the water's pull was too strong. All at once, the current pulled them over the edge.

They tumbled head over heel as the waterfall threw them from the top. Blurs of light surrounded them as they fell into the pool of water below. As they plunged below the surface, the force of the waterfall pushed them even further down. Damien found his bearings and shot straight up toward the surface, but the others were completely disoriented. Damien broke the surface taking big gulps of air. He looked around, hoping to see his friends doing the same, but he was the only one above water. As the seconds ticked by, Damien's face began to show signs of panic.

He took a deep breath and, in a quick and fluid motion, dove back down in pursuit of his friends. What light there was quickly dissolved into black as he swam deeper. Damien swung his arms around, feeling for anything. He was getting desperate. It had been too long. They had to be running out of air. He continued swimming down with breast strokes then pausing to feel around, but with no luck. Still moving his hands around, Damien's wrists began to glow in the pattern of the golden bands. With a slight tingling sensation, two balls of light sprang from his palms, propelling down toward the bottom of the pool. The light found three bodies struggling frantically to find which way was up.

Damien stopped swimming. They were still so far away and he was beginning to run out of air himself. Without thinking, he twisted his body so that he was upright, with his feet a little wider than shoulder width apart to keep him steady. He extended both arms out in front of him, elbows slightly bent. His fingers were spread and extended. He had no idea what he was doing, but something deep inside, like a gut instinct, was telling him that this was going to save his friends.

Suddenly his hands began to shake. Streams of bubbles escaped from the sides of his mouth as he strained and grunted. His wrists began to glow again, this time with more intensity. The entire pool started churning as though it had been brought to a boil. The force emanating from Damien's hands was creating some kind of vacuum. Graham, Kel, and Ailey were forced upward by the current. Holding his position, Damien strained harder, letting a large cluster of bubbles pour from his mouth as he yelled. His wrists were glowing like iron rods in a furnace. The force of the current grew stronger, propelling all four of them up to the surface with such intensity that they shot out of the water a couple of feet into the air like playful dolphins. They all fell back into the water, emerging a few seconds later flailing about and heaving air into their lungs amidst gagging coughs.

They looked at one another with perplexed expressions.

"What the heck just happened?" asked Kel as she continued coughing.

Graham and Ailey continued to hack and cough. "I don't know. Something shot us out of the water… some kind of current, maybe."

"I don't think it was natural, whatever it was," said Kel.

Damien remained quiet.

"Right now, I don't care. I just want to get out of here," said Graham.

Once Graham realized they were not going to drown, he was able to calm down and look around. There were lights. Not natural light, but electric lights. There were floodlights mounted around the perimeter of the cave spaced out every thirty feet or so. Over to his right, Graham could see a wide-open area beyond the edge of the pool. A flicker of light revealed a small room on the other side of the stone floor, which was carved into the rock.

One by one, the small group waded over to the edge and pulled themselves up on the rocky ledge. Exiting the water, they stood to their feet, taking in the construction of the cave.

"This is part of it," Graham said. "Everything." The compound stretched out well beyond the warehouse. The entire section of forest they had been in was probably a part of Catalyst Grove. Aegis had gone to great lengths to carry out their experiments.

"It doesn't matter what we do or where we go. They have rooms everywhere. It's like we're in one big rat maze," Graham added.

"Whatever they did with Casey, they're apparently still doing. How did they build all of this without anyone knowing about it?" asked Damien.

"I guess money can buy anything. Even silence," said Graham. "Mr. Alexander was the richest man in town. He could do whatever he wanted."

Graham's mind flashed back to the photograph from the warehouse. He could still picture Mr. Alexander posed with his hands on the lapel of his overcoat. His large top hat. The radiant smile shining from behind his large beard. Something kept bugging him about that picture– about his face. He couldn't put his finger on it, but he felt like he had seen him somewhere else. It had been grating on his mind ever since he had seen that picture.

Ailey shuffled over to Kel and wrapped her arms around her waist, trying to keep the trembling at bay. Kel did the same and began rubbing her hands up and down Ailey's back, trying to produce some heat. It was not as cold down in the cavern as it was above ground, but the chill was still seeping in through their wet clothes.

Graham was shivering, too. He walked toward the room carved into the wall of the cave as the light flickered on and off. It looked like an office from the warehouse, with the same type of door and large window. Before he reached the entrance to the room, Graham looked to his left and saw a small metal table against the rock with three oval mirrors hanging above it. They were the same type of mirrors that he remembered seeing in Portfield Manor. They even had the same four divots carved into the wood along the right side of the glass. Graham reached out his hand and placed his four fingers into the oval divots in the wood.

"Well, isn't that cute. They even coordinate their decor," he mocked.

Walking back to the door, he checked the knob. It was unlocked. He looked above the door for any sign of a siren. No red lights. No speakers. He twisted the knob and opened the door. Silence. With a sigh of relief, he stepped inside.

Damien stood there completely focused on his wrists. He had no idea how it had happened. Curling his fingers in again, he tried to reproduce the light and the current that he had just done underwater, but nothing happened. He grunted and strained to the point that veins began to bulge from his temples and neck. He held his breath for a few seconds, and then let it out in one big disappointed huff.

Kel caught a glance of Damien trying to recreate the underwater lightshow.

"What are you doing over there?"

Lowering his hands, Damien let out another heavy sigh. "Nothing."

Kel's eyes narrowed as if trying to decipher a code. She reflected for a moment, then her eyes widened.

"That was you?"

"Yeah, it was. At least… I think it was."

"You didn't tell us you could do things, too!" Kel's excitement was palpable. All four of them had now shown a supernatural ability.

"There was nothing to tell. That was the first time it's happened," said Damien.

"What was it? What did you do, other than the light?" asked Kel.

"I…well, I remember thinking that I could help if I could see, and that is when the light shot from my hands. Then, something inside just told me to hold out my hands and try. Just try. I can't really explain it. I just strained like I was pushing a heavy object out of the way, and that is when that current forced us all to the surface."

Kel let go of Ailey and walked over to Damien. She noticed the confusion brewing beyond his excited exterior. It was in his eyes. She gave him a firm hug and then put her hands on his shoulders. "You saved our lives. Thank you." She gave him another tight squeeze.

Damien shrugged, "I really don't feel like I did anything. I just reacted." It was obvious, though, that he enjoyed the appreciation. His normal smirk returned to his face. "*Gracias, amiga.*"

"Hey guys! There are clothes and towels in here!" yelled Graham from the other room.

They all ran into the small room to see Graham searching through a free-standing metal closet. He had already retrieved five or six pair of crimson red sweatpants and hooded sweatshirts. Each shirt had the same yellow sun emblem printed on the back.

"I am not putting that on," said Kel.

"Would you rather tromp through the forest in those?" Graham pointed to her clothes. Large drops of water continued to fall from them, forming a small puddle around her feet.

Ailey didn't care what they were. She was wet and freezing. There were dry, and she wanted them. Her lips were purple and her teeth would not stop chattering. She sifted through the pile of clothes on the floor that Graham had pulled out, finding some that fit her.

Damien also found his exact size. "Um, guys. These all fit us. Perfectly."

"I know. I noticed that, too," said Graham. "I think this is where Chase was trying to make us run to. If they intended us to ride this waterfall down here, then they knew we would be freezing. I guess they knew if they needed us to make them stronger, then they needed us alive."

Kel held up the sweatshirt at eye level. "Say we make it out of here and back up into the woods. These things are bright red. We'll literally stick out like sore thumbs."

Damien looked at the clothes in silence. His mind was churning. It was evident that he was sorting out the details and events of the last couple of hours. His unfocused eyes darted back and forth as his mind continued to race, until a smile curled the sides of his mouth. "Oh, that is good."

"We don't really have a choice," said Graham, in response to Kel. "It's either wear these or freeze to death. We'll just have to get a little creative to stay hidden…wait, what?" Damien's remark sunk in. "What do you mean 'that is good'?

I'm pretty sure this is the exact opposite of good."

Damien looked directly into Graham's eyes. He held up the red clothing. "I was just thinking that it's a little ironic that the clothing meant to trap us is actually going to set us free."

"I don't follow," said Graham.

"You said it yourself. We are in a maze, and we are doing exactly what they want us to do. This whole place is their playground. Do you really think we can hide from them?"

"Well, when you put it that way…"

"You know I am right. They chose you two because you already showed signs of unnatural abilities. They are probably always on the lookout for people like you. I guess you give them the most bang for their buck, but Ailey and I never had anything like that happen to us before. But for some reason, we can now." Damien pulled back his wet sleeves enough to expose his wrists and forearms. "It makes sense then, that those bands were their initial experiment."

Graham pulled back his sleeves to look at his wrists. There was nothing visible, but he knew it was there, lying just beneath the skin.

"It reminds me of something my dad used to do," Damien continued. "Before my parents died, my dad used to collect sap from maple trees to make syrup. It was a much different trade than what he did back in Peru, but he was always good at adapting to the new skills that were needed in the area. When we moved here, in the northeast, he got this new job collecting maple syrup. He would go out mid-morning during the latter part of winter. As the temperature would rise, he would drill holes in the trees. He had a bunch of these small metal spiles that looked like little tubes with a spout at the end. We called them the 'sap taps'. He would take those sap taps and hammer them into the trees where the holes were drilled. Once they were in place, the sap would begin to run out of the tube, and he would collect it in a big bucket."

They all turned to look at each other, trying to figure out

if anyone was getting the point of the story.

"Really, guys? Do I need to write it in crayon? These bands let them take our energy, or life force, or whatever you want to call it. These are sap taps. I think they allow our energy or power to come out. The thing is, we can use them for ourselves."

Damien pointed to each of them as he spoke. "Kel, you used it to break Graham's chair and uproot those trees at the bottom of the hill. Graham, you used it to make a mess in that hallway."

"Gee, thanks for the compliment," said Graham.

"You know what I mean. I even used them to light up the water and pull you guys out of it." Dropping the clothes, Damien held up his arm in front of him. He pointed to his wrist. "We can use these to our advantage."

"Wait. You made the water push us to the top?" said Graham. "I thought it was just another current from the pool. That is amazing!"

Kel was deep in thought. "That sounds great in theory, Damien. It really does, but I can't control these 'powers', and neither can you. I just watched you try."

Graham had never seen Damien this determined or serious. "What choice do we have? Even if we escape this maze, do you think we are just going to run up to Ms. Winstone and tell her about all of this? She knows Chase. She knows Cavaness. There is no way she will believe our word over theirs."

Kel looked at Ailey, then at Graham. Graham shrugged. "He has a point."

"Of course I do. And that is just it." Picking up the shirt from the floor, Damien held it up in front of everyone.

"The *point* of these red shirts is that we can't hide or run anymore. They expect us to keep running. We obviously cannot hide any longer. We have to turn the tables on them. We have to fight. We have to win and expose what they are doing. It is the only way to end this..."

Graham looked over at Kel to gauge her reaction. Her eyebrows were arched in surprise and a hint of curiosity, which surprised him. He would have bet that had been what she wanted. His resolve about her motivation softened slightly, but even still, he could not take the chance and trust her. Not yet.

Damien yanked off his wet shirt and threw it to the floor. He took a towel and quickly dried his upper body before pulling on the dry shirt.

"…and it will be the one thing they do not expect."

The Calm Before The Storm

Graham and Damien collected their new apparel and walked out of the room, letting the girls change in privacy. They made their way over to a dark corner so they could also get out of their wet clothing. Graham was surprised at how comfortable the clothes were, once he was able to get past the fact that they featured the sun emblem he now despised. They were not cotton like normal sweats. They felt like they were made of polyester and elastic, but as soft as silk. There was also a thin, insulated liner sewn to the inside that kept him warm and comfortable in the cold, damp cave.

Graham looked over at Damien as he finished pulling his pants up to his waist. "I'm sorry I dragged you into this. This is my fault. We probably wouldn't have needed to come if I'd told you about my problem in the first place. I'm going to get us out of here, amigo. I promise you that."

"No, you won't. *We* will get out together. I wanted to come here just as much as you did, so don't go whipping yourself, alright? Besides, I've got a plan."

He whispered into Graham's ear. Graham's eyes grew big and his jaw dropped a little.

"You are crazy. I can't even...I mean, I haven't done anything yet. I think I'm broken or something."

"You will. I know you haven't let loose yet, but you will." Damien smiled. "When the time comes."

The girls walked out of the room in their new clothes. Kel hated them, Graham noticed. She kept tugging at her shirt, awkwardly adjusting it in frustration. Ailey, on the other hand, seemed to love them. She was all smiles. They were warm, and most importantly, they were dry. For the first time since being in Portfield Manor, she looked as though she was comfortable.

Damien gathered everyone around and let them in on his plan. He went through the list of the known 'special abilities' and then described how they could work together in a surprise attack. When he was finished, he was met with silence. Kel looked very uneasy. It wasn't Graham's favorite either, but he could not come up with anything better. Finally, Kel broke the awkward silence.

"We could get hurt doing this, Damien. Injured, maybe even killed. How do you know we won't get wounded while doing this? How do you know if we can even use these bands to do anything?"

"I don't. I can't know that we will all make it out of here in one piece, but I think we should act on what we already know."

Kel remained unconvinced. Her brow was furrowed and her arms were crossed over her chest.

In a spontaneous dash, Damien sprinted toward Kel and shoved her violently to the ground. Without thinking, Kel reacted. She held her hand out and shot a beam of light from her hand as she fell backwards, her wrist lighting up with a golden shimmer. Damien flinched but did not move. He just stood there with his eyes shut tight and his head turned to the side as the force hit him right in the chest. It knocked him down on his back at the water's edge with a loud thud.

Graham stood there in total shock. Did Damien suspect

she was one of them, too? Would she finally show her true colors?

Kel pushed herself onto her elbow, looking up to see what happened to Damien.

"WHY DID YOU DO THAT?" yelled Kel, her words echoing throughout the cavern.

Damien pushed himself up to a seated position. He held his chest with his hand and tried to massage the pain away. "I told you. I had to make a decision based on what I already know."

Graham's eyes darted back and forth between Damien and Kel, trying to decipher what was happening.

"Good *gosh* that hurt!" said Damien. He put both hands to his chest and rubbed it fervently. "Look, I admit we can't do these things on command, but we can when our instinct takes over. If we don't think, and just react, the bands work. They let us attack. I knew you would have a hard time believing me, so I thought I would just show you."

Kel lay there trying to process what Damien was saying, Graham assumed.

"But...how did you know I would do that?" she asked.

"I didn't. It was an educated guess," said Damien.

A look of curiosity slowly replaced the fire of anger in her eyes. Kel pulled her hand back so she could get a good look at it. She could not deny what had just happened, and it was true her wrists had lit up. They still had a fading glow.

Graham could not believe what he was seeing. Two different emotions fought inside him like lions. On one hand, he was thrilled to see others like him. The burden and shame of secrecy seemed like a distant memory now. The answers he had been seeking did not come how he'd wanted or expected, but they were unfolding, and now, he shared this rare bond with his best friend.

On the other hand, a looming sense of dread waged war on his newfound joy. As he continued to watch, he could see that Damien was right. They could not run any longer, but he still could not perform. How ironic that he previously shunned human interaction because he could not control his power, and now he couldn't use it when he needed to protect his friends. All he could do was make things hover, and that wasn't going to get them out of anything. Sure, he worked with Kel to blast Chase, but that was her power, not his. He could feel himself holding back with each opportunity to act, but he didn't know why. He was scared that his hesitation would end up hurting the others.

Damien stood up, still trying to massage the pain out of his chest. He walked over to Kel and helped her to her feet. "Sorry about pushing you like that. I had to do it hard enough to make it seem real."

"Don't apologize. That was probably the best thing you could have done."

They all walked back toward each other. Ailey grabbed Kel's hand, studying it to see where the energy could have come from.

Graham spoke first. "Okay, so we have a plan to get away from this compound. That's great, but it's not going to do us much good if we can't get out of this cave." Turning to Damien he said, "Do you have a grand plan for that, too?"

Damien shook his head. "No, I haven't gotten to that part yet."

Ailey walked away from the group. She began making her way around the edge of the water, then around the perimeter of the cave.

"If this is part of their compound, then they have to have a way in and out besides that waterfall," said Kel. "If there is a way out, Ailey will find it."

Graham was surprised at how comfortable he was letting Ailey search. It was rare he was able to trust someone so fully and so quickly. As she made her way around the cave, Graham realized that he was repeating his past mistake. By not telling Damien about his powers, he had pulled him into this mess. Now, he was keeping his self-doubt from everyone.

He was ashamed to admit it to the others, but he knew it had to come out. He was not willing to make that same mistake twice. Surely they had already noticed that he had not yet been able to contribute to the group. All he had done so far was lead them into more trouble. Plus, this would be a good test for Kel. He would try to get a read on her as he opened up.

"Guys, I don't know about this. I don't think I'm going to be able to help when the time comes."

"Don't start doubting yourself now, amigo. You just saw what Kel did. Do I need to push you down, too?"

"I know it's coming now. Nice try, though. But seriously. I couldn't get us out of that room, I just stood there as you got captured. It was Kel's blast that knocked Chase unconscious. It was Kel that kept us from falling over the edge of the gaping hole in the ground, and it was you who saved us from drowning. Even Ailey has helped us by finding the picture of Alexander, the floor plan and the path through the woods. You guys have done all the heavy lifting here. If this plan is going to hinge on anyone, it should be you or Kel. Not me."

"It's not going to work that way. I have to create the distraction. Ailey is too young to fight, and besides, I am not really sure what she can do anyway. She has to stay hidden." Damien took two steps forward so that he was face to face with Graham. He placed a hand on Graham's shoulder, looking at him until Graham finally made eye contact. "I have to be beside the water. I don't know why, but I can feel it. That only leaves you. It will be your time to shine. We can all feel how strong you are. If anyone can give the final K-O punch, it is you, my friend. You just have to get past your self-doubt, that's all."

Graham huffed in disbelief. "I don't know. What if I can't? What if it won't break loose? I've only ever been powerful when I react to the nightmares."

"It will. It has to. You will not let us get captured. I know that, and somewhere in that head of yours, you know that, too."

Graham continued inspecting Kel's reaction as he spoke with Damien. She seemed genuinely concerned about this plan, and he could detect her empathy after he admitted his own hesitations. Maybe he was being too hard on her. Perhaps he was being blinded by the cut of betrayal from Chase, but why was her power so much like Cavaness'? One way or another, he had to discover the truth before they arrived in the clearing. There was enough to worry about already.

Ailey came rushing out of the office where they had found the dry clothes. She seemed excited, waving her arms about. As Damien finished his pep talk with Graham, they all followed her into the small room. Ailey led them past the desk and over to the free-standing metal closet. She pulled the door open, revealing the clothing rod with bare hangers swinging slightly side to side. Kel looked at Ailey.

"What do you see? I don't see anything."

Ailey rolled her eyes and took hold of the side of the closet. With the closet door still open, she shook it as hard as she could. She stopped after a few seconds and walked back over to the front, pointing inside. Graham looked intently into the closet, but still couldn't see anything. Ailey huffed and stood on the bottom shelf and pointed at the farthest clothes hanger to the right. Everyone leaned in to look. It was not moving. All of the other hangers were swinging from the disruption, but this one was perfectly still. Kel reached up and pinched the hanger between her thumb and index finger. She tried to wiggle it, but it would not move. It was fixed into place.

Graham then reached up and slid his finger along the top of the rod to investigate why this one was stuck. There was a groove on each side of the hanger in the metal rod. Graham's brow furrowed. Curling his fingertips around the hook of the hanger, he pulled back, forcing the hanger to slide along the grooved track. The back wall of the closet clicked, then creaked, coming slightly ajar.

"What the…"

Graham shook his head in unbelief. Ailey had again proven to be a valuable gift. Her power of perception was incredible. Kel pulled the door back all the way. Behind the back wall of the closet was a narrow stone staircase leading upwards. It was only wide enough to fit one person at a time. The treads of each stair were carved directly into the stone of the mountain. Electrical wire ran along the top of the right wall with a small light mounted every ten feet or so.

Graham went first. He wanted a chance to prove himself to the others. If there was danger at the top, he would be the first to confront it. The others did not seem to question his loyalty, or even his ability to use his gift when the time came. He knew he was loyal, but he had a hard time understanding why they trusted him to be able to use his power. There was no justifiable reason to trust his ability to act, but he did not want to let anyone down. In an effort to prove himself trustworthy, he was set on throwing caution to the wind. All caution that is, except letting Kel take the lead. That was something he was not yet willing to risk.

The lights had an iridescent shine that brought new life to the stairwell at each turn. They all twisted and turned up the stone staircase until they reached the top, where a weathered, wooden door waited to greet them. A beam of light stretched underneath the door like a golden carpet. It was almost as though it was welcoming them back home. Graham felt for a knob, but there wasn't one. He put both hands on the door, searching for a way to open it. The light shining on the door was dim, especially when compared to the light coming from underneath it. Graham moved his hands upward until he felt a metal latch inset into the wood just above his head. He stuck his index finger into the metal groove and found a small ring. He put his ear to the door and listened for movement until he was convinced that it was safe to proceed. He then pulled the ring until he heard a click, followed by the creaking of metal hinges.

Graham slowly pulled the door open until he could fit through, and realized that they were at the back of another closet, with hangers full of tattered clothing. He pushed the random articles to the side in order to pass through. He continued cautiously, stepping out into the bedroom, noticing that every wall was made of wood. The bedroom was small, and so was the closet. It couldn't have been any bigger than the free-standing closet from the cave. The door to the bedroom was open. Graham quietly made his way across the room as the others emerged from the hidden closet door. The wooden floor creaked and moaned under Graham's feet. He immediately slowed his pace and bent his knees in an attempt to take more pressure off of the floor as he crept across. The others took notice and did the same.

Reaching the door, Graham braced his arms and chest against the doorframe, peeking his head around the corner. The room in front of him was a small kitchenette. A tiny living room lay beyond it. There was one more room beside the bedroom, but that was it. The cabin couldn't have been more than twenty feet wide. Seeing that the kitchenette and living room were empty, Graham eased his way out of the bedroom, shuffling with his back against the wall over to the adjacent room. Treading lightly, he made it to the next room. He poked his head around the open door and saw a small pedestal sink and a toilet.

Graham's shoulders sank as he let out a big sigh of relief. He turned around and walked back over to the bedroom, motioning to everyone that they were safe to come out. They came out one by one. First Damien, then Kel and finally Ailey crept out to meet Graham. They all looked around at the tiny cabin. By the look of things, the place had been here for quite a while. The whole place was run down.

"I think this may be one of the cabins from the picture. It certainly looks like it's been here that long," said Graham, standing in front of a small couch. The cushions were all torn and stained with age. Graham looked at the three mirrors hanging on the wall.

"What is with these mirrors? Did they get a bulk discount or something?"

They all walked over to where Graham was standing and looked at the wooden decor mounted to the wall.

"Yeah, I think I remember seeing these back at Portfield Manor," said Damien.

"Why three? It's always three," said Graham.

Shrugging it off, Graham turned around to face the others, but the windows looking out into the woods caught his attention. Graham quickly shuffled back over to the bedroom and waved the others to follow. Kneeling on one knee, Graham pointed toward the windows.

"We don't have much time. If they knew the river swept us away to that cave, then they certainly know that we will have made our way to this cabin."

They all nodded.

"Ailey, do you remember that picture?"

Ailey nodded.

"Good. I want you to close your eyes and picture the woods behind Mr. Alexander. Can you see them?"

Another nod.

"Great. How many cabins are there?"

With her eyes still shut, Ailey held up two fingers.

"Two? Okay, now think back on how far we have traveled from the warehouse. I know it's just a guess, but do you think we've gone far enough to reach the second cabin, or have we only reached the first?"

Ailey held up two fingers again.

"You think this is the second cabin?"

Ailey motioned no. With her eyes still shut tight, she pointed to her chest, and then pointed to the side of her head. She then pointed to the floor and extended two fingers again.

"Sorry, Ailey, can you do that again? I don't follow," said Graham.

"She said she knows that this is the second one," said Kel.

Ailey opened her eyes, smiled and nodded.

Graham glanced at Damien, and then turned his attention back to Ailey.

"Good. I was worried we were way out in the middle of the woods somewhere. If we are really in the second cabin, then that means we're closer to the clearing than we thought." Graham looked up through the small bedroom window. The sun was making its way well beyond its midday position in the sky. The angle of the sun was casting long, eastern bound shadows as its rays enveloped the trees and rocks around them in a warm embrace.

"It's getting late. If we're going to do this, it needs to happen before it gets dark. We're fish in a barrel here, and they have the advantage at night since they know this place like the back of their glowing hands."

With each discussion, the plan was becoming more and more real. Graham sat on the damp wooden floor, staring at the others. Damien had been like a brother for years. It had been less than twenty-four hours since he met Ailey, but she felt like a sister already. He wanted to like Kel. Her reactions to Damien's little stunt as well as his plan to fight back were still compelling.

Graham watched Kel as she held Ailey close to her side, picking tiny pieces of debris from the younger girl's hair. It was evident that she was like a mother to Ailey by the way she cared for and protected her. She couldn't turn on Ailey now. It wouldn't make sense. Maybe she was just self-conscious about her power. He wanted to let it go and embrace her friendship, especially now that their lives were dependent on each other. He swallowed hard as the pit in his stomach grew deeper. As he watched them nod their heads in agreement with the plan of escape, he hoped that he would still have his new family after tonight.

Kel let go of Ailey and looked around the room for supplies. Walking back into the bedroom and over to the closet, she rummaged through the moth-eaten clothes, tossing shirts out as she continued her search. Not wanting to waste any time, she continued to chuck clothes out of the closet. Like a dog flinging dirt out of a fresh hole in the ground, ragged clothes kept flying out of the closet as Kel stripped it clean.

"Ah-ha! Yes!"

She emerged from the closet with a small, black backpack. She pulled the zipper to open the pack and reached inside.

"Ailey, I need you to take that blanket off the bed and fold it up for me. Graham, why don't you go into the kitchen and look for something to carry water in? There was a pond in that clearing, or at least there was when the picture was taken. We are going to need water and blankets if we survive this thing. I hope we can make it back to town, but we have to be prepared to stay in the woods during the night if we need to."

Graham nodded in agreement and walked out of the bedroom, being mindful of the two windows in the living room. He walked over to the small kitchen and began rummaging through the cabinets and drawers. As he pulled open the top drawer, he reached in and sifted through a few sets of rusted silverware, measuring spoons, and miscellaneous cooking utensils until his hand landed on a large knife. He retrieved it from the drawer and slowly pulled the blade from its leather sheath.

Chase's betrayal was consuming him. He had felt a strong bond with Chase and was struggling to understand how a person could misuse a relationship like that. He was so happy to finally have a big brother figure in his life, and Chase had used that to bring him here. He was seething with anger as he inspected his new weapon.

Though he was now armed, Graham had never been a violent person. He did not like this new, raw emotion, but in the face of such an abuse of his trust and friendship, it only made him more protective of Damien and his new friends. If he could not break free tonight, this would have to do. He didn't know if he even knew how to fight with one of these, but he was hoping that just the sight of it would be enough to buy some time.

Damien was on the floor, looking under the bed for anything else they could take with them. Kel turned around to face him.

"Have you thought about what we are going to do once we get out of here? Who are we going to tell? I know that Director Pitman from our orphanage won't believe us. You said this 'Ms. Winstone' won't believe you. Actually, from what you said earlier, these people are friends of hers. They're probably even well known in this community. With our luck, Alex is probably the Mayor."

Damien half-heartedly chuckled. "Let's just get past this first bridge, alright? We can regroup later and figure out who to go to. Right now, I just want us to make it out of these woods alive."

Kel reluctantly agreed. She started to rummage through the small chest of drawers near the door until she saw the expression on Damien's face. She put down her bag and turned toward Damien.

"We are going to make it out. You have a good plan, despite the reliance on these sap taps." Kel forced a smile on her face as she pulled back her sleeve.

Damien wanted to smile back, but he couldn't. Kel was about to speak again, but was cut off by Graham's return to the bedroom. Graham looked at his friend and could immediately tell that he was really second-guessing himself now. Once they stepped foot out of that cabin, there was no going back. The gravity of his decision was weighing down on him. He looked like he hadn't slept in days.

"Cheer up. This is going to work," said Graham. As he

spoke, Kel noticed that Graham had found a few plastic bottles, some cloth hand towels and a large filleting knife.

Kel's eyes grew big at the sight of the long, curved blade in Graham's hand.

"What in the world do you need that for?"

Graham held the knife up, looking at his reflection in the rusty metal. He twisted it back and forth, mesmerized by the streak of light dancing up and down the length of the blade. He kept telling himself that he would not use it unless it was the last option. Refocusing on Kel who was staring at him, awaiting a rational response, he waved his hand dismissively. "Relax, it's not for them. It's for food. Like you said, we need to be prepared. If we have to stay in the woods, we need to be able to eat. Squirrel, fish, whatever we can get our hands on."

Kel relaxed and let out a sigh of relief. "Good. I thought you went off the reservation there for a minute."

"I'm fine. I just want to get this over with." Graham slid the knife back in its sheath and then tossed it to Kel to put into the backpack.

Kel packed up the backpack with all the supplies and swung it over her shoulder. Graham reached out his hand and said, "Let me carry that. You don't need to be the one hauling it around."

"I've got it, Graham. It's not that heavy."

"Really, let me carry it."

Softening her voice, she took on a more serious tone as she leaned toward Graham.

"Ease up. You don't need to carry the world on your shoulders. No one here is blaming you for anything. We are not mad and we are not disappointed that you haven't 'saved' us. It's not a competition, okay?"

Graham was a little taken back by the blunt delivery. He wanted to defend his actions, but she wouldn't let him.

"You don't have to be a hero to earn our trust. It's already there. Just accept it and let's move on."

Evidently, Kel wasn't one for sugar-coating things. Taking

Graham's silence as confirmation, she said, "Okay, then. It's settled. We go out there and we stick to the plan."

Graham wrestled with his conflicting emotions. He wanted to trust her, but something inside would not allow him to. He needed more proof that she was not one of them, but there was no way to get that proof. Not until it came time to face their captors. With a heavy sigh, he locked eyes with her.

"Tell me you are on our side."

"What's that supposed to mean?" asked Kel, clearly offended.

"I still haven't figured you out, so I'm just going to ask. You haven't sugar-coated anything so far, so don't hold back now." Kel crossed her arms and arched her eyebrows, waiting for Graham's next words. "You lied about your power. You were timid about telling us, and I get that… sort of. But now, I've seen you use the same power that Cavaness has, and that can't be a coincidence. I had you pegged as one of them, but I just can't see you throwing Ailey under the bus, so just tell me straight. Are you with us or against us?"

Kel stood silent, weighing his words. She slid the backpack off her shoulder and onto the floor. Taking a few steps toward Graham, she said, "You're right. I lied. I wasn't ready to talk about it, because I didn't know you two yet. Ailey is my number one concern, and I just didn't trust you."

Graham looked intently into Kel's eyes as they grew misty. "I can't prove to you that I'm not one of them. Yes, I think I do have powers similar to Cavaness. I don't know how or why. Maybe they gave me the same kind of bands or something. I really don't know, but it doesn't matter." Kel wiped away a single tear. "Ever since the day that Ailey arrived at Oak Ridge, she has been like a sister. Ever since my real sister–" Kel choked back more tears. "Well, let's just say that the bond is the same. I would die for her, and that is something I can prove if it comes to it." The determination in her voice caused the tears to dissipate. "If we can't trust each other when we walk out of this cabin, then we'll fail. I don't know how I can make up for the lie, but I am on your side, Graham. We're all in this together."

If she was lying now, she would be the most deceptive person on the planet. Graham looked over to Kel. She was looking at him, waiting to see what he said next. It wasn't until Graham saw the look of pain and vulnerability in her eyes that it finally sank in. His resolve broke.

"Okay, we are in this together." Without thinking, Graham wrapped his arms around her. She hugged him back and they both squeezed tight, knowing that no words were needed. Kel was right. They had to trust each other. There could not be any room for doubt. Graham gave one final squeeze in affirmation. "I trust you. Let's just hope you don't have to prove that second part tonight, okay?"

Kel backed up a step, smiling as she wiped away another tear. "Yeah, let's hope nobody has to."

Just as they had finished making up, Damien came back into the room. Though the seriousness of their conversation was tangible, he could not resist trying to lighten the mood.

"Hey, you can flirt with each other later. We've spent too much time here already. Let's go."

Graham's cheeks turned red with embarrassment, but mostly with anger. "Hey! We weren't flirting…"

Kel just rolled her eyes and walked out the door, passing Damien.

"Typical boy," she said, as she nudged Damien with a swing of her hips, knocking him into the doorframe.

"Oww." Damien cracked a small grin.

Graham quickly followed, shoving Damien back into the doorframe with his shoulder as he walked by. Damien just grinned even wider.

"Come on. Lighten up. I was just kidding."

Damien followed them to the front door where Ailey was waiting patiently. They all gathered in a circle on the floor. The heavy silence immediately stripped all the playfulness from the room. Graham could see the grim expressions. The realization of reality had hit them all at the same time.

"Ailey, do you know which way it is to the clearing?" asked Graham.

Ailey pointed out the window on the western side of the cabin. Closing her eyes, she visualized the cabin in the picture. She held up a finger and traced a winding path, assumedly the path from the picture at the warehouse, mapping out their route to the clearing in the trees. Once she felt confident in her assessment, she opened her eyes again. She raised her arm again to point out the window, then traced the same path in the air.

They all took note of the curves Ailey was making with her finger. After she was done, they sat in silence for a few moments. The dread and unwanted anticipation were palpable, hanging in the air like a dense fog. Damien looked down at his red shirt, reminding himself of what he had said in the cave. He had to convince himself again that this was the right move. "No more running," he said.

Graham stood and reached to open the door. There was no point in waiting any longer. The decision was made. He looked at Damien and Ailey as they walked through the door with what he hoped was confidence, though even to him it felt forced. Kel gave him a tentative smile and nod as she ran out the door. They were now exposed. No going back and no way to retreat.

Running to catch up with the others, Graham left the door wide open. It was his way of showing Aegis that they were not going to hide anymore. It was time for them to stand their ground and fight.

PERCHED

Chase sat up in the tree behind the cabin like one of the stone gargoyles from Wellington. He put his hand to his throat mike. "They've left the cabin and are heading west."

Through the static of the radio, a gravelly voice answered on the other side. "Roger that. We'll cut them off at the clearing."

Chase waited a few more minutes, letting the small red dots disappear into the trees. Sliding from his perch, he descended to a lower branch. He continued slinking down branch by branch in one fluid motion until his feet hit the ground. He bent his knees to absorb the force of landing from the final jump and slowly stood up, gazing in the direction of the clearing.

"Ah, the best-laid plans of mice…"

Chase pushed his earpiece further in as he spoke. "I'm guessing they'll make their way to you in about twenty minutes. Stand your ground, fellas. They have an extra pep in their step. We've all seen that before, haven't we? If I'm not mistaken, I believe we have some fighters on our hands."

Speaking in a calm, commanding voice, Cavaness said,

"Murphy, Branson. I will take the older girl. It is apparent that we have something in common. Chase, you concentrate on Damien, and make sure that the little one is separated from the rest. We don't want her touching the others again. As for Graham… don't underestimate him. He needs to be isolated. If that cork pops and all that bottled up energy comes out at once, then we are all in trouble. Chase, once you take care of Damien, make sure that Graham gets nice and dizzy."

"Roger that," said Chase.

"They've been out here long enough," Cavaness continued. "They should be ready to take back to Alex now. The catalysts have taken full effect in each of them, all except for Graham. Hopefully tonight's events will draw it out."

"We are ready, sir," said Branson.

"Same here," replied Murphy.

"Ready when you are, boss," said Chase.

In anticipation of what was about to take place, Chase took off. He ran with supernatural speed and jumped forward, grabbing the edge of the cabin's roof. Pulling himself up and tucking his knees to his chest, his momentum was strong enough to carry him all the way to the ridge. His sleeves were pulled back to his elbows, letting his glowing wrists show. His eyes had turned a deep, amber color. As he stood gazing toward the clearing, a faint glow began radiating from his body.

"Stop holding back, Graham. Just let go," Chase murmured, as if the winds could carry his message through the woods.

Cavaness stood with Murphy and Branson among the trees. Graham and the others were approaching the clearing from the east; whereas, Cavaness and his men were drawing near from the south. If Chase's bearings were correct, they would reach the clearing about the same time.

"We are in the final stage, and we need to be 100 percent sure that the catalysts are solidified," said Cavaness. "Now spread out. We need them contained."

Branson started moving through the trees westward with military precision. Though he was a stout man, he could move silently. His black fleece coat formed to his broad shoulders. His brown cargo pants were old and worn. His thin, black combat boots moved carefully through the underbrush, feeling for twigs and dry leaves on the way down. If anything that could create noise was detected, his foot would divert and find a new section of ground to fall on. His footfalls were so precise that he could keep up with the others and be completely undetectable.

Murphy, on the other hand, had no intention of sneaking around. Not until they got closer. Continuing forward, Murphy held a hand to his mouth and whispered a few words into it. Once done, he revealed an opaque ball that had formed in the palm of his hand. It was almost completely transparent, yet still maintained a faint glow and reflective property. Satisfied with the result, he held his hand up toward the sky and watched as the orb sprang upward from his hand.

Murphy turned to Cavaness, his eyes fading from their natural dark brown to a deep amber.

"Looking now."

He used Cavaness' shoulder as a guide as he focused on the scene from the sky, watching faint yellow forms run through the forest. The animals always had such an interesting look to them, never glowing like humans. They were always more of a dim, yellow color. It was always shocking to see exactly how many woodland creatures were around at any one time, though they were rarely ever seen with the naked eye. The yellow outlines grew smaller and smaller as the orb ascended into the sky. Murphy did not have to hold his hand out to control the orb; he was now able to move it with his mind.

The orb glided to the east and then slightly north. More animals were scampering through the trees. He was about to move the orb further north, when a bright yellow form crept into the picture from the left. Murphy refocused.

"I got 'em." He raised the orb higher in the sky until he could see the edge of the clearing. "They're probably about five minutes out now."

"Okay. That's good enough. Get into position," said Cavaness.

Murphy removed his hand from Cavaness' shoulder as his eyes faded back to brown. His pupils refocused and the orb in the sky dissolved.

"Yes, sir."

Murphy ran off toward the east, disappearing into the trees. Cavaness headed straight on, wanting to approach the clearing directly from the south. He'd made it another forty feet, maybe fifty, when he saw Chase leaning against a nearby tree with his arms crossed.

"It's about time you showed up," said Chase.

Cavaness kept walking. "Aren't you supposed to be farther east, closer to the kids?" It wasn't a question.

"I'll get there. I think I can make it on time," said Chase. "I wanted to talk to you first."

Cavaness stopped.

"I've seen his type before. You can't push him too hard. If you do, Graham will pull back into his shell. Either that, or he'll blow up and we'll all go up in a flash of light. This kid is stronger than anyone I have ever come into contact with. He's definitely the one we've been searching for, but that said, he's still a wild card."

Cavaness grunted. "If I were a betting man, I would say you have a soft spot for him."

"So? What if I do?"

Cavaness moved forward until he was within inches of Chase's face. His expression was emotionless. "Keep your feelings at bay, you understand me? I've been doing this longer than you have been alive. I know how this works, and I have dealt with his kind more times than you could count."

Chase stood expressionless. Cavaness took a step back.

"Change of plan. You take the girl. I will deal with Graham. I don't want you handling him with kid gloves."

"But he *is* a kid," Chase said bluntly.

Cavaness continued walking to the clearing.

"Not anymore. None of them are. They no longer have the luxury of a childhood. They will return to Alex as recreations. They all will. You know that, so stop pretending this is just a game. None of us like the final push, but it is a necessary step. You have to do what is necessary no matter how it may be perceived."

Chase followed behind Cavaness. "I know the system, Cavaness. I don't need a lecture. I'm just saying go easy on Graham if you want him to have his breakthrough."

"Sometimes a tame dog will only attack when backed into a corner."

"You're not listening. Stop being so stubborn. You have to—"

"Go. Get in position. That's an order." The words might as well have been etched in a boulder. In a blur, Chase ran eastward into position.

Cavaness looked toward the clearing. His expression remained emotionless.

"Let's get this over with."

19

Now Or Never

Graham and Damien knelt behind the bushes at the edge of the clearing. Kel and Ailey were close behind. Once they caught up, Kel dropped beside Damien and slid the backpack off her shoulder. Damien unzipped the pouch and retrieved two empty water bottles. He poked his head over top of the bush, looking to see how far the pond was from their resting spot.

Sinking back down, he turned to face the others. "It's about fifty feet. I'll go fill these up."

He studied the surroundings, searching for a good hiding spot. Pointing to his right, he said, "Why don't you take Ailey over there to that big cluster of rocks? Maybe she can wedge herself in between them."

Ailey silently nodded. They all fell silent again, just like in the cabin. A wave of nerves hit Graham as the anticipation turned his stomach into knots. His blood pressure began to rise, creating a rhythmic pounding in his skull. The silence enveloped the forest like a looming storm. Not even the wind was stirring.

"Are you guys ready to get out of here?" asked Damien,

trying to cut through the tension.

"I'm just ready for this to be over with," said Kel.

Graham could hardly move. He was numb with fear as the time for him to act drew near. He had serious doubts about his ability to do his part, but he refused to admit his heightened fear to the rest of the group. He swallowed the lump in his throat, hoping it would push the fear down with it. Everyone needed to be confident now, and that is what he was going to focus on. Confidence. "This is going to work."

Cavaness could see the field ahead. He glanced to his right and saw Murphy off in the distance, crouching and inching toward the treeline. Murphy pushed his sleeves up around his elbows as he crept toward the clearing, pushing branches out of his line of sight. Once he got close enough, he laid down on his stomach and crawled, arm over arm, until he was wedged underneath a cluster of branches. Like a tiger, he lay in wait behind the bushes, ready to pounce.

The sun was creeping closer to the western horizon, taking the temperature down with it. Chase sat ten feet up in a tree blowing hot breaths into his hands to keep the edge off the chill. As the puffs of white vapor poured from between his fingers, he began to feel the butterflies fluttering in the pit of his stomach. He had done this enough times to know the importance of shutting off his emotions, but for some reason, he couldn't shake the concern he had for Graham. He did not intend to rescue him. They needed him, but he felt like he had to soften the blow somehow. Knowing that Cavaness had already shut him down, he tried to focus his energy on watching and waiting.

Branson was already in position. He was stationed to the right of the pond. He, too, was peering through the branches into the small field, keeping his trained eye focused on the treeline to the east for any sign of movement. He saw a little head poke out from over the top of one of the bushes and then disappear moments later. Branson whispered through the radio.

"I've got them. They're due east, positioned between two large pines, with a small patch of shrubbery at the base. There's at least one kid behind it."

"Roger that, Branson," said Cavaness. "They will not separate. They would be too vulnerable on their own. If there is one behind the shrubs, then they are all there. Hold position until I give the green light. Let's see what their next move is."

"10-4," said Branson, followed by the others. "Waiting for your signal."

Damien looked at his friends. "I want you guys to stay here."

As he got up, Graham grabbed him by the arm and pulled him back down.

"Wait. What if they're out there already?"

"The longer we wait, the more likely they are to find us. Someone has to be the bait. This was my plan. It's me. I need to be the bait."

Graham let go of his arm. Damien was right. They needed to act fast, and time was of the essence.

"Don't worry, Graham. I've got this."

Damien pushed the branches of the bush aside to move through them. Still in a crouched position, he ran out into the clearing toward the pond with a plastic bottle in each hand. Graham watched Damien run out into the open. He did not have his normal easy stride. Damien could always keep a calm and relaxed demeanor, but Graham could tell that his friend's nerves were frayed.

Damien forced himself to look straight ahead instead of

all around him as he fumbled the bottles between his fingers, trying to get some feeling back in his hands.

"Ease up, Damien," whispered Graham. He couldn't say it loud enough, though, in fear that he would give away their position. Damien was so focused on his nerves, that he almost didn't notice the edge of the water as he approached.

Meanwhile, Graham and Kel took Ailey over to the cluster of boulders. Graham dug his fingers into the ground behind a few rocks and rolled them to the side. Kel took Ailey by the hand and led her to a small groove between two huge slabs of rock.

"I don't care what you hear out there. *Do not* come out, okay? You must stay hidden. We'll come back for you once this whole thing is over," said Kel.

Ailey nodded as she stepped over some rocks and wedged herself into the gap. Graham took hold of one of the bigger rocks and rolled it back into place, so that it would not appear as if anything had been disturbed. There was a big enough gap in which Ailey could retreat if necessary, but also small enough so that an adult would have a hard time reaching her.

Digging his heels into the ground, Damien came to an abrupt stop at the water's edge. He wobbled a bit, until he was able to catch his balance. After steadying himself, he knelt in the cold grass to fill up the first bottle.

Cavaness watched Damien closely. Without turning, he gave his command.

"Branson… move in."

FACE YOUR FEARS

Pushing the branches aside, Branson emerged from the woods, his arms swinging slightly from his broad shoulders. He did not make any further attempts to be stealthy.

The fog was beginning to settle into the clearing, hovering over the ground like a thin, misty blanket. The evening rays of the sun filled the fog, giving the air a sinister glow. The sun would be settling down behind the horizon soon. The warming hands of the sun would soon let loose the chill of the night.

Damien was filling the second bottle, unaware of the approaching threat. Small puffs of breath came out of Branson's mouth as he walked toward Damien. He was about fifteen paces away before he broke the silence.

In a deep, smooth voice he said, "You guys have really kept us busy with all this running around."

Adrenaline surged through Damien's chest as he whipped his head around to see Branson approaching. He had known they would eventually come face to face, but nothing could have prepared him for it. He had hoped he would have more time to build up his nerve, but they had found them too fast.

Damien tightened the cap on the second water bottle and stood up to face Branson.

"Maybe this was a good thing," he whispered. "Don't think. Just react." He kept repeating this over and over as he stepped down into the pond. The water was frigid. The shock of the cold felt like tiny knives stabbing him all over his feet and ankles as he waded further in. Damien kept a tight grip on the bottles, squeezing them in reaction to the cold water as he made his way toward the middle of the pond. He continued walking backwards, keeping his eyes on Branson.

"That's an interesting strategy. Are you hoping that I'm unable to swim?"

Damien said nothing.

"Well, I hate to be the bearer of bad news, but swimming is a prerequisite for a Green Beret."

Branson walked to the water's edge. He held his right hand up to display the bolts of electricity flowing around each finger and down his glowing wrist. The blue of his eyes changed to a deep amber color as he stared at Damien.

"I've heard you have a Pusher with you. That's a raw force, kind of like an earthquake sending ripples through the earth's surface. Mine is more… electric."

The bolts of electricity grew more intense, sending sparks flying from the sides of Branson's hand. Keeping his eyes on Damien, he moved his hand closer to the surface of the water.

"Do you know what happens when water and electricity meet?"

He bent down further and put his non-electric hand into the water, feeling its chilly bite. Damien saw this as his time to strike. Dropping the bottles, he held up both arms to the right side of his body as the water beside him began to churn. A large wave formed under his arms. It began to twist and turn in a circular motion, under Damien's unspoken instruction. He scrunched his nose and bared his teeth. In a quick motion, he flung both arms toward Branson, commanding the huge wave to follow. Branson barely had time to look up from the water before the large, spiraling tidal wave slammed into his chest.

It hit him so hard that his feet flew up in front his face. As the water surrounded him, the electric sparks from his hand surged and engulfed the wave. Gargling screams echoed through the valley as the fog lit up like fireworks. Branson's body tensed under the surge of electricity flowing through him. He rolled to the side, curling up into a ball, and then straightening his legs, going stiff as a board. He writhed in pain and shock for a few more seconds until he finally fell unconscious as the water soaked into the ground.

Damien was concerned that he'd killed him, but the faint puffs of visible breath coming from Branson's mouth told him otherwise. Murphy sprang from his post at the sight of his fallen comrade, and ran toward Damien. Damien now stood near the middle of the pond with the water around his calves. With his teeth still bared, he lifted both hands up, bringing the remaining water in the pond up with them.

Damien screamed again as he flung both hands in front of him. The water gathered together in two huge streams and shot toward Murphy. The force was so strong, that even the moisture from Damien's clothes was stripped from the fabric.

Murphy anticipated the move and whispered something into the air, holding both hands up in front of him as he sprinted. Two massive walls of light formed in front of him, acting as a dam between him and the water. The streams of water slammed into the wall of energy, diverting the water to each side. Once the wave was gone, he pulled his arms down, causing the light to disappear.

Damien took a fighter's stance. He put one foot back and braced himself against the dry earth. What once was a pond was now just a dry hole in the ground. With his arm drawn back, Murphy was the first to shoot a blast of light from his hand. Damien reacted by doing the same. The blasts met in the middle, creating a blinding light and the sound of booming thunder. The blasts flattened into discs, then faded away into the thick fog. Damien reared back for another blast, but before he could release, the ground erupted beside Murphy, creating a mound of earth protruding out and upwards. The dirt and rock crashed into his face, propelling him over Branson's crumpled form, and into the vacant pond. He rolled past Damien like a ragdoll, out cold.

Damien looked up to see Kel running toward him with an outstretched hand. They locked eyes. Two down, two to go. They looked around them for any sign of the other Aegis members, but the fog was too thick, and the light of the sun was beginning to fade behind the horizon. Damien hopped from the hole in the ground. The two of them ran over to Branson and pulled him into the empty pond beside Murphy.

Kel stood shoulder to shoulder with Damien, looking for any sign of Cavaness or Chase. Starting left, they searched the perimeter of the woods, looking for movement. A gust of wind began to blow, forming goosebumps on their arms. They both shrugged their shoulders in reaction to the chill, as the hair on the back of their neck began to stand up.

The fog in front of them started to whip and whirl. The gust grew stronger, carving a channel in the fog. Before they could process the abnormality of the wind, they saw a blur of movement through the path in the fog. They barely had the time to breathe before the blur began to glow and a blast hit them both in the torso. They both crumpled over in pain, falling back onto the dry earth. The motion stopped at the edge, and once the fog separated, they could see Chase looking down at them.

Chase had his hand up with the same yellow, fiery flame dancing around it. He looked over at Murphy and Branson lying in the dirt and shook his head.

"Now that wasn't very nice. Though I've got to say that I am impressed. No one has ever knocked one of us out, much less two." Chase studied the two kids with a slight expression of admiration. "But please don't tell me this was all you had to your little plan."

Damien stared at him defiantly.

"Good. I was hoping for a little more flare."

"Get away from them, Chase." Graham's voice carried through the clearing, echoing through the trees, making him sound much bigger than he really was.

"Graham! I was wondering when you were going to make your entrance."

Graham felt sick to his stomach. It had taken all his strength to stay hidden at the treeline while his friends took the frontline. He had to remind himself repeatedly to stick to the plan. Timing was everything. Damien and Kel were so powerful. How could he ever do more than what they had already done? His pulse was racing so much that it felt like it was going to leap from his chest. His breath was shallow and sporadic as he tried to control his nerves. The last thing he wanted to do was have a death match with Chase, who was older, faster and stronger. But it was his turn to save his friends. Graham swallowed the lump in his throat and continued toward Chase.

"I'm done with your games. Whatever you're doing here, we will not be a part of it. If you want to take us, you will have to go through me first."

Chase's eyes widened. "Wow, such authority! If I didn't know you better, I would actually think that you were serious. It is a good facade." Chase took a step closer. "But we both know that deep down, you are freaking out."

Chase looked back over to Kel. "He is so stubborn. Did you teach him that?"

"HEY! Don't look at them, look at me." The blood rushed to Graham's cheeks as small sticks and rocks around the edge of the woods lifted from the ground and began to hover around him. A faint glow appeared, surrounding his body. His eyes began to flicker and a deep, amber color began to overtake the blue.

"And put your hand down."

Chase obeyed. The light around his hand faded away as

he turned to face Graham. "That's it. Keep going," Chase said under his breath.

Tilting his head back toward the pond, Chase said, "You two stay put. I need to show Graham how playtime really works."

Chase calmly walked toward Graham. Not backing down, Graham matched his pace until they were face to face. His fists were balled up and his jaw was clenched tight. Chase opened his mouth to speak, but before he could, Graham shoved him with small blasts of yellow light that launched from his palms. Chase stumbled backwards a few steps, and then regained his balance. He smiled as he patted at his chest, as if to dust off the light from the blast.

"Come on. Surely you have more than that."

Graham quickly realized that there was hardly any force behind his blast. He was still holding back. He wasn't trying to, but something inside was blocking his ability to let go. *Why can't I use this power outside of my nightmares?* He glanced at Damien and Kel, who were both watching hopefully, then focused back on Chase. *Maybe I just need to warm up the old-fashioned way.* He sprang toward Chase and sank his shoulder as hard as he could into Chase's gut. Chase fell backwards, his surprise at being tackled evident. Before his back hit the ground, he brought his legs to his chest, doing a backward roll and popping back up on his feet.

As soon as he landed, he fired a blast at Graham. Graham reacted by firing another blast at Chase. The two blasts collided, and, as in the previous collision, the two balls of light slammed into each other, flattened into small discs, and disappeared in a flash of light and a thunderous crackle.

Chase fired again and again, throwing blasts at Graham's legs. Graham jumped up, tucking his legs as the blasts bolted underneath him. Chase's wrists began to glow and his eyes started their gradual transition to amber. Once Graham landed back on his feet, he stretched out his hand, but there was no blast. No glowing of the wrist. He grunted and strained, but nothing happened.

"Stage fright?" asked Chase.

Not waiting for an answer, Chase whizzed behind Graham, held his hand to the small of his back and fired a blast. In a millisecond, Graham was flung forward onto his chest, feeling like a hot iron had just smashed into him at fifty miles an hour.

He noticed that his wrists had a very faint glow. It wasn't what he had hoped for, but at least it was a start. He stayed on the ground as Chase walked up behind him. When he was close enough, Graham shot two short blasts into the ground, propelling himself quickly upwards. He twisted around with a glowing fist and landed a solid punch to Chase's face.

Chase took the punch in his stride, letting the force of it twist him a full 360 degrees so that he ended up face to face with Graham again. He hovered a hand in front of Graham's ribcage and fired another blast, sending him crashing to the ground. Graham crumpled into the fetal position, holding his side. The pain from his back merged with the fresh sting in his side to create an overpowering throbbing throughout his entire mid-section.

Chase walked over to Graham and knelt beside him.

"Come on, Graham-y." He poked Graham in the shoulder a couple of times as he continued talking. "Open the floodgates. Why are you holding back? Don't you want to save your pals?"

Graham could hardly speak through the surges of pain. He winced as he sat up to face Chase.

"Why do you want me to open up so bad? So you can take my energy for yourself?"

Chase looked up to the sky and shrugged his shoulders. "Hmm. Interesting theory. Did the Casey file give you that idea?"

"Maybe. Among other things. Is she dead?"

Chase chuckled. "Well… yeah."

"Did you kill all of them, once you were done with your

sick experiments?"

"What makes you think I want you dead? According to you, I need your energy. I'm curious. How exactly did you see me taking it? Was it something like this?"

As Chase spoke, he quickly grabbed Graham by the wrists. His grip was so tight that Graham thought his bones were going to crack. The amber of Chase's eyes grew more intense as glowing vapor began to rise from his hands. Graham felt lightheaded. His arms tingled as he felt a steady flow of energy flow moving from his wrists into Chase's hands. The glowing vapor rose in circular motions around his forearms. Graham's rebellious stare gave way to fatigue as his eyes began to roll to the back of his head. Just as the darkness began to overtake him, Chase released his grip and fell to his side with a grunt.

Damien stood at the edge of the bank with his hand stretched out. Chase rolled over to see what had just hit him in the back of the head and found a water bottle lying beside him. He blinked to refocus as he picked up the bottle and got to his feet.

"Nice arm, amigo! You had some heat behind that one. That actually hurt a little."

"It wasn't a throw," said Damien. His wrist was beaming with light. The bottle ripped from Chase's hand and hovered in the air for a second before slamming into Chase's face, then his gut. The bottle was throwing jabs at Chase like a professional boxer, mimicking Damien's arm motions. After the fifth hit, Chase shot a blast from his right hand, disintegrating the bottle; letting the water splash into the grass.

Looking over at Damien, Chase said, "Not bad! Not bad at all." He turned to walk toward Damien. "You know, Aquatics are pretty rare. Actually, I don't think I've seen one come through here before."

As Chase walked past Graham in mid-monologue, Graham made his move. His wrists lit up as he fired a blast at

Chase's feet. The force was not strong, but it was enough to send Chase's feet into the air, making him fall flat on his back. Graham leapt from the ground and straddled Chase, pinning his arms to the ground, with a tight grip on his wrists. Chase tried to get free, but Graham reared back and slammed his forehead into the bridge of Chase's nose, making blood spray from his nostrils. Graham focused all his energy on his hands. As he concentrated, the bands of Graham's wrists slowly began to glow like the light from an oil lamp. Faint, translucent vapor began to rise from Graham's grip. Chase struggled under Graham's weight, but found that it was too taxing as the energy left his body.

"Doesn't feel so good, does it?" mocked Graham through bared teeth.

Blood continued to run out of Chase's nose, making a small stream that flowed down past the corner of his mouth and pooled in the hollow of his neck, just below his Adam's apple. He fought against Graham's grip, but as the energy from his body continued to escape, he felt his head hit the grass as the starlit sky and fog began to fade.

"ENOUGH!"

Graham whirled around to see Cavaness walk out into the clearing. He was holding a small girl under his arm who was kicking and mouthing silent screams. Hearing his voice sent waves of fear through Graham, making him loosen his grip on Chase's wrists. Forgetting his current battle, Graham stood up, dismounting Chase like a horse. Chase's eyes rolled back to consciousness. He flexed his fingers, trying to regain the feeling in his hands and slowly sat up. As he did, he brought his hand up to his face, cradling his nose and forehead in his palms.

"Let her go, Cavaness," said Graham.

"I don't take orders from little boys," replied Cavaness in his usual calm, authoritative voice.

Cavaness looked over at Chase, who was still inspecting the damage done to his face.

"We tried it your way. Now we do it mine."

Not bothering to even look at Graham, Cavaness shot a blast into the ground a few feet in front of him. The ground rumbled and a small mound of dirt shot up, sending Graham into the air. Before he could go too high, Cavaness fired a blast into his chest, sending him violently back into the ground. Cavaness never broke eye contact with Chase. Chase let his head sink and reluctantly nodded in agreement.

Graham didn't move. He lay in the wet grass in complete shock from the intensity of the last blast. It was much worse that Chase's hits. Kel and Damien rushed toward Cavaness at the same time, firing blasts from their hands as they sprinted. The first two hit Cavaness in the shoulder, but with one huge blast from his hand, he countered their attacks. Cavaness then shoved his hand forward, hitting both Damien and Kel with an invisible force. It hit them so hard that they flew back at least ten feet before crashing into the dry pond bed.

Ailey was still dangling at his side, punching at his stomach and kicking the air. Cavaness did not flinch. It was as if he did not even notice her at all. He remained focused on Kel and Damien as they slowly got to their feet. Cavaness held his hand back up. His wrist was glowing like fire, and another ball of light was forming around his hand.

Graham watched in shock as Ailey grabbed Cavaness' massive, scarred forearm and glowing band. Her eyes immediately began to turn amber. Her wrists lit up and she clenched her jaw. She flung her other hand toward the ground, shooting a beam of light into the grass underneath them. The ground erupted like a small volcano underneath Cavaness, hurling them both through the air. Ailey was flung back toward the treeline and Cavaness landed near Chase.

Cavaness rolled over to his stomach and brought one foot up, resting his elbow on his thigh. He shot an angry look at Chase.

"Hey, don't look at me. I told you she was a Bridge," said Chase.

Cavaness was not used to being knocked down, especially by a little girl. He stared at Ailey as she pushed herself up, sitting Indian-style in the grass. His snarl turned into a small grin. She was a feisty one. She had a lot of spunk and good reactionary skills. She was a good find. Still wearing the grin, he fired a blast, hitting Ailey in the legs while she tried to get to her feet. The force knocked Ailey back to the ground. She grabbed her knee and gritted her teeth.

"GET AWAY FROM HER!" screamed Kel, reacting like a mother whose child was under attack. She threw a blast at Cavaness, but with a simple flick of his wrist, Cavaness countered her blast with his own, sending it back into her chest. Kel fell to the ground, hitting her head on the hard dirt. Damien looked down beside him and saw the other water bottle lying on the ground. He held his hand above the bottle, and, as if throwing a baseball, he flung his hand forward. The bottle sprang from the ground and shot toward Cavaness, but before it could hit him, he raised his hand and snatched it from the air. His hand radiated light and with a vicelike grip, he squeezed the bottle, causing it to burst in his hand. Without expression, Cavaness threw the crumpled bottle to the ground and turned his attention back to Ailey.

Walking over to her, Cavaness put his fist in the palm of his other hand. Light from his palm formed around his fist in the shape of a small bowl. He then removed his fist from the light and a bowl-like glow remained in the palm of his hand. Cavaness then grabbed Ailey's wrists and held up her hands. He set the glowing bowl-like object over her hands. The light then contracted, binding her like handcuffs.

Ailey looked down in panicked breaths, fighting against her illuminated shackles. She twisted her arms and pushed against the light, but the bonds were too strong. Cavaness wrapped his arm around her waist and picked her up again as. Ailey kicked and slammed her arms against Cavaness, trying to escape, but it made no difference. Evidently her power came from grabbing others with her hands, which was impossible now. Cavaness continued to walk over to the hole in the ground where Damien and Kel were.

Kel was still trying to stand up and Damien took his fighting stance again. As Cavaness approached, he held up his free hand as swirls of flame like light engulfed it. Instead of holding it out to blast Damien or Kel like Graham expected, he bent his arm at a ninety-degree angle and held his hand to the side of Ailey's head.

Ailey immediately ceased her kicking and flailing, her fear-stricken eyes reflecting the golden light. Damien and Kel stopped moving. Graham caught his breath and froze, not wanting to put Ailey in further danger.

Cavaness raised his right foot in the air, holding it a couple of feet above the ground for a moment, then stomped the ground with the intensity of a small earthquake. Damien and Kel felt a rumble of energy flow past them, making the earth around them tremble. The quake surged to where Murphy and Branson lay, and then pushed its way to the surface, cracking the ground beneath them. The force looked as though the ground were giving the men CPR; their bodies rising up a few inches and then falling back to the ground. As they hit the ground again, they both grunted and opened their eyes.

"Get up, you two," said Cavaness.

Following orders as best they could, they got to their feet, both holding their heads and looking around, trying to process what had just happened.

"Murphy, bind these two and stand guard over Kel. Branson, you take Damien."

Murphy and Branson walked over to the two worried figures, who both kept their eyes on Ailey. Murphy held his fists side by side with his thumbs touching, as if he were about to pull a sword from its sheath. As he moved his hands away from each other, golden chains of light formed between them. They appeared to be a mixture of light and mist, but as Murphy wrapped them around Kel's wrists, Graham could tell they were as strong as real chains. Murphy did the same to Damien, binding his hands with the luminous chains, and then moved behind Kel to stand guard. Branson was already positioned behind Damien, with his hands on Damien's shoulders. Tiny bolts of electricity danced across the back of Branson's hands ready to flow into Damien at his command.

Damien and Kel swallowed hard and looked over at Graham, who was just now beginning to stand.

"Time to shine, amigo," he muttered under his breath.

Cavaness sat Ailey down in front of Kel, laying her gently on her side.

"Chase, take the little one. It's time to pop the cork!"

Chase looked over at Graham with a glint of sorrow and compassion in his eyes. He walked past, not breaking eye contact. His eyes were a little swollen from the headbutt, and the corners were beginning to turn purple. His wrists were still glowing, and his eyes retained the odd amber color. Graham looked beyond Chase to Cavaness, Murphy, and Branson. They all looked the same: wrist bands radiating through their skin and their eyes a deep amber.

Chase walked past Ailey, positioning himself between her and Kel. The board was set and the pieces were in place. Damien's plan, though they had misjudged some of the details, had succeeded. All four men were together and Graham could make his move.

Graham stood facing the others. Cavaness had his back to everyone else as he stepped from the edge of the pond bed. He continued walking toward Graham until there were only a couple feet separating them. The two kings stood face to face, and Graham had the feeling they each believed they had checkmate.

"Your move, Graham. It's time to show us all what you've been holding back this whole time."

Graham said nothing. His quickened pulse led to short, shallow puffs from his mouth. Graham clenched his teeth and balled his fists as the bands on his wrists began to illuminate.

The storm churning from within manifested with streaks of lightning-like flashes darting around his body as his entire form began to radiate with an iridescent glow.

"Now that's more like it," said Cavaness.

A streak of confidence sprang from Graham's core. "No more games. You wanted a way for our energy to be released—well here you have it. But I will not let you or anyone else take it from us."

Cavaness grinned. "Then I suggest you stop holding back."

Holding back? This was more than he had ever done. Graham let this fuel him even more. The streaks of light and the glow became more intense as it began to slowly swirl around him. The winds created by the force emanating from Graham made Cavaness' clothing flap.

"I said stop holding BACK!"

Cavaness threw a ball of light at Graham. Graham ducked to the right as the blast shot over his shoulder. He flung his hand forward in retaliation, shooting a thick ray of light at Cavaness. Not trying to avoid it, Cavaness shot an even thicker ray at Graham, overpowering Graham's and deflecting it straight up into the sky. Cavaness darted to the side, positioning himself so that their blasts were perpendicular to the other kids, out of harm's way. Cavaness fired again. Graham leapt into the air, letting the light fly underneath him as he fired at Cavaness. He fell to the ground, ducking his head into a forward roll, and then popping back up on his feet, completely amazed at his reactionary skills. Blast after blast, the two waged war on one another, dodging and deflecting the attacks.

Cavaness kept his feet planted, but twisted his body so that Graham's blast flew past his head, letting it crash into the tree behind him, causing the entire trunk to explode. Cavaness watched Graham carefully as he finished his roll, then fired another shot, hitting Graham in the chest. The force knocked Graham to the ground, but it did not hurt nearly as much as the previous blast. *This glowing force around me must be absorbing some of the shock.*

As Graham fell to the ground on his back, he pulled his arms back, cupping the heels of his hands together with his fingers curled to the sides. Light swirled around in his hands and he fired a shot directly at Cavaness. The force of the blast sent Graham's shoulders digging into the ground and his muscles tensed under the extra force. The beam of light hit Cavaness in the shoulder, causing him to stumble to the side.

Finally, a hit!

Cavaness regained his balance, holding his injured shoulder in his hand. Not wanting to waste the moment, Graham fired another beam of light from his hands. This shot was more intense, sending Graham scooting backwards a few feet in recoil, leaving a trail of mud and dirt underneath him.

Cavaness was surprised at how much power was coming out of such a little kid. The strength of his shots was beyond most adults; however, they were still no match for his own. Shaking off the pain, Cavaness fired back, but this time the light did not deflect into the sky. Like Robin Hood's arrow splitting the competition's arrow in half, his blast penetrated Graham's. Graham did not know what to do, but there was no time to react. The beam tore through his own until it hit the palms of his hands, exploding in a giant flash of light. The force sent Graham flying backwards into a tree behind him. The glow around him faded away as he crumpled to the ground.

Chase winced as he watched Graham slam into the tree.

"Cavaness, that is enough!"

"Hold your tongue! He is strong, stronger than anyone else that has come through here. He can take it. He is going to have to."

Kel looked over at Chase, perplexed by his compassion for Graham.

Cavaness walked over to Graham, watching him trying to get to his feet. Before he could stand fully erect, Cavaness fired another shot straight into Graham's gut, sending him back down into the base of the tree. Graham held his stomach as he fell to his side. He cringed as Cavaness fired another shot into his ribs.

Graham cried out in pain, but Cavaness did not stop. He hit Graham three more times with blasts of light, until Graham felt like he was going to pass out. Cavaness reached down and grabbed Graham by the collar and picked him up off the ground. Graham grabbed Cavaness' hands as his feet dangled in the air. He carried Graham over to the others, flinging him to the ground at the edge of the pond bed.

Graham looked over to see Kel's backpack lying beside him. He shuffled his body next to it, quickly opened the front pocket and retrieved the knife he had taken from the cabin. He pulled the blade from the sheath and held it in front of him.

"Get away from me, or I swear I will use this."

Cavaness stood there unimpressed. "I am disappointed, Graham. Murder isn't your thing."

"You have hurt us enough for it to be self-defense," said Graham with shallow breaths. He was dizzy from the pain. The metal blade in his hand was multiplying into three as his eyes crossed. He drifted to the side a bit and then forced himself to refocus. His wrists were still glowing, though they were fading with each attack.

"There's a big difference between close combat weapons and long-range weapons." Cavaness extended his hand, firing a blast of light from his palm. The light hit the knife, sending it spiraling into the air. "Now you know the difference."

Graham recoiled from the attack. The knife had taken the bulk of the hit, but his hand was stinging from the aftershock. As he pulled his hand to his chest, his heart sank into his gut. There was no way he could win this.

"Fight back," said Cavaness.

Graham remained motionless.

"I said fight back!" Cavaness fired a blast into the ground, just in front of Graham, sending dirt and rock into the air.

Graham wanted to fight, but he was so fatigued that it took all his strength to remain upright on his knees and not succumb to the dizziness.

"Fine. Have it your way."

Cavaness reached out and shot a blast just in front of Kel and Damien, making the ground erupt in front of their feet. They shuffled back in reaction to the explosion, but were held in place by Murphy and Branson.

"STOP IT! Why are you doing this?" yelled Graham.

Cavaness did not respond. He just stared back into Graham's eyes as his hand illuminated again.

"Hit me! Leave them out of this!" Graham's chest was wracked with pain as he pleaded.

"You need to fight. The catalysts have taken effect. You should be able to use your full strength, but you're still holding back."

Cavaness let the ball of light loose, hitting Damien in the gut. Damien shrieked in pain, doubling over to his knees.

"Does everyone have to get hurt before you let go?"

Graham tried to react, but it was no use. His mind was numb with the pain surging through his body. He could not focus. He could hardly even breathe. Trying to stand back up, he braced on one foot, but it gave way, sending him back onto his side. All Graham could do was lie there in pain, wrapping his arms around his stomach.

"I see. This is your play, then? Giving in to pain and fatigue?" Cavaness paused, letting his words seep into Graham's conscience. Looking over at the others, Cavaness nodded his head, giving them the authority to act.

Damien was the first to fall. A bolt of energy surged through his body from Branson's hands until he fell flat to the ground, unconscious. Kel was not far behind. A wave of energy flowed from Murphy's hands, through Kel's shoulders, to the rest of her body. Her knees gave way as she fell beside Damien. A tear ran down Graham's cheek as he watched

Ailey's eyes roll to the back of her head, before she fell on top of Kel. They were all unconscious and he had failed. Everyone had done their part but him.

No. It can't end this way. I will not let it end this way. Closing his eyes, Graham pressed his face against the wet grass. In his mind, he saw a wave of black smoke. He heard his parents screaming to keep away, and then his own screams filled the air as the light surrounded him. Taking a deep breath, Graham let the memory empower him.

His nightmare that had once infused him with fear had now given him an odd sense of bolstered confidence. With his eyes now open, he braced his weight on his hands and pushed himself upright. His head was swimming, but he forced himself to focus. In slow movements, he swung his legs around so that he was on his hands and knees. Graham's wrists began to glow as he painfully got to his feet. He clenched his jaw as he made eye contact through the fog. His fingers curled up into fists, making the light around his wrists intensify.

"Yes, now you are beginning to understand." Cavaness took a step back into a fighting stance. "Now we are getting somewhere." The chill in the air caused his breath to form white puffs of vapor as he spoke.

The pain that had wracked Graham's body was subsiding. He could feel his energy levels rising with his anger as the light around him grew brighter.

"This ends now."

The once faint light that encircled Graham had now intensified so that the surrounding fog was illuminated. With one final surge of energy, Graham yelled as loud as he could. The wind around him picked up speed and his wrists began to glow as brightly as the light he emitted. For the first time, he was able to will this power to happen. He was learning to control it.

He felt like he had just been plugged into a power plant. Pure energy was flowing through his veins. It was exhilarating.

Finally, Graham thought that he just might have the upper hand. The same raw power from his dream was finally manifesting at his will. His whole body was tingling.

Now was the time to strike. Graham pulled back a hand to fire, but just as he thought the power within was going to overtake him, a wave of fatigue started to take hold. The light around him quickly began to fade along with the bands and his body began to tremble. The pain that had dissipated moments ago, came back with full force. The power was too much for his body to handle. Instead of an eruption of pure energy, his body was handling the shock by shutting down. Graham immediately collapsed to his knees, the momentum carrying him over onto his hands. It was over. His body continued to tremble as he watched Cavaness walk closer and kneel down beside him. He put his mouth to Graham's ear.

"You gave it your best shot, kid. You really did. I'm proud of you."

Wait, what? Graham thought, but before he could verbalize his question, a warm wave of shock flowed from Cavaness' hand. It was not a painful shock, but a soothing one. The whole world spun in circles as Graham's eyes rolled to the back of his head.

Graham's head hit the ground. Guilt, failure, and confusion filled his mind, before everything went black.

21
COMING FULL CIRCLE

The bright light of dawn penetrated the windowpanes, making Graham flinch and pull the covers over his head. He held them there for a moment, not wanting to leave the warm embrace of the mattress, while he tried to shake off terrifying dreams of monsters and glowing wrists. Groggy, Graham blinked a few times.

Wait a minute. Glowing wrists?

Graham's head shot off the pillow, excited at the possibility that he had just woken up from a horrific nightmare. He sat upright expecting to see the other kids of Greenwood asleep and catch a glimpse of his belongings hovering in mid-air before they all crashed to the ground. He saw neither. He looked to his right, flinching again at the bright morning sun. He held a hand up to block the light as he looked to his left. There were other beds near him, but he was definitely not in Greenwood. Damien was in the next bed with his back to Graham. He watched Damien intently to make sure that the blanket rose and fell slightly with each breath. *Good, he's alive.*

Graham then turned around so that he was facing the foot

of his bed. There was a small aisle between his bed and the next row of four beds lining the opposite wall. The two nearest the door were vacant, but Kel and Ailey were lying in the other two. Graham made sure they were breathing, too, before letting himself relax. They were sound asleep, and looked as peaceful and content as a dog curled beside a warm fireplace.

Graham flung the sheets off and twisted his legs around to the side of the bed. He held his breath, expecting to be wracked with pain, but there was none. He moved his hips side to side, and then started to cautiously tap his chest, stomach and arms with his fist. He felt like a million bucks. Not a single ache or pain. He looked down to see that he had a fresh pair of logo sweats on, except these had golden fabric sewn into the sleeves to mimic the bands around their wrists. He pulled up his sweatshirt to inspect his bruises, but there was not a single scratch on him. *What in the world was going on?*

Alex sat at a table with one hand resting on top of the other. Cavaness sat to his right and Murphy sat beside him. To his left were Chase and Branson. Alex turned toward Chase.

"How's the nose?"

Chase turned to face Alex. There was no sign of trauma on his face.

"Good as new, sir. Never felt better in my life."

"I am glad to hear that, Chase. How are the children?"

"They were pretty frazzled when it was all said and done, but they are resting now, and it's well deserved. I have never seen a group like this one before. They really gelled as a team."

"Then I suppose that is the way they will stay, should they accept."

Alex got to his feet. He brought his fist to his mouth, clearing his throat to speak.

"Gentlemen, before we begin, I would like to take a moment and congratulate you on another successful venture. The stage of the catalysts is a difficult one. A lot of time and effort goes into the planning and execution of Catalyst Grove, and you all have done a marvelous job, as usual. You are men of integrity and impeccable character. Well done."

Alex took the wooden goblet from the table and held it high in the air, giving acknowledgement to the efforts of each man.

Graham put his feet on the cold, wooden floor. He crept over to where Damien was sleeping. Placing his hand gently on his friend's shoulder, he shook him. "Damien. Wake up."

Damien did not move, except to shrug Graham's hand off his shoulder. He smacked his lips as he snuggled down further into the covers. Graham opened his hand and gave a few small pats to Damien's cheek. Damien did not move a muscle.

"Damien, for the love!" Graham's voice was louder but Damien still did not stir.

"Alright, fine. You want to do this the hard way?" Graham asked with a huff.

Placing both of his hands on Damien's back, he sent Damien rolling over the edge of the bed. Damien yelled as he hit the floor.

"Ahhhh! Fang face!"

Kel and Ailey bolted out of bed and ran over to Damien.

Graham could not help himself. He doubled over, holding his stomach in laughter. He would pay for this later, but he didn't care. After last night's events, he had needed that. "What in the world were you dreaming about?"

Damien jumped to his feet. Both fists were balled up. He

was standing like a boxer in the ring, ready to strike. "Wha… Who? What just happened? Where are we? Where is the lion?"

"Lion? What are you talking about?" asked Kel, looking around the room. She furrowed her brow as she studied the unfamiliar surroundings. Ailey's head was on a swivel, combing the room for clues, or anything familiar.

"You, um, fell out of bed," said Graham, still trying to control himself.

"Where the heck are we?" asked Damien. His eyes were still adjusting to the light. As Kel and Ailey came into focus, he let down his fists. "Was I just in bed?"

"Yeah, we all were," said Graham.

Thoroughly confused, Damien looked over to Kel and then to Ailey. His mind flashed back to the field, where they had been held captive. He remembered seeing Graham being tortured by Cavaness. He remembered seeing Kel and Ailey with the glowing bonds around their hands, then shuddered as he felt the waves of electricity flow through his body and the darkness that followed. Damien looked back to Graham.

"Did we win?"

Graham's smile melted at once like wax under a flame of guilt. He could not even look at them. His countenance grew dark as he hung his head. "No."

The others looked at each other, then down at their clothes, checking out their new apparel. Their hearts sank at the sight of the golden bands woven into the sleeves.

"If we haven't been rescued, then where are we?" asked Kel.

"I'm not sure," said Graham. "I just woke up myself."

Not wanting to face the others, Graham stepped back and sat on his bed.

Kel's heart sank, and her eyes began to water. She walked over to Graham and wrapped her arms around his neck.

"You did all you could. You can't blame yourself for that. We certainly don't."

Graham sat silently, trying to suppress his emotions. He really didn't know what to do next, so he just awkwardly placed his hands on Kel's back. He expected to feel another wave of shame overtake him, but something else came in its place. He felt compassion. Kel was beginning to tear up. The jolts of her sporadic sobs seemed to pound a foreign emotion into his chest. It was something he had never experienced before.

Damien walked over to Graham and put his hand on his shoulder. "You were tortured for us, amigo. There is not much more you could have given."

Ailey also had tears in her big, green eyes. She ran over behind Graham and put one arm around his waist, and the other around Kel.

This is what having a family must feel like. Graham wanted to convey his gratitude, but he lacked the proper words. All he could muster was a nearly silent "Thank you."

The group hug lasted a few more moments, until Damien removed his hand from Graham's shoulder. Ailey let go, then finally Kel.

"Do you guys hurt anywhere?" asked Graham.

It was an odd question, but after looking themselves over and twisting their bodies in all sorts of odd angles, they shook their heads.

"Me neither. I took a pretty good beating last night. I shouldn't even be able to move right now," said Graham.

Ailey held her leg up by putting her hand behind the crook of her knee. She extended her leg up and let it back down a few times. The smile on her face grew wider, revealing the fact that she was also pain free.

Damien and Kel both patted the areas of their bodies that had been hit by the blasts. They, too, were completely restored.

"Graham, what's going on?" asked Kel.

"I dunno. I wish I could tell you."

"None of this makes any sense. No drug in the world

could heal us like this, not to mention that we're in a strange bedroom. Last time, we woke up tied to chairs. I don't understand."

Damien twisted his head in disbelief.

"Let's figure this out later, okay? I think we need to figure out how to get out of here first."

The five men guzzled down the contents of the goblets. After letting them finish their drinks, Alex broke the silence.

"If we have indeed found the one we have been searching for, this is truly a cause for celebration."

"I really don't think there is any question about it, sir," said Chase.

Alex smiled, placed his goblet back onto the table and excused himself.

Chase looked over to Cavaness. "Do you think they will be convinced?"

Cavaness thought for a moment. "Time will tell, though it is hard to believe anything else once Alex has spoken. I don't remember it taking very long for you to believe."

The right side of Chase's mouth curled upwards. "Yeah, I guess not. Even after the beating you gave me."

Cavaness grinned at Chase with a warmth not usually found on his face. "You were the first person to knock me to the ground. I didn't expect the speed."

As Chase and Cavaness continued to reminisce, Alex emerged from the side door carrying the same silver platter that had once held the catalyst bands. In their place were four golden envelopes spaced on top of the platter. He walked across the room and set the tray on the table.

Alex looked at them with pride. "The time has come."

"We've got to get out of here," said Damien.

"I know, but we don't even know where *here* is," said Kel. "We might as well be back in that warehouse."

Ailey looked out the window, but all she could see was a small courtyard between two sections of the building.

Placing his hand on the doorknob, Graham looked above the door for another siren. With a half measure of confidence, he said, "Here goes nothing." The knob twisted and the hinges groaned as the door creaked open.

On the other side of the door, Alex got to his feet followed by Cavaness, Chase, Branson, and Murphy. As Graham and the others walked through the door, each person gave a salute by bowing their head slightly and putting their fist to their chest, each with a gleaming wrist.

22

Explanation

Graham was thrown off by the entire scene. He continued into the room, but once he had made it all the way in, he wanted nothing more than to leave. The scene seemed frozen in time. The room was elegantly decorated and the table adjacent to them was filled with all sorts of meats, bread, cheeses, and fruits. Cavaness, Chase, Branson, and Murphy, the men who had been pursuing and injuring them, were all at the other end of the room welcoming them with a salute and standing ovation. Graham looked over to the left side of the room, where he recognized the ornate wooden table with three mirrors hanging above it. They were back at Portfield Manor.

Once the room had its fill of applause, all the men took their seats except for Alex. A hush fell over the Aegis members in anticipation of Alex's next words. In a booming voice, Alex spoke.

"Welcome back. I trust you all had a good night's rest. You had more than earned it. No doubt your desire is to be as far away from here as possible, but if you would do us the honor of extending your attention for a few moments, I believe you will be satisfied with the answers that follow."

Alex extended his hand. "Please, take a seat. Help yourself to some food if you would like." His words were warm and inviting.

He was correct. Graham wanted to run, to see anyone standing in front of him but Cavaness. He wanted to show his rage over the torture he had endured and fire a blast in the man's smug face, but he couldn't. None of them could. There was a very odd atmosphere of peace and warmth in the room that Graham could not explain. It was as if there was a force around these four walls that held back the feelings of fear and anger.

Graham found himself walking over to one of the four chairs placed in front of the table where Alex stood. It was like his legs were obeying Alex's command rather than his own. The others did the same. The way Alex spoke commanded respect and obedience, but not in the same way as Cavaness. Alex had a more regal tone. His words were spoken with a similar finality to them, yet they also echoed with deep compassion.

The tone was so familiar. Graham searched his mind trying to understand why. Sifting through memories like files in a cabinet, he suddenly recalled his dream and the tone in his father's voice. *"You are a special little boy, Graham. You make Mommy and Daddy very happy and very proud."* That was it. This was the distinction. Alex had a fatherly tone to his voice. It was this tone that kept Graham in his seat.

Looking up, he focused back on Alex.

"Thank you for your trust. I promise not to waste it. Your purpose in being here these past twenty-four hours comes from a story passed down from generation to generation since the beginning of recorded history. Perhaps you have heard of it. It is called *The Unseen War*. This particular story begins with the provision of two men, who were given to all of mankind as leaders and protectors of the human race. The one known as *The Ancient* fashioned these men himself, one after the other, and ordered them to shepherd his new creation of humanity. He christened them for service by giving them the gift of immortality and equipped them with special powers to fulfill their purpose. For hundreds of years after their christening, the two men were seen as brothers who ruled with great strength and authority, allowing the human race to thrive and multiply. Under their stewardship, cities were built and kingdoms were established. They were given wisdom to govern and a vast knowledge of all aspects of life: nature, economics, morality, engineering and even the inner workings of the human heart."

Graham looked at his friends. They had all heard the legends before. It was an age-old story developed to warn the reader of the consequences of greed and the misuse of power.

"As I am sure you know, greed and jealousy crept into the heart of the younger man. Instead of stewardship, he began to strive for dictatorship. His compassion for those under him was poisoned with pride and an unending lust for sole authority. He was angry with *The Ancient* for being made second and it made him feel terribly inferior. So, in the fulness of his pride and envy, he launched a mission to destroy the only other one like him, though he could not wage a physical war. Instead, using his knowledge of human nature, he used deception to lead his rebellion. Through his craftiness, he led a large portion of the human race to believe that he alone was the rightful ruler, but even with the power of the masses behind him, there was still one final roadblock to his ultimate success."

Alex let that statement linger for effect.

"Back then those two leaders, the Elder and the Younger, were able to take the power that they were given and bestow certain giftings to a select few for benefit of the community as a whole. Each nominee was given a gift, an object, which enabled them to serve alongside their fellow man. Knowing that this delegated power could pose a potential threat to his rulership, the Younger slowly convinced them through the years that this mantel of power was more of a burden than a gift. He was able to appeal to the sense of fear for the unknown, to portray the bands as dangerous and an unwanted obligation for any who possessed them. It took years to lay out the proper story and supporting arguments, but as the people grew to fear these powers, they begged and demanded that they be removed. *The Ancient* granted their plea and destroyed the objects that provided the power."

Kel, Damien, and Ailey were enthralled, leaning in to hear what came next.

"Different cultures have varying versions of what this object was. Though not much was written about how this *power* was bestowed or removed, the description of its existence has been spoken of throughout history. The most famous version is illustrated in Greek mythology. The Greek god, Zeus, possessed a shield with enhanced protective qualities. It was known as The Aegis. Some say it was crafted from the hide of a monster defeated by Athena. It was used by Perseus to defeat Medusa. Once slain, her head was displayed in the middle of the shield to further enhance its magical properties.

In the Roman Empire, they named their breastplate armor after the Aegis, thinking it would give them increased protection. I am sure they also used that name to strike fear into the hearts of their enemies. Anyone who had been familiar with Greek mythology would have understood the power of protection that the Aegis held.

"This, however, is not the only version of the object. In the ancient Egyptian culture, their account of the Aegis did not depict a shield, but a wide golden necklace, usually in the possession of the goddess, Isis. Moving throughout history, other cultures attempted to describe this powerful object as a leather sash or a breastplate. In *The Unseen War,* this unique power was given in the form..." Alex looked directly at Graham, "...of wristbands."

Graham immediately pulled back his sleeves and looked at

his wrists at the mention of the bands. How could he forget? Of course the story had wristbands. Even the depictions showed the fighters with illuminated wrists. They just looked so different from what was actually given to him, that he had not made the connection.

Alex smiled. "Yes. Your assumptions are correct. Most legends are birthed in truth, though the vague details are usually amplified by the imagination of the storyteller."

Alex walked behind his chair, pushing it under the table.

"When you first came here, I told you that magic did not exist. Today's culture uses magic as a way to describe the unexplainable. What these bands provide is power, not magic. The same type of power that initiated the human race was handed down from *The Ancient* in order for mankind to serve and protect each other. You think the story of *The Unseen War* is a myth– a fairy tale perhaps. Or even a simple parable of morals. Maybe now you can see that there is more truth to the story than you originally thought."

Alex waved a hand in the air as he did a day ago, illuminating their wrists. "All those stories throughout history tried to explain a very real truth. At least one version of the story remained correct."

They all looked down at their illuminated skin. The sun emblem radiated brighter than the rest of the band. Graham felt a surge of energy rush through his body. Feeling exhilarated, Graham looked at the others to see if they had all felt the same thing. They each shared the same look of wonder.

"So, you don't want to take our energy?" asked Graham.

Alex turned to address Graham with a smile and soft, joyful eyes.

"No, son. I have no intention of taking anything from you. Quite the contrary. I mean to give you more than you could possibly imagine."

Smiling at the confusion that his statement had caused, Alex continued.

"It is amazing what the mind can create when stressed and presented with ill-defined details. Almost every group of people that come through Catalyst Grove have a different explanation of what we are. Take Chase for example. If memory serves me well, he thought I was some variety of alien."

Chase laughed as his cheeks turned red. "Yes, sir, I did. And until now I thought we were the only two who knew that."

Alex laughed with him. "Well, don't worry. It is not the worst story. I believe Casey had the best one."

"Casey Hagan?" asked Graham.

"Yes. Do you know of her?" asked Alex.

"Sort of. We read her case file. She was the first one to have the bands. It said she was seen here, engulfed in flames. She died here."

"And what makes you think she died here?" asked Alex.

"Who could survive being in a fire? Plus, Chase said she was dead."

"She is dead, but not because of the fire. She died in 1987 at the ripe old age of ninety-three."

"Ninety-three? You mean the fire that almost burnt this place to the ground happened over one hundred years ago?"

"It most certainly did. The Aegis armbands were a new development at that time. Ever since the removal of the Aegis from human history, we have been trying to find ways of bringing it back."

Alex turned back to the rest of the group. The smile faded from his face and a more serious tone took over as he spoke, as if from memory.

"Once the Aegis was taken from humanity, all of the power rested solely with the Elder and the Younger. The Elder never broke his oath to watch over and protect the human race, while the Younger grasped for complete control over them. He would use his followers as pawns in his fight against his so-called brother, and as generations came and went, he was eventually seen as a god because of his power. Many versions of the Greek and Egyptian gods were developed from the different ways people viewed the Younger. His anonymity ensured his survival and enduring operations. Seeing the evil and deception, the Elder knew that there had to be a way to reintroduce this power to the human race. That is when *The Aegis* group was formed, and ever since that time, we have been searching for ways to bring the power back. We looked for centuries, all over the world for a sign, for a way to reintroduce the bands. It wasn't until Casey's generation that we stopped looking externally and finally decided to look within the body itself."

Alex paused for a moment to let them process all the information.

"We scoured the earth for any sign of the source of power, but we found nothing. Without it, the group was powerless to stop the domination of the Younger. He was too well protected by the people who viewed him as a god. We finally learned that all those centuries ago, *The Ancient* did not remove the power from history, but instead hid it within each person. The gifts and feats mankind once possessed through the bands now lie dormant within each and every one of us.

"Once we realized that, we built the warehouse as a type of training facility. We thought that given the right circumstances and education, each person would learn to draw it out, but with each person came failure, time and time again. After years of willing participants, we discovered the need for a catalyst. We needed something that would bring the dormant power to life again. It was at that moment that we saw the flaw in our thinking. The bands were no longer the Aegis. *We* were. The bands now serve as the key, or catalyst as we call them, enabling us to access the gifts inside. Through the knowledge originally given by *The Ancient*, we were and are now able to craft the bands."

"So... we are superheroes, then?" snapped Damien.

Chase cringed at Damien's response. "If he only knew

who he was talking to," he whispered to Cavaness.

"I do not blame you for your unbelief, Damien. Truly I do not. Casey did not believe either until her catalyst erupted in flames. It wasn't until afterwards, when she remained unscathed, that she understood. She was the first to become activated."

Alex grinned. "I guess for some, seeing is believing."

Alex stretched his hand out again, causing their wrists to illuminate. "These past twenty-four hours have been a time of activation. The catalysts activate the power coded in your DNA so that the Aegis power can be accessed. It happened last night when you first put them on, but it could not take full effect until your specific gifting was drawn out. Think of it as a needle from the doctor, drawing out blood. Catalyst Grove was designed to do just that."

Alex could feel their confusion. Looking to the other men, he signaled for them to come over to the new recruits. Cavaness, Branson, Chase, and Murphy all walked over to the small table, pulling up their sleeves. Each balled their fingers into a fist, forcing their bands to appear. With their forearms facing up, Graham was surprised to see that the circle portion of the bands were not empty. There were strange symbols filling them, different for each one.

"Now, if you will, please turn your arms over so that your palms are facing upward."

Each one did as Alex asked. Their bands were still illuminated. The once vacant circle that lay on their forearm was now filled with a symbol like the others. Beginning with Ailey, Alex walked over to each one. Ailey's circle was filled with a small line connecting two semi-circles.

"Ailey, you have the gifting of a *Bridge*. Your purpose is to serve the others by helping them use their powers together. I am sure you remember the odd feeling in your hands when you grabbed Graham and Kel's shirt in the warehouse, and the confusion of seeing both of them shoot a similar beam of light from their hands."

Ailey nodded, remembering the experience.

"And I'm sure you will never forget grabbing hold of Cavaness and causing the ground to erupt."

Ailey grinned and motioned a quiet no.

"It is a wonderful gift being a *Bridge*. It suits you. You are good at building up others. You would rather let the light shine on someone else as you work in the background using that creative mind of yours. Don't you agree?"

Ailey nodded again. Alex moved over to Kel next.

"Kel, you have the gifting of a *Pusher*."

The small circle in Kel's band had a sort of a 'V' in it, which was inset into a small arch resembling the ground.

"It is not unlike a normal mode of attack, though the energy you use when you *push* is more like the shockwave of an earthquake. What makes your gift unique is the fact that it can change trajectory."

Alex looked into Kel's eyes as if peering into the intimate parts of her mind and soul.

"You are a math and science person, are you not?"

"Yeah, those are my favorite subjects in school," said Kel.

"Alright, let's use a basic rule of physics. For every action, there is an equal and opposite reaction. Now, let's apply that. Your favorite game back at your orphanage is billiards, correct?"

"Well… yes," Kel admitted, sounding surprised.

"Let's say there is a ball close to the pocket, but you have to use the side rail of the table because there are other balls blocking a direct shot. When you strike the cue ball into the side rail of the table, you do it at a calculated angle so that it collides with the other ball in just the right way to make the shot. That is the strength of a Pusher. Do you remember your reaction to falling down the embankment?"

"Sort of. It all happened so fast. I remember shooting the ground, then the trees blowing up into the air," said Kel.

"And what was the distance between the entry and exit points?"

"Umm, I don't know. Fifteen or twenty feet, maybe?"

"Twenty-three feet. Based on your position and elevation, you calculated the exact angle needed to uproot the trees so that they would span the gap in the ground. You already have such a keen sense of the spacial relations of your surroundings. As long as there is a surface to absorb your shots, you will be able to deflect it back at any angle you wish. Cavaness has the same gift, and will be your mentor."

Kel's shoulders sank. "Cavaness? He almost killed us."

Alex smiled softly. "I wouldn't say that. If you had ever felt the full force of his attack, you would be very thankful for his restraint last night."

Alex turned and addressed all four of them. "I hope you will not hold these acts against the men sitting behind me. Everyone in this room has acted on the desire to draw out and develop your skills. Putting someone in extreme circumstances with the understanding that you will be hated and despised for it takes a great measure of courage and love, if they truly believe the final outcome is for the best."

"Why not just tell us what it is from the beginning and help us develop it that way?" asked Damien. "Wouldn't that be a lot less drama for everyone?"

"Indeed it would. That is exactly where we started. Those case files you found were the records of each attempt to draw out the power with willing participants, but we came to discover that it simply does not work that way. Let's use your words, Damien. I think you put it best when you shoved Kel to the ground while in the cavern. You said, and I quote, 'Sorry about pushing you like that. I had to do it hard enough to make it seem real'."

Instantly, the lightbulb went off in Graham's head. Without even knowing it, Damien had realized what Alex had long ago. It was all about perception. Graham immediately looked at Chase, who had been staring at him the entire time.

Had Chase kept these things in mind while he'd been scaring the life out of them these past twenty-four hours? Did he want Graham to become one of them as a friend and team member? Chase's eyes evidently displayed his wishes, because as he watched Graham's facial expressions, he gave a nod of confirmation.

"Since you have spoken up, Damien, let's discuss your gifting," said Alex.

A three-pronged trident was illuminated in his circle. Damien traced all three prongs with his finger.

"An *Aquatic* is a rare strength. There has only been one other to come through Catalyst Grove. And I've only seen a handful in the past twenty years, and none of them were able to drain a large pond from the very beginning." Alex looked directly into Damien's eyes. "I am curious. Once you saw the others display their power, did you already know where your strength lay?"

"Well… in a weird way, I kind of did. How did you know that?" asked Damien.

"I know you look out over the lake every night before you go to bed. Lima was quite the arid place to live, and your family did not have the means to take you down to the port much, did they?"

"No, they didn't. They took me once when I was like three or four. I remember how good it felt to splash around. It was so cool and refreshing. It was like nothing I had ever felt before, but we were never able to go back."

Graham looked up at Alex, vexed by his knowledge. Lima might as well be on the other side of the world from Portfield. There is no way Alex could know about Damien's past, and besides, he had never told anyone of his love for water.

"How do you know about our pasts?" asked Damien, bluntly.

"I know a great deal about each of you. No one comes here to be developed without my acceptance, so naturally, I must know who I am dealing with."

Alex walked up to Graham. Taking hold of his wrist, Alex turned his arm over to show his gifting. As his forearm twisted upward, he could see that his circle was still vacant. Graham's head sank almost as far as his heart. He couldn't make eye contact with anyone, especially Alex. He barely knew the man, but for some reason he felt as though he had let him down. Alex put his hand under Graham's chin and gently lifted his head up.

"You've nothing to be ashamed of. You have a lifetime ahead of you to develop your gifting."

Graham listened but still could not bring himself to look Alex in the eye.

"Graham. Look at me."

Graham didn't want to, but he could not disobey. He slowly looked up at Alex, who lowered his voice so that only Graham could hear what he had to say next.

"You've had a difficult past. I know you feel abandoned and have always questioned what you may or may not have done to your parents. I promise you, I will help you unravel this mystery. For now, you must understand that you bury things inside, building walls around your personal life. That is how you have learned to cope. Somehow, your true strengths are chained to those walls. We will learn together how to break them down. I promise."

Graham sat speechless, choking back tears. Not wanting his voice to break, he simply nodded.

"Good. It is settled then," Alex said, winking at Graham. Straightening up, Alex raised his voice for all to hear. "Graham, Chase will be your mentor. I hope you will find that agreeable. You may not have the same gifting, but Chase is extremely knowledgeable and an expert at drawing out strengths."

Alex walked back over to his table and picked up the silver tray he had brought in earlier. He walked back over to where the kids were, and, beginning with Graham, he lowered the platter so that each of them could take a golden envelope. Graham examined it while he waited for Alex to explain what they were just presented with.

"Cavaness has reported that you have worked extremely

well as a team. Your strengths compliment one another's and, as I can now see, you have all grown very close. Like men and women of war, you have all created a tight bond by way of the trials you have just experienced. These types of bonds are so tightly woven, that they are nearly impossible to break. You are a team, but I must warn you that accepting our offer will come with the certainty of danger. These powers have been activated in you to serve as protectors. You cannot protect someone unless there is something to protect them from. We form a very real alliance of able men and women under the name of Aegis, who are at war with a very real enemy. I want you to be aware of this right from the start."

Damien raised his hand.

"Yes, Damien?" asked Alex.

"Who are we protecting, and what does that have to do with this envelope?"

"The *who* will take some time to explain. More time than we have right now, although I gave you some detail in the story. As for the envelope, the last thing I want is for you all to be separated now. Time and distance are the only tools capable of tearing this bond you all have with each other, and these are relevant factors, since you come from different orphanages. It is not up to me to arrange a transfer, nor do I have the legal authority to request your presence here on a daily basis."

Graham had been so caught up in the previous night's events and the explanation of it that he hadn't thought about the reality of having to go back home. They had been through so much. He hated to think that he would never see Kel or Ailey again.

"By the law of the land, I will never have that type of legal authority. That is, unless you are my children to train."

They all looked at Alex, thoroughly confused.

He smiled back at them. "These are adoption papers. If you accept, I would like to make you permanent members of Aegis, and of my home."

Graham looked at the others in complete shock. Every orphan dreams of the day when they will be chosen and accepted. Year after year, he had seen others chosen instead of him. What he held in his hands was the physical manifestation of his heart's desire. This was the hope he had been waiting for. The hope of being part of a family and to be genuinely loved by someone other than people paid to do so.

"I will only turn these in if you are in agreement. I have already been in contact this morning with Ms. Winstone of Greenwood and Mr. Pitman of Oak Ridge Orphanage. They know that you have made your way here to Portfield Manor, and I assured them you were all in my care until your return in a few hours. So, between now and then, you have a decision to make. We will leave you to talk amongst yourselves and make a final decision."

Alex walked a few steps back toward his table, then turned back around to face the kids. He grabbed the bottom of his vest and adjusted it. Graham leaned closer. He finally realized why he recognized Alex.

"You are a remarkable group. Whatever your decision, please know that I hold you all in the highest regard. Now, please help yourselves to food and drink. I know you are famished."

At that, Alex turned toward the other members and motioned for them to leave the room. Branson and Murphy got up to congratulate Graham and the others, followed by Chase and Cavaness. After the first two had shaken hands and given high fives, Chase walked up to Graham and placed a hand on Graham's shoulder.

"You were a hard one for me to draw out. I hope you aren't too shaken up."

"I'm okay. You really had me going there," said Graham, feeling a bit sheepish.

"Well, I'm glad to hear it. Trust is a funny thing. I know I had to break yours to help you realize your gifting. I hope we can repair it once you accept."

"Yes, I'd like that," said Graham.

"Atta-boy," said Chase with a wide smile. "I'll see you on the other side."

With a pat on the back, Chase moved on to the others, giving his apologies for the hardship they'd endured, while expressing his excitement to have everyone on board. Cavaness stood where Chase had been in front of Graham. His large form blocked out the light from the chandelier, making his face hard to read.

"How's the stomach?"

"Uh, surprisingly okay. I don't hurt at all. It is odd."

A slight smile broke through his hardened leathery face. "Good. You are a strong young man. I pushed you as hard as I did because I knew you could take it. With the potential you have inside, you will be able to move mountains if you want to. It may not have released fully this time, but it will."

Cavaness patted the back of Graham's head. It was surprising to see a hint of compassion in his eyes. What was even more surprising was that Graham felt close to him now. This guy had a heart. Hours ago, Graham wouldn't have believed it.

Cavaness made his way over to Kel next. "Kel, you are already quite the Pusher. I look forward to our time together."

Kel blushed and gave him a smile.

Making his way down the line, he came to Damien. "Mr. Ortega," he said with a nod.

Before Damien could respond, he made his way to Ailey. Damien frowned, but quickly shook it off.

Cavaness knelt beside Ailey and gently took hold of her leg. "You are full of fire, little one. I hope it didn't hurt too badly."

Ailey gestured no.

"Good girl. I am anxious to see what you are capable of. There is a lot of strength in that little body."

He gave her a quick pat on the back of the head as he had

done with Graham, and then made his way to the door, closing it behind him.

There was a moment of silence before Graham spoke. For him, there was only one choice to make. Soon, Greenwood would be a distant memory.

"Guys, Alex is one of *the* Alexanders. It has been eating at me this whole time. I knew he looked familiar, but I couldn't put my finger on it. It wasn't until he adjusted his vest that I realized he looked exactly like Mr. Alexander from the warehouse picture and the portrait at Greenwood. He must be the great grandson or something. When he kept saying *we*, he must have been talking about his whole family line."

"Are you sure about that? That would mean his name is Alex Alexander. I really don't think his parents hated him that much," said Damien with a chuckle.

"Alliteration aside, I'm sure. He's the most powerful man in this state. What are you guys going to do?" Graham then addressed Damien directly. "I hope you're staying. I don't want to gain a family and lose my best friend."

"Are you kidding me, amigo? I just drained a whole pond with a blast from my hands. I am not going anywhere," said Damien.

Kel smiled at Damien's remark, and then turned to Graham. "We don't have much to go back to. All we do there is exist. Here, we can have a reason to exist. Danger or not, we're in!"

Ailey bobbed her head in agreement with Kel.

Graham could hardly contain his excitement as he thought about his new home and family members. "Okay, then. I guess it's settled."

Damien gave Kel and Ailey a big hug, then turned to Graham and gave him a thump on the back as he started singing "We are family…"

"Stop that," said Graham.

Damien stopped singing, but continued humming the song as he strutted over to the table filled with food.

"You've gotta watch him. He gets trapped in his own world sometimes," said Graham. Kel smiled as the food on Damien's plate slipped off and onto the floor as he continued humming.

"Kel, I never got a chance to say I'm sorry for not trusting you. It's a thing with me."

Kel shrugged it off. "We all have our thing. Plus, it looks like you'll have a lifetime to make it up to me."

Graham blushed and nervously scratched the back of his neck. "Yeah, I guess so."

Ailey was still standing beside Kel, picking at her wrist, trying to make it glow again. "That goes for you too, sis," said Graham. Ailey looked up at him with a grin. She threw her arms around his waist, squeezing tight.

Graham returned the hug and squeezed her even tighter. "Come on. Let's go tell them our decision."

IMPLOSION

Once Alex and the others had taken their seats at the table, Graham stood to address the group. "You really don't know what this means to us. I still don't know why or how you knew what we are capable of, but none of that really matters. I can speak on behalf of all of us when I say that we accept your offer. We want this to be our home."

"That is music to my ears," said Alex. "I will submit these papers first thing in the morning. You will still need to go back to your orphanages until the paperwork has been processed. Once the process is complete, you will officially be members of my household." Alex pulled back his sleeve to look at his watch. "We still have some time before you are expected. There are a few things I would like to show you."

Alex led the four of them over to the three mirrors.

"There are many unique qualities to our powers that are difficult to explain. I want to take you back to the warehouse where you were first kept. We will be going there using this," Alex said, pointing to the first mirror.

"Sweet! Is this another secret passage like the one in the cabin?" asked Damien.

"Not exactly," said Alex. "It is a passageway, but not a normal one. These are called Transit Mirrors. Among the variety of gifts we are able to possess, there are some who are able to infuse their power into objects. The power injected into the object will remain there for as long as that person is still alive. We call them *Weavers*. Only the most masterful of Weavers can craft these mirrors. Their power is infused into the rear of two mirrors at the same time. This forms a bond between them. Once that is complete, the mirrors are placed back to back and a passage is formed. Next, the mirrors are placed in the two desired locations where the weaver wants to travel."

Graham reached out to touch the dimples in the wood. Alex gently grabbed his hand to keep him from making contact. "You only want to put your fingers there if you intend to take the mirror with you to the other side. Since you are all new to this, I want you to hold on to one of us as we go through. We don't want anyone left behind." Alex reached out and took Ailey by the hand. He then placed his other hand to the center of the mirror. His wrist illuminated and, in a fading mist, they both vanished.

Graham, Kel and Damien were speechless. Noting Graham's expression, Chase chuckled.

"This is only the tip of the iceberg, my friend." Taking hold of Graham, he placed his hand on the mirror.

Branson took Damien, and Cavaness took Kel. Within seconds, they were miles away in the warehouse at the top of the hill. The feeling was exhilarating and gut-wrenching all at the same time. Going through the Transit Mirrors felt like the first drop you experience on a rollercoaster. Graham noticed that Cavaness and Chase emerged as if it were nothing. He, however, had come out on the other side with every muscle in his body tensed.

"You get used to it," said Chase, grinning.

They were now in a large office. Alex opened the door and led them down the hall to a small foyer with two elevators. All the furniture in the foyer was turned over on its side.

"Recognize anything?"

"Yeah! This is where we crawled down that elevator shaft," said Damien.

"Yes, which was a great plan, I might add. Very inventive," said Alex.

They continued to walk down the hall toward the larger rooms, where Damien had found the files and pry bar. There were other people in the building now, straightening up the place. One lady had a manila folder in her hand. Alex asked the woman if he could see the papers. He flipped through a few pages until he found the one he was looking for. He removed the piece of paper and handed it to Damien.

"Casey Hagan. That is the one you read, correct?"

"Yeah, but we took that with us. Kel had it folded up in her pocket."

"We are restocking the facility. We want to be sure that everything looks as real as possible. It was Chase's idea to add the files. He did not want anyone else to go through the trauma of believing they were being abducted by aliens. This gives Catalyst Grove a more down to earth feel."

Graham and the others chuckled as Chase began to blush. "Hey, I'm a Star Trek fan, what can I say? I have an overactive imagination."

"These rooms were our training areas when we first tried to develop people's giftings. That is why you see our sun emblem on the floor of every room. Like I said before, it took us years to realize that the power only surfaced when the subject reacted to a perceived threat. We did not want to send new members to the frontline to draw it out, so we purchased this entire estate and the surrounding acreage to be our development center."

They continued down the hall to where they had first been held captive. There were two men in the room, removing the broken chair and bolting a new one to the floor.

Alex pointed to the dangling wires and the leaky pipes. "Each stage along the way has the necessary elements in place to develop the various types of giftings. We wanted every type of power to have the opportunity to move the subject from point A to B and C. Damien, you mentioned that you felt like lab rats in a maze. Well, you were not far from the truth; however, it was for the benefit of the rat, not the one conducting the experiment."

"These mirrors. I noticed them in every place we went. Even the cave," said Graham.

"Yes, we have placed Transit Mirrors at each stage along the way. It is how we keep tabs on you while also staying one step ahead." Alex looked at Chase. "Not all of us have supersonic speeds. While the others were out moving you through the various stages of the Grove, I was monitoring everything from the mirrors. Not only can you move through them, but you can also observe and listen as well."

Alex walked back toward the office. Once they had all returned to the room, he held his hand up to the middle mirror. As he did, the reflective properties of the mirror faded away to reveal a small, dark living room made completely of wood.

"I heard all about your plan to fight back. It was I who let the others know about your intentions at the clearing," said Alex.

Graham peered through the mirrors. He'd wondered why they'd been able to stay one step ahead. Now, it made complete sense. As he looked into the old cabin, he began to feel awkward and self-conscious. *What did Alex think of me? Surely he watched as I took the knife?* His sense of wonder began to fade as he thought about Alex's watchful eye. He had seen everything. *What does he think of me now?*

Alex held his other hand up to the mirror on the left. The reflection faded into a view of the underground cave. "Let's go here." They paired up as they did before and, within seconds, they all appeared in the underground cave.

"I bet it seemed rather harsh to make you all tumble into the river, not to mention extremely dangerous. What if you could not swim?"

Alex walked over to where the edge of the cavern wall met the edge of the pool. A rock the size of a basketball, sat in the corner. He bent down, retrieved the rock and threw it in the water. A few moments went by, until the surface of the water began to bubble and the stone returned floating to the surface.

"I mentioned earlier that there was one other Aquatic to come through here. As she advanced in her power, she helped develop a reaction based current below the surface. Nothing can stay underwater for long. Even in the stream where you originally fell, you were protected."

Damien's demeanor instantly changed. Graham noticed that his excitement over the Transit Mirrors faded quickly into a new expression of disappointment.

"So you are saying I did not help my friends get out of here?"

Alex looked over at Damien. "On the contrary, you tapped into the power of the current. Did you notice how that rock only just broke the surface?"

"Yes."

"And what happened to your friends? They went airborne, didn't they? Because you are an Aquatic, you intensified the current, getting them to the surface quicker. There is no doubt that you were able to help your friends in a time of need."

Damien's smile quickly returned.

Mirror by mirror, Alex took them around the facility, showing them the various stages and how each section had options to develop certain gifts, as well as explaining the safety protocols they had put in place. Wanting to show them one final location, he took them through another mirror, which led to a dusty cellar. Alex opened the wooden door to expose the edge of a cliff.

"Are we at Greenwood?" asked Graham. He looked behind him to see three small mirrors hanging below bundles of dried leaves suspended from the ceiling joists.

"Yes, we are. This is where you almost fell to your death, or so you thought," replied Alex.

Graham took one step out of the doorway and then sidestepped to the left along the narrow path, starring out over the towns below. Alex looked over and motioned to Chase, who immediately jumped over the edge.

The kids all reached out as if to stop him. "WAIT! What are you doing?" yelled Kel.

Graham peered over the edge of the cliff as a strong wind blew upwards. The seconds that ticked by seemed like an eternity while he contemplated why Chase would jump. As the wind grew stronger, a voice carried in the squall. "Whoohoo!" It was faint at first, but the sound of Chase's voice grew louder as the heavy wind lifted him upwards through the air and back onto the ledge.

Alex smiled at the kids' perplexed expressions. "You see, you were protected even before you arrived. Everything you have encountered up to this point has been under our complete protection."

"Unbelievable," whispered Graham. This was stuff he had only read about in books. He could not believe what he was seeing. He half expected to wake up at any moment back in his bed, snapping out of a dream. Two different worlds were before him. One was the world he had always known; a world of predicable, daily routine behind the walls of Greenwood. The other was filled with superhuman abilities that should not exist, yet here they were, right in front of him.

Walking back into the cellar, Alex moved a hand back and forth as if creating ripples in a pond. As he did this, the view of the cave faded and the reflective properties of the mirror were restored. He then poised his hand over the third mirror and Portfield Manor appeared. Alex placed his hand on Ailey's back.

"I do not think you need any further evidence. I hope this makes up for the temporary pain you endured last night. Come, let's head home."

Alex placed his hand in the center of the mirror. Two by two, they all emerged from the mirror into a different room of Portfield Manor. Graham and the others again emerged tense and rigid from the rollercoaster feeling. As his feet hit the floor, Graham's eyes were shut as tight as his clenched fists. Once he realized it was over, he opened his eyes and took a deep breath of relief.

Graham looked at Damien with a grin. "That was awesome!" he whispered.

"I know, right? I want to do it again!"

Kel was still doubled over a little. "Not me. I hate that feeling. Who in the world would want to keep doing that?"

Ailey silently laughed as Kel tried to shake off the nerves. She shuddered as goosebumps ran up the length of her arms.

Alex watched the kids mingle, enjoying their energy and the joy of the moment. It wouldn't always be like this, though. He knew that eventually the time would come for them to use their powers for the purpose for which they were given. Times were growing increasingly evil, like a looming storm. He was burdened by it, but for now, that knowledge would remain his own. True joy and contentment was hard to come by these days. He wanted them all to enjoy it, because it's joyful times like these that give people perseverance during hard times.

Alex pulled a pocket watch from his vest pocket. He put his other hand to his mouth and cleared his throat. The sound carried throughout the room, causing everyone to turn around. "You will need to depart in an hour's time. As much as I would like to stay and hear all about your adventures in the Grove, I must be on my way to New York for some urgent business matters."

Alex clasped his hands together as a wide smile spread across his face. "I am so thrilled that we will be together. I truly am. I look forward to spending time with each and every one of you. Until then, be safe, and guard your power. We are not keen on broadcasting who we really are, and you will discover that everyone else will be unable to see your catalysts. For something like this, prudence is our best ally."

Alex turned to leave, but Graham spoke out before he had a chance to open the door.

"Are you an Alexander? It's been bugging me this whole time. You look just like the picture of Mr. Alexander, both from the warehouse and the painting that's in my orphanage."

Alex raised an eyebrow. "You have a keen eye for detail, Graham. How much do you know about the Alexanders?"

"Not much, really. I know that they pretty much own this whole town. Mr. Alexander built our orphanage, and was one of the founders of Wellington. He was pretty rich, and evidently had a lot of power. That's about all I know."

"You are right on all but the ownership. He did purchase the land that is now Portfield, but as his town grew, he delegated responsibilities and land to other families. It was always his desire to work with and through the people. But enough with the history lessons. To answer your question, I am. Now, if you will excuse me."

Graham watched as he left the room.

Damien turned to Graham in unrestrained excitement. "This is crazy, man! Can you believe it, amigo? We have a home! We have super powers! I have a trident on my arm! I am glad you kept going to Wellington, amigo. We would not be here or have all this if it weren't for you."

Graham smiled half-heartedly at Damien. He turned his arm over and traced the small vacant circle on his forearm with his finger.

Damien's excitement carried him all over the room, talking up the new powers they all had. Taking notice of Graham's disappointment, Chase walked over to him.

"It will come with time. You're not the first one to have to wait. It happens."

"I guess. I just hate feeling inadequate, that's all. I've held back all my life, and this is no different." Feeling uncomfortable, Graham changed the subject.

"So, what does your catalyst look like?"

Chase pulled up his sleeve, baring his forearm. He tightened his hand into a fist as his wrist began to glow. Within the small circle was a horizontal lightning bolt, with the points extending just beyond the rim of the circle.

"How did you do that?" asked Graham.

"Do what?"

"Just make it light up like that? I thought you had to use your power to make the bands show up."

"There are a lot of things you will be able to do once you develop. Making your bands illuminate is only level two. Just wait until you get past level ten. You think a glowing wrist is cool? You just wait, my friend. There's a lot more to see."

"Levels? What's a level, and how many are there?"

"It's pretty simple, really. The more you learn and train, the more advanced you become. The levels are a pre-designed metric that helps you understand how far along you are. As for the number of levels, I couldn't say. I don't think there is a cap. I have heard of people getting up into the fifties before, but that would take a lifetime of dedication."

"So, what are you? Are you at level twenty or something?"

"Twenty? I wish. No, I am at fourteen right now. Cavaness is working me pretty hard, so that I can move up to the next level, but it is pretty intensive. Plus, I've been a little distracted lately with chasing kids through the forest."

"Yeah, well, your blasts did seem a little weak to me," Graham replied. "Speaking of the forest, how did you get started in all this?"

"Now that is an interesting story. As you have probably figured out by now, I was also a lonely kid at Greenwood. I was a perfect picture of the stereotypical problem child. And I'm probably single-handedly responsible for most of the gray hair on Ms. Winstone's head. It took a very long time for me to come around, but she was diligent with me. I think she made it her life's mission to set me straight. Almost every day, she would tell me, 'Those who spend ample time in the shadows know the true value of light'. It was her mantra for me. Now, I can see the wisdom in it, but before I changed, I hated it. She was good at that sort of thing. It's like she kept planting little seeds in me that would push me in the right direction later. As a matter of fact, it was something she said to me that led me here. I remember one night when I–"

Before Chase could finish, the wall beside them exploded, sending both of them flying backwards across the room. They both hit the ground hard. Their arms instinctively shielded their faces from the rock and rubble that flew through the air like shrapnel. Graham tried to look around, but his mind was in a tailspin. Squinting through the smoke, he could see that everyone had been knocked to the ground, even Cavaness. Through the fire and smoke, Graham saw six men in black coats step through the gaping hole in the wall. Before he could react, blasts of purple fire shot from their hands, hitting Cavaness in the chest.

More blasts filled the room like fireworks as Murphy and Branson retaliated. Branson reached out with both hands. One hand fired a steady stream of light toward the unknown attackers, as electricity sprang from the other. His yellow stream was met by a purple one, creating a shockwave that knocked everyone within a ten foot radius to the ground. Branson's electric blast hit one of the other men in black, making him convulse and crumple to the ground. Chase fired at him, knocking him into the wall so hard that he fell into the surrounding rubble, unconscious.

Graham was still trying to process what was happening. His first impression was that this was yet another attempt to bring his power to the surface, but before he could form the thought, a purple blast hit him in the side. His legs flew out from underneath him and he crashed to the ground with a thud. He grabbed his side and rolled over in agonizing pain.

This was different. This was real.

The blasts continued to fly around the room, lighting up the smoke that permeated the Manor. Graham spotted Kel and Ailey curled up underneath the large table with Damien's arms wrapped around them. *Thank God.* Graham looked around for Chase, but he was gone. There was a faint path through the smoke where he had run. Graham followed the path with his eyes until he saw two of the invaders fly through the air and crash into the walls.

As he lay there, looking through the smoke, he could see Cavaness' large form in hand-to-hand combat with two of the others. Murphy was trying to form what looked like a glowing net to capture one of them, but before he could cast it, seven or eight blasts hit him. His body went limp as he fell backwards and his head connected with the wood floor.

Branson was still locked in his streaming blast with one of the others. His stream was growing shorter and shorter as the dark purple blast was growing longer. In a split second, Branson was overtaken by the purple stream as the invader's blast met his hand, and in a huge flash of purple, he was sent crashing into the table where Damien and the others had taken shelter. Branson hit with such force that the table broke in half, sending shards of wood everywhere.

"Run, Graham! Get the others and run! NOW!" Chase's voice echoed through the room. Graham's adrenaline kicked in. The pain in his side faded and he jumped to his feet, running over to his friends. He grabbed Damien by the arm.

"Come on, we have to get out of here!"

"Where? I can't see anything!" yelled Damien.

Graham desperately searched for an exit, spinning around until a glare to his right caught his eye.

"Get off him!"

Graham could hear Chase trying to help Cavaness. The glare hit his eye again.

"The mirrors! We have to get over to the Transit Mirrors!" shouted Graham.

Small stones peppered his face as the fighting continued behind them. Graham heard another body hit the ground. His heart sank and he prayed it was one of the invaders and not Chase or Cavaness. Graham could now see a faint outline of one of the mirrors through the smoke. He stretched out his hand as his wrist illuminated. They were almost there. He was just a few feet from the mirror when a large hand with a glowing purple wristband took hold of his arm.

"Where do you think you're going, boy?" The voice was deep and cold. "Over here. I have them!" the man yelled.

The smoke was beginning to clear, just enough for Graham to make out one of the invaders forming thick black chains between his hands. Cavaness was already bound, and Chase was in the process of being shackled. The chains around their bodies looked like smoke. The Former placed his hands over Chase's and Cavaness' mouths. Once his hand was removed, a thick black substance remained. There was one other invader still conscious. He fired two blasts into their chests. Their muffled grunts of pain echoed through the room. Graham struggled against his captor, but he could feel his energy being syphoned from his wrist. Damien reached out to fire in retaliation, but the stranger held his glowing purple hand to Graham's temple. "That would be a mistake." Damien swallowed hard and put his hand back down.

The element of surprise had been too much. All the members of Aegis were either unconscious or bound, and once again, Graham could not help but feel despair over not being able to help. The remaining men in black walked over and picked up their fallen comrades. They carried them over to where Graham and the others stood. One by one, the taller stranger grabbed his teammates by the wrist. Their bands began to glow as he transferred some of his energy to the others, bringing them back to consciousness. They all stood up, shaking off the pain.

The man holding Graham looked at Cavaness and Chase as they fought against their bonds. He then looked back at

Graham. "So, this is the one. The bottomless well." He tightened his grip around Graham's wrist and turned it so that his forearm was facing the ceiling, taking notice of the vacant circle. "He is strong, no doubt about that. I guess we will find out soon enough."

He looked over to one of the others and gave a nod of approval. The man then removed two of the Transit Mirrors from the wall and threw them to the ground. With two swift stomps, he shattered them beneath his boot. A few of the men grabbed Kel, Damien, and Ailey by the arms and placed their hands to the center of the final mirror, vanishing. Only Graham, his captor, and one other man in black remained.

"Time it right," said Graham's captor to his comrade. The other man raised both hands and shot a large pulse of energy into the ground, turned around, and exited the room through the mirror. The entire house began to quake and tremble and the floor began to crack beneath them.

Graham's captor looked over to Cavaness and Chase. "I won't kill you myself. I would, but I have my orders." His gaze remained fixed. "Consider us even."

Cavaness clenched his jaw and furrowed his brow, murmuring something behind the strip covering his mouth. Graham looked behind him at his captor's face.

"Silas?"

Bits of the ceiling began to fall around them. The walls were beginning to buckle and the beams from the ceiling were cracking and caving in. Silas shifted his gaze from Cavaness to the ceiling above. The corner of his mouth curled up into an evil grimace.

"A little ironic, don't you think, Cavaness?" Silas reached his free hand toward the final transit mirror. "Best of luck, old friend."

Silas leaned further toward Cavaness, in a taunting manner. With his ominous grin becoming even more sinister, he continued.

"Vae Victus."

At that, he placed his four fingers into the small divots carved into the wood surrounding the mirror. Still having a firm grip on Graham's arm, he placed his thumb to the mirror, and with a fading mist, they were gone, taking the mirror with them.

Within minutes, Portfield Manor imploded into a large heap of rubble as Silas' sinister laugh lingered in the air.

REVELATION

Graham's feet landed on the cold stone surface as he realized that the attack on Portfield Manor had literally knocked him right out of his shoes. The light from the bulbs around the cavern danced along the surface of the water in the pool. Graham tried to get his bearings as he looked around. Six of them, with enough skill to take out Cavaness and the others, against four kids who had just learned about their powers. Their chance of survival was very grim.

Thick smoky chains had already been placed around the hands of Kel, Damien, and Ailey. The Former was in the process of extracting more chains from his hands so he could shackle their feet as well. They were lined up in a row near the edge of the pool, with one of the men in black standing guard behind each one.

Silas shoved Graham, making him almost fall to his knees. He looked at his friends, his mind racing. *What do they want with us? Are the others even alive? Surely the house has crumbled by now?*

"I've been told you are the one that can tip the scales in our favor. Is this true, boy?" asked Silas in a controlled, icy voice.

"I don't have any idea what you're talking about. I'm a nobody. If there was someone strong enough to give you an edge, there's no way it could be me. Please, just let us go," said Graham.

Silas laughed. "We didn't get to finish our conversation the other day. I don't think I even got to give you my full name. My name is Silas Serene. You know, my offer still stands. I can still help you if you would like, though I can see that you have already gotten started."

Silas grabbed Graham's arm and twisted it so that his forearm was facing upwards. He held his hand above Graham's wrist, making it illuminate. Silas stared at Graham's band and the empty circle that was supposed to house the emblem of his gifting. He released Graham's arm, letting it fall back to his side. "Not there yet, I see. No matter. We will make it come to the surface one way or another. These things can be tricky. Alex might have created your little training facility to develop you, but I have found the direct route to be more effective. You see, the real key is to find the proper motivator. The most difficult part is in finding the right fit when there are so many to choose from."

Silas paced around Graham as he spoke, his hands joined together behind his back in a sophisticated strut. "Public humiliation, physical harm, destruction of personal property, injury to loved ones. These are all effective methods. Which one do you think will draw out your ability, Graham?"

Graham's blood ran cold at the mention of injury to loved ones. He could take pain. He would prefer torture over seeing his friends being hurt. His pulse quickened as his eyes combed the cavern for anything that would get them out of this.

Silas must have noticed Graham's change in demeanor, because he stopped his pacing and smiled. "Ahh, something struck a nerve, did it? Now, it's just a process of elimination. Very well."

"Wait! Just tell me what you want me to do and I'll do it. What is this special person supposed to do? I can't claim to be someone I don't know about," Graham said, trying to buy some time.

"Let's just say that there is one special person who is rumored to have a gift of unlimited potential. We will leave it at that."

"And you think I'm this holy grail of limitless power? I can tell you right now that you have the wrong person." Graham pointed to his friends. "Ask them. They'll tell you. I haven't been able to save anyone or do anything to help this entire time."

Silas never took his eyes off Graham. "So modest and humble. I'm touched. Of course, no one will think they have such power. That would be arrogant. Besides, you have only just stepped into our world." Silas put a hand on Graham's shoulder. "I wouldn't expect you to know your potential right from the start. It must be revealed. And that is what I am here for… to help you."

His grip tightened, making Graham's knees buckle. "Now, you have bought enough time. Have you been able to find a way out yet?"

Graham was silent.

"No, I didn't think so. You could not find a way of escape, because there isn't one. Now it is time for me to follow through with my promise. Based on your earlier reaction, I'm guessing it would be better to start with the last option. Let's begin, shall we? I will not take you back with us until I am certain you are the one. Don't worry, though. Our methods are much faster than Alex's. It will be as quick as tearing off a band-aid."

Silas held up a hand. It ignited into a ball of purple energy. He held his hand close to Graham's head as he leaned in to whisper in his ear. "Ladies first."

Graham gasped.

Silas fired a blast, hitting Kel directly in the stomach. Kel yelled in pain as she doubled over and fell to the ground.

"Stop! Just take me with you and do whatever you want to

with me! You don't have to do this!" Hot tears pricked Graham's eyes.

Kel lay there, curled up in the fetal position, as Silas threw two more blasts, hitting her in the small of the back and thigh. Kel cried out in pain and curled up tighter to shield herself from the attack.

Graham threw a punch at Silas, but the man's reflexes were too fast. Silas moved his head to the side, dodging Graham's paltry attack. He then fired a blast into Graham's ribs, making Graham stumble to the side.

"Physical harm won't do. You are much too stubborn for that. Don't worry, though. I can see what needs to be done."

Silas walked over to the others. Kel was still on the floor. Ailey tucked her head into her shoulders, shifted her shackled feet away from Silas, and threw herself on top of Kel to protect her. Damien tried to summon the water from the pool, but the chains seemed to be blocking his ability. He frantically swept his hands from side to side, trying to make the water rise, but the power of the Former's chains was too strong. Not knowing what else to do, he sprinted toward Silas and barged him in the side, knocking him to the ground.

"Stay away from them, you freak!" Damien tried to use his chains as a weapon. He laced his fingers together and used them as one big fist to hit Silas, but one of the other men in black fired a blast, sending Damien flying through the air and onto the edge of the pool.

Graham's bands began to glow, and he fired at the man who'd hit Damien, but the man deflected his shot. The blast hit the rock wall, causing a small explosion that created a hole in the cavern. Small chunks of rock hurled through the air and fell into the pool.

Graham sprinted toward Silas, throwing his arm forward and sending a huge wave of energy in his direction. The blast hit Silas in the leg, causing him to fall forward onto his face. Graham sent blast after blast at him, not stopping until he could no longer see through the cloud of dust and rock. At least twenty shots had been fired at Silas as Graham roared in anger. He stood with one hand still extended, panting for air. Beads of sweat rolled down his forehead as he waited for the dust to settle.

Fifteen or twenty seconds went by. Graham expected to see Silas' body lying on the ground, but instead a shadowy figure darted from the rubble and fired a purple blast into his chest. Graham fell backwards, letting his momentum carry him into a backwards roll, and then sprang back to his feet. He braced himself for another attack, but nothing came.

Silas swept the dust from his black shirt. "You are strong, I'll give you that. You have just begun, and are already advanced beyond the average novice, but you're going to have to do better than that if you want to save your friends. You think I will stop after a couple of hits?"

Silas' voice grew deeper. His eyes seemed to have a flicker of madness in them. "I will do whatever it takes to draw it out, Graham. *Whatever* it takes." Another purple wave shot from Silas' hands. Graham shifted his weight and ducked his head as the purple wave of light darted over his shoulder. He stood up straight again and looked Silas right in the eye.

"This will not work! I told you. Take me and leave them. As long as they are in danger, I cannot concentrate. I know that about myself. This isn't the way." Graham had a pleading tone to his voice, but what he was saying was true. He had to keep the others safe at all costs, even if it meant paying for it with his own life.

Silas slowly walked over to Graham, lost in thought. He reached down to retrieve his cane as he weighed Graham's words. He continued walking until his face was inches away from Graham's. "I'll tell you what. Why don't we do this…"

Silas swiftly extended his cane and fired a purple ball from its tip into Graham's chest. His teeth were bared and his eyes were lit up in a consuming rage.

Graham slammed into the stone floor. He held his chest with both hands. The pain was so intense from being hit point blank that he could hardly move. He felt like he had just been hit by a train. He wanted to cry out, but the breath had been knocked out of him. All he could do was gasp for breath as Silas walked away from him toward the others.

The other men in black must have anticipated what was going to happen next, because they all moved together behind Kel, Ailey, and Damien. The men behind Kel and Ailey both grabbed a handful of hair and pulled the girls' heads backwards, forcing them to their knees. One of the others walked over to Graham. He grabbed him by the collar and pulled him up to his feet. Graham's knees were weak. He did not know if he could stay standing, but somehow, when the man let go, he stayed upright.

Silas grabbed Damien by the hood of his shirt, pulling him to his feet. He dragged him sideways over to the edge of the pool. Letting go of the hood, he then took a firm grip around Damien's throat. Damien's eyes widened in shock, his heart beating faster as his air supply was being cut off.

"Enough of the games, Mr. Dawson. It is time for your emancipation. Does your best friend need to perish, or will you break free?" Silas' grip tightened even more. Damien's mouth widened and the veins bulged from his neck as he struggled for each breath.

"STOP THIS! I will do whatever you want, just stop!" Graham barely managed to get the words out through the lingering pain in his chest. A tear fell down his cheek as he pleaded for his friend's life.

"Just get out of here, Graham! Save yourself! Oww!" The echoes of Kel's whimper hovered in the air as her hair was violently pulled back again.

Silas loosened his grip, allowing Damien to take a few deep breaths before constricting his grip again. With teeth still bared and eyes wild with anger, Silas said, "I hear you're an Aquatic. It's a pity your salvation lies at your feet, waiting to be commanded." The water still had ripples lapping at Damien's foot, caused by the fallen rocks. "These chains are a bit of a block to your power, I'm afraid."

Graham watched Silas, trying to decide whether he was more afraid of the threats, or of the calm and collected voice that traveled through a face engulfed in such evil and rage. Silas continued.

"You like the water, don't you? You're like a fish, drawn to its natural habitat." Silas took his free hand and cupped it over Damien's mouth. Purplish-black steam rose from his hand, and when he removed it, a black seal was covering Damien's lips. Damien squirmed and murmured, but could not get the seal off his face. Damien grabbed Silas' arm as he was lifted off his feet. Silas held Damien up in the air by the throat.

"Ok, then. Swim… little fishy."

He threw Damien into the water and watched as his writhing form sank toward the bottom.

"NO!" Graham yelled. He struggled with all his strength against his captor, but the grip was too strong. Graham felt a boot slam into the back of his knees and found himself on all fours, facing Kel and Ailey.

Graham was screaming at the top of his lungs. "Let go of me! Damien! Come on, swim!"

Kel and Ailey also struggled to get free, but a blast hit them both in their backs, making them crumple to the ground.

"Time is ticking, Mr. Dawson. How long do you think poor Damien can hold his breath?"

Graham was wild-eyed. His entire body went numb. Panic flowed through his veins. He continued to struggle against the man behind him, wishing his bands would activate, but nothing was happening. His friend was going to die, and he could not save him. He held his breath and strained so hard that the veins in his head began to bulge. He wanted so badly for the power to surface, but it was no use. Graham looked over to Kel and Ailey with a look of sorrow and defeat on his face. They looked back at him with tears in their eyes. It was hopeless. They knew that they were next, and there was nothing to be done about it. This was the end.

"Tick. Tock. Tick. Tock. One minute has passed by. I think poor Damien's fate may be sealed," mocked Silas.

Graham's breath was rapid and shallow. He looked over to see a small cluster of bubbles break the surface of the water. Damien was drowning. For all he knew, that was Damien's final breath escaping his body. Graham held his breath again for one final attempt to strain, when suddenly, the numbness melted away. The storm of panic inside subsided, replaced with an eerie calm. His breathing slowed down and deepened. A spring began to well up inside. It felt as if liquid energy rushed throughout his entire body.

"Let go of me," said Graham in a slow and calm tone.

"Let go… or what, exactly?" questioned the man behind him. In irritation, the man fired a blast into Graham's back, knocking him back onto his hands. Graham grunted, but did not retaliate. Now on all fours, he calmly repeated his request.

"Let go."

Electric sparks began to fire all around him. Gusts of wind emanated from within, stirring the dust around him. His fingernails dug into the stone surface beneath him, turning his knuckles white. The force around him was so intense that the man behind Graham started to get nervous. Small pebbles and debris around Graham began to hover like the dust ring of Saturn. A perfect collision of righteous anger and love for his new family collided within him, creating a perfect storm that shattered the wall of self-doubt and restraint. In a flash, a blinding yellow light shone all around him as he screamed:

"LET GO!"

The light around him exploded in an inferno of energy, hurling his captor into the cavern wall. Kel and Ailey ducked their heads, trying to shield themselves from the intensity of the explosion, but it was too much. Both of them, along with the men behind them, were also sent crashing to the wall.

The entire cave shook and the walls started to crumble

and crack. Graham never shifted his gaze from the floor in front of him. All he could do was scream and allow the power to flow. As Graham continued yelling, the energy around him shot straight up, blowing the ceiling to small pieces. The ground above erupted in light, sending dirt and rock mushrooming into the night sky. The cavern, now open to the ground above, began to shake violently under the surge of power. The cracks in the walls grew wider as chunks of rock began to fall.

As Graham stopped yelling, his eyes began to cross. His body trembled as the dizziness made everything around him spin. He had nothing left. All his energy was spent. The wall inside him had finally crumbled, but the outcome would be the death of them all. His arms felt like thin rubber. He tried to focus his eyes and find his friends. He could make out Kel and Ailey lying on the ground. They were not moving, but he knew their chains were gone, because he could see their arms sprawled out to the sides. Darkness faded in and out as Graham felt himself slipping in and out of consciousness. The sound of his blasts had muffled his hearing, as though a grenade had just gone off beside him. He fell to his side, completely exhausted.

"What have I done?" he whispered, as his eyes began to close.

Before Graham gave in to fatigue, the surprise of an object darting out of the surface of the pool made him come back to life.

"D…Damien?"

Graham's eyes began to cross again. Dirt and rubble fell on his face. The faint sounds of someone talking beside him made him open his eyes again. He could not make out the words, only bits and pieces.

"Am…go. Et up. It is… ime to go."

Damien tried to pull Graham to his feet, but he was too heavy.

"ELP! Chase… here!" yelled Damien.

Graham turned his head to see Chase run toward him. Chase was talking, but Graham's ears were still throbbing. All he could hear were murmurs. Chase bent down and grabbed Graham under his arms and legs. He picked him up and ran away from the edge of the pool.

"Ch…Chase? What's happening? How are you here? I'm sorry, I–"

Before Graham's eyes rolled into the back of his head, he saw Cavaness running toward him with Kel and Ailey over each shoulder. The scene faded to black for a few seconds, then Graham returned to consciousness, looking up at the stars through the hole he had created in the top of the cave. The scene went blurry again and the black velvet sky gave way to a haze of gray as Graham felt his body go limp.

FALCON HQ

Graham slowly opened his eyes, blinking as the ceiling fan above his bed pushed dry air down onto his face. For the first time in years, he had slept an entire night without a single dream. He shifted his weight, rolling over on his side to see Damien asleep in the armchair next to his bed. He looked terribly uncomfortable curled up in a ball, with one foot continuously slipping off the edge of the cushion. He had a small blanket that was hanging over him like a cape. It wasn't even long enough to cover his feet.

"Damien," Graham said groggily, sitting up. It was then that he remembered what had happened, because pain wracked his body, sending him back down into his pillow.

"There you are! You had us scared for a while. What on earth happened to you?" asked Damien.

"I thought you were dead! I thought I'd never see you again. How did you escape the chains?"

Damien thought for a moment. "I don't know what happened. All I could see from the surface of the water was a bright burst of light. That light penetrated and lit up the entire pool. I watched the chains dissolve and my bands reappear. I tried to kick and swim to the surface, but I couldn't hold my breath any longer. I inhaled a large gulp of water, gagging and freaking out, because I knew that was it, but I kept breathing. I was floating there in the middle of the pool breathing water! I can breathe under water, Graham!"

Graham was clutching his side as the pain ricocheted through his body. "You've lost it. You couldn't use your powers, remember?"

"No, I completely forgot about being kidnapped, chained up and almost killed," said Damien, sarcastically. "Of course I remember. Weren't you listening? The chains faded away and I was able to use my powers again. The light made the chains dissolve. What was that light?"

Fragments of memories flashed through Graham's head as he tried to remember what happened. "Um… I think it was me. I remember freaking a little when you were tossed into the water, and when Kel got hurt. I tried to use my power, but I couldn't, not until I saw the bubbles come to the surface of the water. I thought I'd just seen your last breath come to the surface." Graham grabbed his throbbing head. "I just remember a strange calmness, followed by an explosion and a lot of yelling. The last thought I remember having was that I'd finally broken free, and that I'd killed everyone in the process."

"Well… you didn't kill us. You saved us. You saved me. If that light came from you, then you were the one who made the chains disappear."

"What about Kel and Ailey? I saw Cavaness pick them up. They looked like they were in pretty bad shape." Graham paused and looked up at Damien. "Wait. How did Cavaness get there– and Chase for that matter? Did I dream that up?"

"No, Graham. That was not a dream," said a gravelly voice. Cavaness walked through the door and into the bedroom.

"Looks like you finally came through. That was quite the display of power you put on back there."

"How did you find us? I thought you had all been crushed," said Graham.

"We'll get to that. First, let's try to alleviate some pain." Cavaness took hold of Graham's wrists with his calloused hands. He then closed his eyes in deep concentration. His wrists began to glow, followed by his hands. Graham began to feel a wave of heat flow through his body. He took a deep breath in anticipation, flinching with pain. He slowly let out his breath and cautiously took another, less painful breath. A few minutes ticked by as Cavaness infused Graham with his energy. The light slowly faded. Cavaness opened his eyes and took a deep breath.

"It will take a few more sessions to get you back to normal, but your pain levels should decrease with each one. Nobody should have been able to sustain that much energy flowing through them. You're lucky to be alive." Cavaness leaned in closer so only Graham could hear him. "You should not have any further reason to doubt yourself." He gave Graham's shoulder a squeeze. "Now, let's get you downstairs. Everyone is eager to know how you're doing."

At that, Cavaness walked out the room. While Damien watched him leave, Graham quickly looked down and grunted. He tried to illuminate his bands to see if Cavaness was right, but evidently, he was still too weak to make them appear. His heart longed to see that circle filled with his gifting.

"Not much of a talker, is he?" asked Damien.

"No, he isn't," replied Graham. "But I kind of like that about him."

This was the third time Graham had seen a more caring side to Cavaness, though one of those times happened to have been just after the man had seemingly beaten him to death.

Graham twisted his torso around, and then tilted his head from side to side. He felt like a new person. He still hurt, but not nearly as bad as he did when he had first woken up. He sprang from the bed and ran through the bedroom door.

"Hey! Wait for me," called Damien, chasing after him.

Graham felt the smoothness of the wooden handrail slide beneath his hand as he made his way down the staircase, jumping down to the landing at the bottom of the living room. He looked around at the strange new surroundings. The room looked like a mountain lodge with thick wooden beams lining the ceiling. The posts that held the floor system in place looked like huge tree trunks.

"Whoa, what is this place?" Graham asked.

"Welcome to Falcon, our Regional Aegis Headquarters," replied Alex, who was walking in from the other room.

"Alex! You're back!"

Graham had never been an outwardly affectionate person, but he found himself running to Alex without hesitation. Alex gave Graham a big squeeze.

"Yes, I am here. I'm only sorry that I was not with you earlier," he said in a tender voice.

This world of emotions was new to Graham. He was so used to keeping others at a distance that he had a hard time controlling the new things he was beginning to feel. Focusing on these new emotions went against his natural instinct, but he was learning to embrace them. He didn't know why he felt so safe around Alex. Logic would have told him to keep Alex at a safe distance until he could figure it out. Now, he was able to accept the fact that things don't make sense sometimes, and he would enjoy the comfort until it did.

Graham pulled away enough to look at Alex. "Did everyone make it out of the Manor alive?"

Alex smiled, though it was not entirely filled with joy. Graham could detect a measure of concern. "Yes, they all made it out alive. Once I felt the quaking and heard the rumbling, I returned in time to help."

Graham breathed a sigh of relief. "What about the Manor?"

"Portfield Manor is gone, along with the entire training facility. It has all been laid to waste." It was evident that Alex was holding back some heavy emotions. "But never you mind about that. You are all safe and alive, and that is all that matters right now." Alex stood up and patted Graham on the shoulder. "Come. I know of a few people eager to see you."

Alex draped his arm around Graham's shoulders, ushering him into a spacious living room area. Kel and Ailey were sitting on a leather couch positioned beside a massive stone fireplace. They were in the middle of a board game when they heard Graham and Alex walk into the room with Damien close behind. They both sprang from their seats, spilling the board and game pieces all over the floor. Kel ran to Graham, throwing her arms around him.

"You're okay! Thank God you're okay!"

Graham squeezed tightly. "Yes, I'm okay. Better than ever, actually." He bent down and kissed Ailey on the top of the head, then looked Kel in the eye. "You took some pretty hard hits yourself. Are *you* okay?"

"I am now," she said. "You've been out for a while. You had us all worried. We were starting to think you were in a coma or something."

"How long is a while? Was I out all day?"

"Try three. You never moved a muscle unless someone was trying to give you water or soup, and even then it was only a flinch or a moan," said Kel.

"Three days? Holy cow. No wonder I feel like a million bucks. I've never slept more than seven hours at a time. We never even got to wake up on our own at Greenwood. Anyway, I'm glad to see that you're both okay. When I saw you both slumped over Cavaness' shoulder, I thought the worst."

"We were pretty beat up when we first got here, but Alex fixed us up. Remind me not to get on your bad side from now on. What was that, anyway? I thought you had exploded."

Graham shrugged. "I don't know. Everything pinned up inside just broke loose. That's about the only way I can describe it."

"That's as good an explanation as any," said Alex. "Except for one small detail." He lifted Graham's arm with both hands and rotated it, so that his forearm was facing the ceiling. Two small ripples of light flowed from Alex's hands into Graham's arm, causing his band to glow. Everyone gathered around, staring at the Aegis sun emblem filling the previously empty circle in the catalyst band.

Alex held Graham's arm up a little higher so that everyone could see the emblem. "Congratulations, Graham. Your catalyst is finally complete."

Graham's entire body began to tingle. He had finally come through for once. He stared at the sun in the circle for a few seconds until his excitement turned into curiosity. Looking back to Alex, Graham traced the outline of the sun with his finger.

"What does it mean? This is the same emblem that's on the other side. It's the Aegis Sun."

"It means that within you lies the full measure of the Aegis Power. It means that once you are trained to use and control what you have, you will be without limit. It also means that you will have a very different life than what you are accustomed to. Silas has seen what you are, and now, they will stop at nothing to get you. Your life is no longer your own. It will now be lived serving your fellow teammates and fighting the battle that is sure to come. It's a lot to ask of a fifteen-year-old boy. Is this something you're prepared to accept?"

Graham weighed Alex's words carefully. He did not really know what hardship looked like. He had always been sheltered at the orphanage, though he knew perfectly well what purposelessness felt like. If this meant being a part of something bigger, something worthwhile, then he was willing to accept any danger that came with it. He may regret it later, but right now, as he looked into the eyes of his new family members, he was willing do anything for them.

"Yes, I am," he said. "Not that there's much chance of going back now anyway," he added with a grin.

Alex returned the smile. "You don't know how glad I am to hear it. We are all here to help you carry the weight of this new responsibility."

"I do have one question," said Graham. "We were lucky last night that everyone didn't get buried after the explosion. How long will it take me to control this?"

"Believe it or not, you already are controlling it, though I think it is on a subconscious level."

"How? I almost killed everyone."

"You did more to protect them than you realize. When you let loose, the magnitude of your transformation should have extended out in every direction, but it didn't. Somehow you were able to channel the power upwards, only destroying the ceiling of the cavern instead of everything around you. You have great instincts, Graham. This will not be an easy or quick process, so you will have to give it some time."

Detecting Alex's desire to speak with Graham alone, Cavaness herded the others back into the living room.

Alex's tone turned more serious as the smile faded from his expression. "From what I gather, Silas has made clear the degree of your importance." He lifted Graham's arm once more and ran two fingers over the length of the glowing band. The lines holding the circle in place had changed positions. The two lines above the circle widened into a triangle shape, while the two lines below merged together into a point, making it look like a small dagger.

"This does not happen to everyone. It is the mark of someone truly unique," said Alex. "You are an exceptional young man, Graham. You may not believe it now, but this gifting would not have been given to you unless you had the physical and moral capacity to wield it. You mustn't allow an open door for corruption. A power of this magnitude will sway entire armies at the proper time. Part of your responsibility will be to keep yourself and your motives pure. Do you understand what I am telling you?"

Graham shrugged. "Yes and no."

"Complete devotion is the true force behind the power. It is the degree of loyalty you have to the cause that will keep you strong. You don't have to fully understand it now, but keep it tucked away in your mind. It may prove useful in the near future." Alex straightened up, his usual smile returning to his face. "Now. Enough serious talk. Let's celebrate your return to the land of the living before I take you and Damien back to Greenwood."

Graham had forgotten all about needing to go back to the orphanage. He had almost forgotten about the destruction of the Manor as well. Graham looked all around him, at the timber-framed architecture and the grand fireplace.

"Where are we, anyway?"

"It is called Falcon, our headquarters for the eastern region of the United States," said Alex. "We have facilities like this all over the world, each named after a bird or type of bird of great boldness and skill. We never know who is listening in on our conversations, so we use these coded descriptions to protect our outposts. Plus, birds are such majestic creatures. I like to see it as a simple reminder of the virtues we should all hold inside."

"Is it safe? Is it part of Catalyst Grove?" asked Graham.

"Yes, it is safe, but it is not part of Catalyst Grove. It is never a good idea to put all your eggs in one basket. This is a secretive, secluded facility, well out of reach of Silas or any of his crones," said Alex. "Why don't you have a look for yourself?"

Alex walked Graham through a few rooms, until they came to a huge lobby and fourteen-foot-tall arched doorway that obviously led outside. Alex grabbed the thick metal handle and opened the door. Graham stepped outside to find himself surrounded by a forest. The entryway of the building was made of stone. It looked oddly familiar. He ran his hand along the cultured stone, inspecting the shape of the rock and the moss that covered it.

Alex smiled at Graham, enjoying his curiosity. Staying

inside, he closed the door in front of him, leaving Graham to inspect the exterior. As the door clicked shut, Graham turned back to see that the door was gone. All he could see were trees and undergrowth. He took a few steps back, and, to his amazement, he realized where he was. It was the stone arch in the woods beyond Greenwood, his place of solace, where he had taken shelter when he had got lost years ago.

"Impossible!" He ran through the opening of the arch where the door had just been, continued around the side, and back around to where he had first stood. "What the heck is going on?"

Alex pulled the door back open, revealing the inside of the Mansion. "I told you it was secretive," he said. Graham ran back inside, then back outside to take another look. He could clearly see the treeline and blue sky, just above the arch, but when he ran inside, he could also clearly see the twelve-foot-high ceilings, knowing there was at least another floor above.

"How? What? I don't understand."

"It's a long story. I'll be sure to explain later. For now, just be glad it's concealed, though I think you have always known that there was something special about this place."

Alex was right. Graham did always feel at peace here. He could never put his finger on the reason, but there was always something magical and comforting about the arch. Now he knew why. There was a secret mansion behind it.

Alex showed Graham back into the living room. He explained to the others that it was time to take them back to their orphanages. The destruction of Portfield Manor had made headline news, and naturally this had caused some concern with the orphanage directors.

"I have met with Ms. Winstone and Mr. Pitman. I assured them both that you are all perfectly healthy and intact. They are eager to see each of you."

"What about the adoption? Where will we go now that the Manor is gone?" asked Kel.

"Everything is still in order. I have many homes here in Portfield. We obviously cannot have the in-home visitations required for the adoptions here in Falcon, so for the next few months, we will have to be at the other end of the county in the Millstone District. Once everything is finalized, we will move here to headquarters. Until then, you will need to be on your guard. No one else will be able to see your powers or catalyst bands, but that does not mean there won't be rumors. Go about your business and daily routine until I return for you."

Everyone said their goodbyes and wishes of good luck for Graham, Damien, Kel, and Ailey during their final days at their orphanages. Alex told them to go back upstairs, where new clothing would be provided for each of them to change into. The sweat suits with the golden sun emblem would obviously raise too many questions.

Once changed into normal clothes again, Graham found that Chase had a car parked at the edge of Wellington, ready for Alex to take the kids back.

Addressing them all, Chase said, "It will go by faster than you think. Trust me. You will all be back here before you know it." Chase looked to Graham. "And what will I do while my new little brother is gone?" He smiled and gave Graham a brotherly hug. "I'll miss ya. Take care of yourself at Greenwood, and try not to get on Ms. Winstone's bad side. It never works out well."

Graham smiled and nodded. "Well, too late for that, but thanks. I'll miss you, too."

Chase walked the kids through the woods and loaded them into the car. He waved goodbye as the car faded into the distance, then disappeared into the woods toward Falcon.

Scattered Pawns

It was late, and everyone had turned in for the evening. Only Alex and Cavaness sat at the long dining table made from two giant slabs of oak. They were deep in conversation. The lights in the headquarters were all off, except for the chandelier hanging over the table, making the seriousness of their conversation tangible and an air of tension filled the room as they discussed what had just taken place. Alex stared at Cavaness, his fingers wrapped around the handle of his coffee mug.

"That is what he said," said Alex, breaking the silence between them.

"Are you confident he was in his right mind when he said it? The boy did have quite a time. When that much power flows through a person, sometimes it makes their recollection disjointed and unreliable," replied Cavaness.

"I am sure, Cavaness. Both Kel and Ailey corroborated his statement." Alex stopped as he lifted his cup to his mouth. He let the steam dance under his nose for a moment before taking a sip. "Graham told me about Silas' remarks. He knew information about their time in Catalyst Grove that no one else could possibly know."

Cavaness sat with one arm on the table and held his other hand to his mouth, smoothing his fingers down the sides of his goatee.

"I just can't imagine it being anyone here. Silas was a psychology professor in his former life. You know how he likes to mess with the mind. Maybe he was mentally trying to tear Graham down."

"Of that I have no doubt, but I also do not believe that's the whole story. Silas knew the giftings of Kel, Ailey and Damien. He knew about Graham's inability to let his power come to the surface, and there's the most obvious fact that they knew about our facility and its location." Alex gently pushed his mug aside, shifting his gaze from the table to Cavaness.

"No, my friend. I know we do not want to believe it, but we must. We have a traitor among us."

Cavaness let out a heavy sigh. "And what of Portfield Manor and the Grove? Are we to rebuild it?"

"No. No, I don't think we can. It has been exposed now. They would just burn it down again. We need to send a message to the other facilities. I will get word to Corbin and he will tell the rest to be on guard. You know as well as I that if you are skilled enough, you can detect the Grove's energy signature while you are here. If Silas had enough time at the Grove, then he will know how to find the rest. Our priority is to warn the others. Only then can we focus on developing our final recruits and flush out the one who has turned against us."

"Agreed."

Alex took hold of his mug and held it up to Cavaness. Cavaness took his cup and clanked it against Alex's mug.

"We dodged a tremendous disaster today, and for that I give thanks. Moments like these are few and far between these days. Let's enjoy them while they last."

"I'll drink to that," said Cavaness.

They both drank from their cups. A trying time was upon them. Tomorrow, they would begin to hunt for their betrayer, but tonight, they were going to celebrate a victory, no matter how small it may be.

He limped through the dimly lit stone corridor in haste, stopping at the large wooden door to knock. Two resounding thuds of the metal ring bounced off the door. Silas impatiently tapped his foot, the scroll repeatedly tapping in the hollow of his empty hand.

"What is it?" said an icy voice. The 's' was drawn out, like the hiss of a snake.

"I bring good news, my Lord," replied Silas.

"Then by all means, come in," said the voice from the other side.

Silas opened the door and shut it gently behind him. Pulling his cane from underneath his arm, he continued walking into the room, his limp pronounced. He flinched with every step, trying unsuccessfully to hide his injury.

"What is this? What happened to your leg?"

"This is proof that the boy, Graham, is the one we have been searching for."

"And where is this boy?"

Silas lowered his head submissively. "He has escaped. We barely made it out alive. We were in a cavern, and when he went off, the whole place imploded."

The man's face grew dark, and his eyes lit with anger. "So, what you are telling me is that you have failed."

Silas' voice was now beginning to quiver. The one thing worse than bringing bad news was to look as though you were making excuses for your failure.

"No, my Lord. We did confirm that he is indeed the one we have been searching for." Silas placed the rolled-up scroll on the vacant table in front of him. "We also have this."

The man in the shadows stood from his chair and walked over to the table. Silas unrolled the scroll, revealing a map that displayed a detailed sketch of the seven continents. Hundreds of small orange dots were scattered throughout the landmasses, most of which had a small purple flame hovering over top.

"We believe we have found all of the training grounds. Forty percent have already been destroyed, and the others will be overtaken by dawn. As soon as I escaped the cavern, I sent the details of their energy signatures to our teams. Every Former blanketed the sky in search of the specific details I had provided. They were all found within hours. The Aegis recruitment pool has just dried up, my Lord. They will be devastated."

The faint glow of the purple flames cast a sinister glow on the other man's face, making his grin look exceedingly evil as the flame's reflection danced in his pupils. "This is good. This is very good."

Silas put his hand to his chest and bowed, almost falling as he shifted his weight from his hurt leg to his strong one. "Thank you, my Lord. It has not been an easy mission, but it has been a successful one." Silas paused, trying to choose his next words carefully.

"May I humbly ask a favor from your Lordship?"

The man was still staring at the purple flames, his grin fading away in annoyance. "What is it?" he spat.

"It's my leg. I've tried to heal it myself, but the injury is too severe. In light of our victory tonight, I was hopeful you might see fit to restore it."

The man looked intently at Silas.

"You have done well tonight. Alex will be most devastated by the news of his fallen facilities and personnel. In this, you have made me proud, and for that I commend you."

Silas stood high, taking pride in his Lord's contentment.

"However, your mission was to verify the boy's ability *and* bring him back with you. In that you have failed. It is only because of the destruction of the training facilities that I will not completely tear your worthless leg from your body. Leave now, and let your handicap be a constant reminder that I expect the orders I give to be completed."

Silas stumbled back in fear, catching his balance against the wooden post behind him. "Y– yes, your Grace. Thank you for your kindness. I will not fail you again." Silas regained his composure and limped to the door, closing it behind him.

The man walked back to his chair, picking up a black bishop from the chessboard beside him. He twisted it in a circle between thumb and finger before swiftly moving across the board, knocking over all of the white pawns on the first row, then throwing the chess piece down on its side. He stared intently at the white king.

"One step at a time, brother. One step at a time."

Power List

The Official Power List Revealed in Catalyst Grove

PUSHER

A Pusher has the ability to fire energy into solid surfaces, then have that same energy deflect at any angle. General application of this gifting is used with the earth. The subject will propel an energy shot into the ground, calculate the desired depth and angle of trajectory, then allow the energy to deflect, causing earth and rock to explode upwards. More advanced methods can use solid surfaces such as metal to either propel the material surfaces themselves, or allow the energy blast to deflect outwards to areas which, from a normal, direct blast, would not be possible.

BRIDGE

The Bridge gifting is normally developed in the introverted personality, whereas the subject prefers to work in the background, not wanting to be the main focus of attention. Fueled by the desire to empower others, the Bridge can make a connection between one or more people, acting as a conduit. This allows the gifting of each person to flow to anyone who is in physical contact with the Bridge. These powers can be used individually or in combination with all participating members. Many Aegis members label the Bridge as the 'Wild Card', due to the exponential methods of attack possible from the group as a whole.

AQUATIC

This is a very rare gifting. An Aquatic gifting gives the subject the ability to manipulate the element of Dihydrogen Oxide: H_2O. Aquatics have been known to be able to absorb oxygen from the water in order to remain submerged for prolonged periods of time, without the need to intake oxygen from the air into the lungs. Due to the properties of electrolysis, the Aquatic subject can use the power provided by the catalysts to control the physical state of water, causing it to move wherever they desire.

SURGE

The Surge gifting is a term to describe rapid movement. Defined by the modern English dictionary, a *surge* is a sudden and powerful movement. The subject possessing a Surge gifting is able to move at supernatural speeds in both mind and body, as well as firing an energy blast at much higher rates of speed than any other gifting.

FORMER

The Former gifting gives the subject the ability to form objects out of the raw power given by the catalyst. The possibilities are near limitless, only restrained by the creativity and imagination of the person. Not only can the Former create offensive and defensive attacks in various forms, but they can also connect their vision to whatever they create, making them most useful as scouts and spies.

SPARK

The gifting of the Spark gives the subject full ability and control over electricity, both in its manipulation and creation. The electric charge may be created from the catalyst band itself, or controlled from an outside source.

 *THE AEGIS*

The gifting of the full power of the Aegis has not yet been found or understood by either side. It is termed, 'The Great Mystery'. Only when the person possessing the gifting of The Aegis is found, can its true power be made known.

CHARACTER SERIES

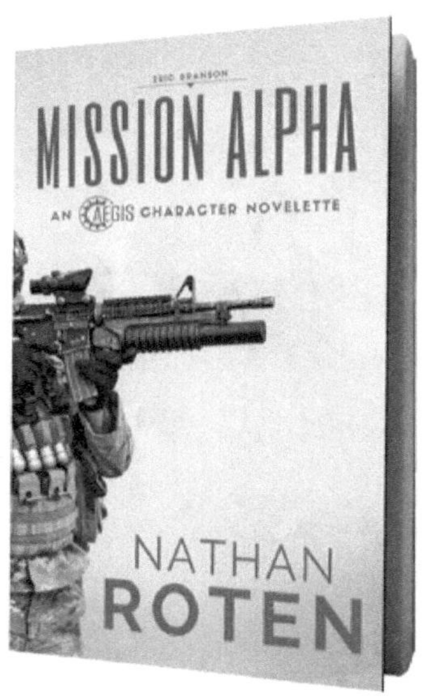

It is 2003 and the mission is to infiltrate an Al-Qaeda compound to secure intel on the whereabouts of Saddam Hussein, underground terrorist cells, and WMDs.

Eric Branson is a seasoned Green Beret but nothing could have prepared him for the supernatural events inside the compound.

ACKNOWLEDGEMENTS

None of this would have been even remotely possible without the support of my God and family. Kelly, Anna Gray, Sam & Eliza, Mom, Dad, Matt & Jordan– I love you so much. Thank you for all your love and support.

I also want to thank my incredible group of friends and supporters who played an important role in making this possible:

David & Beverly Aderhold • Joe & Kim Benson • Andrew Boyter • Jeff & Benita Brooks • Chuck & Patty Blanton • Matt & Amanda Cottrell • Tiffany, Alexander, & Denise Driver • Margaret Edwards • Kelly & Chet Emery • Matt Fitschen • Dipper & Charlotte Garrison • Chris & Stacey Gotwald • Jamie Gough • Scott & Peyton Grissom • Susan & Dan Grissom • Len & Ruth Hagaman • Jim & Grace Harrelson • Cyndi Helton • Vicki and Rick Hodges • Amanda Joe Kern • Jeremy Kilday • Matt & Sarah Long • Todd & Emily Marriott • Samuel B. McGinn • Bob & Vivien McMahon • Betsy Rosenthal Mennona • Brad & Bunny Osborne • Wayne & Donna Pennell • Bryan Prather • Arthur & Hanna Rasco • Margaret Roten • Matt & Jordan Roten • Faith Spinks • Dusty & Sharon Stacy • Jeff Stager • Michael Surber • Bruce & Karen Sutton • Chris & Mara Swanson • Michael Talley • Johnathan & Becky Webb • Dale Williams • Trish Wilson • Jennifer & Allie Woods

Thank you for your valuable feedback and friendship. You rock!

ABOUT THE AUTHOR

Nathan Roten grew up in the mountains of North Carolina, where he spent hours on end acting out the epic scenes playing in the theatre in his head. Knowing that he had to eventually grow up, he attended Appalachian State University, and moved on to be co-owner of two companies. In 2011, he began his official writing career with the publication of his non-fiction book, Embark. Now, with the desire to be that imaginative kid again, he has come back to his love for fiction.

AEGIS: Catalyst Grove is his debut novel. He resides in the mountains of North Carolina with his wife and three children.

Nathan would like to invite you to connect with him wherever you are in cyberspace:

Facebook: facebook.com/TheNathanRoten
Google +: plus.google.com/+NathanRoten
Twitter: twitter.com/Nathan_Roten
Blog: www.NathanRoten.com

And don't forget to join the vibrant community of people who love a little awesome-sauce in their daily lives by signing up for the *Epic Insiders* Newsletter. Get the latest news on the development of the Aegis Series, free books, sneak peaks, connect with Nathan and other fans of the series, and much more. You can sign up here:

NathanRoten.com/epic-insiders